Shades of Time

Books in the *After Cilmeri* Series

A Novel from the *After Cilmeri* Series

SHADES OF TIME

by

SARAH WOODBURY

Shades of Time
Copyright © 2017 by Sarah Woodbury

www.sarahwoodbury.com

To Brynne

Dearest Reader:

While many of you will have a better recollection of the events of the previous books than I do, some readers might be joining us only now (note, if that's you, you might consider starting with the prequel to this series, *Daughter of Time*, which is *free* in ebook at all retailers!) or be struggling to recall some key events from the previous books. If that's you, read on!

The *After Cilmeri* series begins with Meg, a young, troubled American widow, who, at a moment of catastrophic danger, falls through time and into the life of Llywelyn ap Gruffydd, the last Prince of Wales. A strong and charismatic leader, he saves her, and she in turn saves him, thanks to her knowledge of future events. Although powerful forces seek to divide them, by working together, Meg and Llywelyn navigate the dangerous and shifting alliances that constantly undermine his rule and threaten the very existence of Wales.

But before they can create a future which avoids the predetermined death of Llywelyn, Meg is ripped from his world and returned to her own—in time to give birth to their son, David.

David and his older sister, Anna, as teenagers, return to the Middle Ages to save Llywelyn yet again. This time, Norman lords have lured him into the fateful ambush at Cilmeri in eastern Wales. Without warning, David and Anna are thrown into a world they do not understand, among a people whose language and customs are totally unfamiliar. Ultimately, David is recognized as Llywelyn's true son, and he and Anna begin to make a life for themselves in the Middle Ages.

Over the course of thirteen books, it becomes clear that the medieval world is actually an alternate universe, and Meg, Anna, and David (and ultimately his son, Arthur) time travel when their lives are in danger. In the process, many new characters, both medieval and modern, are introduced. These include Math (Lord Mathonwy), a distant relation of Llywelyn, who marries Anna (*Footsteps in Time*); Ieuan, David's captain, who travels with him to the modern world (what ultimately comes to be known to the time travellers as *Avalon*) (*Prince of Time*); and Lili, Ieuan's sister, who becomes David's wife (*Crossroads in Time*).

From the modern world comes Bronwen, an anthropology graduate student who marries Ieuan; Callum, an MI-5 agent suffering from PTSD, who attempts to prevent Meg and Llywelyn from returning to their world (*Children of Time*); Cassie, a Native American woman, who was plucked from the mountains of Oregon in the wake of Meg's plane crash (*Winds of Time*) and must survive on her own in medieval Scotland (*Exiles in Time*); a busload of twenty-firsters, who make the mistake of traveling on the same bus as Meg and Anna and end up in their alternate universe (*Ashes of Time*); and Christopher, David's cousin (*Masters of Time*).

All the while, the combined efforts of Anna, David, and their family and friends are transforming the medieval world. Not everyone appreciates the burgeoning equality, universal education, and democracy, however, and throughout the books, the twenty-firsters face threats both from outside their inner circle and from within it.

The immediate precursor to *Shades of Time* is book 11, *Outpost in Time*, in which David, Meg, and Llywelyn, with friends and other family members, journey to Ireland to attempt to address the ongoing turmoil and warfare there. Unbeknownst to David, however, rebellious barons have colluded with King John Balliol of Scotland to assassinate him—and almost succeeded. David leads a coalition of Irish and Norman allies to defeat the rebels in Ireland ... but because he has no way to effectively communicate with Anna and Math, he remains unaware of the events playing out in England, Wales, and Scotland.

Shades of Time takes place simultaneously with *Outpost in Time*.

Cast of Characters

Anna—Time traveler, Princess of Wales
Math (Mathonwy)—Lord of Dinas Bran, Anna's husband
David (Dafydd)— Time traveler, King of England, Anna's brother
Lili—David's wife, Queen of England
Llywelyn—David and Anna's father, King of Wales
Meg— Time traveler, David and Anna's mother
Christopher Shepherd— Time traveler, David and Anna's cousin
Elisa Shepherd—Meg's sister, Christopher's mother
Ted Shepherd—Christopher's father
Elen Shepherd—Christopher's sister
Callum— Time traveler, Earl of Shrewsbury
Bronwen—Time traveler
Ieuan—Lili's brother, Bronwen's husband
Mark Jones— Time traveler, MI-5 agent

Humphrey de Bohun—Earl of Hereford, Constable of England
Edmund Mortimer—Earl of the March
Roger Mortimer—Edmund's brother
John de Warenne—Earl of Surrey
Cadwallon—King Llywelyn's captain
Bevyn—David's companion
Hywel—Steward of Dinas Bran

The Children

Gwenllian—Llywelyn's daughter by Elinor de Montfort
Elisa and Padrig—Twin children of Meg and Llywelyn
Cadell and Bran—sons of Anna and Math
Arthur and Alexander—sons of David and Lili
Catrin and Cadwaladr—children of Bronwen and Ieuan
Gareth—son of Cassie and Callum

1

19 March 1294

After midnight

Anna

Anna pulled her thick cloak closer around herself, chilled to the bone by the damp air and fog that had enveloped her small company at this higher elevation. The fog also muffled the slight conversation among her companions, which included another midwife, Mair, and five men-at-arms.

The torchlight barely penetrated five feet on any side, and Anna wished she had a torch—or better yet, a flashlight—of her own. She was glad her children weren't here. Though she was only a few miles from home, it was one of those nights when danger lurked around every corner, and the hollow sound of the horses' clopping hooves on the hard-packed dirt of the road forebode the arrival of the old Welsh gods.

Anna shivered and told herself she had allowed the latest enthusiasm of Cadell, her eldest son, to afflict her too. At nearly nine years old, Cadell had developed a fascination with ghost stories. In the evenings, he would pester the men for an endless supply of terrifying supernatural tales. All the men knew them like they knew the legend of King Arthur. The Welsh had a strong superstitious streak, coupled with an innate belief in the mystical, so everyone had one tale or another to tell.

Earlier this week, they'd been entertained by a story of the ghost of King Alexander of Scotland, Anna's supposed great-grandfather, who'd ridden his horse too close to the edge of a cliff one foggy night and died when he'd gone over it. According to the storyteller, the king's ghost haunted the cliffs to this day. Tonight, the story hit a little too close to home. So far, Cadell hadn't been visited by nightmares, though she'd told him in no uncertain terms that if he scared his younger brother by repeating any of the stories he knew, he would be writing Latin verb forms until his hand bled.

Hoping Mair wasn't feeling similarly spooked, Anna put out a reassuring hand to her, but Mair's smile was genuine in the torchlight, and she appeared to be visited by no such worries. Mair knew as well as Anna, when she was being rational, that Wales was safer tonight than at any other time in its history. They hadn't been at odds with England since Anna's brother, David, had taken the English throne.

Just the other day, Anna's husband had told her of a conversation he'd overheard between an Englishman and a Welshman as he was passing through one of the taverns in Llangollen, having taken a moment to check in with its proprietor, a former Crusader:

"So, you're from Chester are you? English?"

"Yes," the Englishman had replied, somewhat defensively.

The Welshman sniffed. "Then I'd better buy your next drink. Lord Mathonwy up at the castle says we have to welcome you."

"I'd be grateful," the other man said, unbending slightly at this unexpected overture.

"We rule your country now instead of the other way around, so it's the least I can do."

Math had gone away laughing and tucked away the story to repeat to David when next he saw him. Anna hoped David would laugh when he heard it. Her brother was far too stiff himself these days—not with self-importance but with the burden of running a country. The two of them had been fourteen and seventeen when they'd arrived in the Middle Ages for the first time. A little more than eleven years on, they'd lived here just long enough for people to treat them as if they belonged—and for young people born after 1282 not to remember the time when England and Wales were constantly at war.

Which was why the road should be safe, not giving her the heebie-jeebies, and the reason they were heading home at two in the morning instead of staying the night back at Heledd's house. Anna had spent the last twelve hours helping Heledd give birth to a baby boy. The birth had gone well, and both mother and baby were healthy, but Anna was a princess, and one who very much liked her own bed. Thus, she and Mair had left a third midwife with Heledd and chosen to return to Dinas Bran.

The five miles from Heledd's house to home hadn't seemed so daunting when they'd left an hour ago, but it hadn't been foggy then. Anna also hadn't realized how tired she was. Now that the adrenaline from the delivery had worn off, all she wanted with every fiber of her being was to lie down.

For once, she hoped the boys had stayed up late, even if it meant Cadell might have a new crop of horror stories in his repertoire. Most of their cousins were visiting, so the possibility of chaos and hijinks in the castle was high. If so, there was a slight chance Bran, her youngest, would sleep in and not come into the bedroom and wake her before dawn. If Cadell woke early, he was happy to read or concoct yet another ghostly adventure in his room, or perhaps sneak down to the kitchen for an early breakfast. But Bran wasn't yet five, and he still came in to Anna every morning, snuggling under the covers and putting his cold feet on Anna's warm legs.

Not that she would have it any other way.

But in the last five years, she hadn't woken in the morning more than a handful of times without Bran's small face peering at her, and she had the fleeting wish that for once the boy would just *sleep*.

As it was, Anna rarely went out on calls anymore, not with an entire university of healers in Llangollen at the disposal of the residents of the area. But Heledd was special: back at Castell y

Bere, she'd been Gwenllian's wet nurse. After Gwenllian had no longer needed her, Heledd had married a small landowner named Gryff, who settled them a few miles to the southwest of Llangollen.

The two women had spent very little time together since that fateful winter when Anna had led her and Gwenllian, along with the stable boy, Hywel, out of Castell y Bere. With Anna a princess and Heledd becoming a farmer's wife, there hadn't been much chance—or much they had in common. But what they had experienced during that cold January had bonded them forever, and Anna had been glad to keep her promise to attend the birth of Heledd's latest child.

"My lady, do you hear that?" The captain, Adda, held up a hand to halt the small company. His concern was apparent in his voice.

Though she'd been telling herself for the last half-mile that they had nothing to fear, it was unusual for anyone to be riding this late at night without a very good reason. Not just anyone could afford a mount either, and from the thunder of hooves coming towards them from the north, more horses than their seven were approaching.

Anna peered ahead. Despite the torchlight, she couldn't see past the next bend in the fog-shrouded road.

"Maybe Lord Mathonwy has sent a troop to meet us, my lady," Mair said. "Your husband does care for you so."

"He does." Anna wanted to believe these men belonged to Math, but she couldn't shake off her concern. Her captain clearly felt the same, since he signaled for two of the men to ride ahead to the bend in the road.

The hoofbeats grew louder, echoing in the windless night. Anna's horse danced sideways as it waited. As Anna tugged on the reins to control it, she wished she'd chosen a mount that was a bit less rotund, though normally he was exactly the kind of horse she liked.

Then one of the soldiers, who'd ridden to the bend in the road, shouted a warning. In response, Adda pulled his sword from its sheath, and the other two men with him did the same without needing a command. As Anna steadied her horse, prepared to flee if she had to, a company rode around the bend. Though the two soldiers up ahead held their ground, the oncoming cavalry was unstoppable. Swords raised high, they swept over, through, and then past Anna's men, tumbling them to the ground as they came. They wore no lord's colors.

"Ride, my lady! Ride!" Adda pointed at Anna and Mair. "We'll hold them off!"

Anna wasn't a warrior and had no pretensions to being one, so she didn't hesitate or argue, even though she could see as well as Adda that no amount of heroism from her men, no matter how well-trained, was going to be enough to overcome the force they faced. Twenty men had come around that bend, and there would be no holding them off for more than a few seconds.

"Come on!" Anna slapped the reins. The riders were here for her. She wouldn't dishonor the sacrifice of her men by throwing away her only chance at escape.

Cadi had been slower to react than Anna, so her horse immediately fell several lengths behind. But she was a better rider than Anna, her horse fleeter, and the oncoming riders had no interest in her anyway.

"They're gaining!" Mair screamed the words at Anna's back.

Behind them, the men following shouted to one another, some orders and some responses. "We need her alive!" These last words were spoken in heavily accented English, as by a Scotsman. If the words hadn't rung clear, Anna could have convinced herself she'd misheard them, but as it was, her throat closed. She couldn't think why Scots had ventured this far south seeking to capture her, but it was hardly the time to inquire. She had to get away.

At first, Anna had hoped—if she'd hoped anything at all— that she could lose herself in the fog, but as she glanced back to see how close the riders were, she was terrified to find them only forty yards behind her. Anna had to assume her men were dead. She was incredibly grateful that, unlike the last time she'd been abducted, Cadell was safe in his own bed.

"We have to split up!" Anna said to Mair as the other midwife came abreast. "They want me, not you. I need you to make your way to the castle!"

"I can't leave you!" Mair's voice was high and frightened.

"You can, and you will!" She motioned to Mair once again, to confirm the order, but Mair had already obeyed, breaking to the left down a track Anna hadn't noticed, or she might have taken it herself.

Which left Anna alone with her pursuers.

She glanced back once again. The men were gaining, which was no surprise, given their skill versus hers. On the other hand, Anna was a good hundred pounds lighter than any of the oncoming men, not necessarily because she was so much smaller, though she might be, but because they were in full armor. Even if her horse wasn't fast, Anna had an inkling of hope his greater endurance might save her.

Unfortunately, that hope was squashed a second later as a second contingent of men appeared out of the fog in front of her, torches blazing. There had been too many hooves on the road for her to distinguish the sound of these newcomers sooner—not that doing so would have done her any good.

She pulled up, knowing she could go neither forward nor back, and in a moment, she was surrounded by grinning men. Though most were English, Anna heard more Scots accents above the general hubbub, as the men spoke to each other or their horses in satisfied tones.

An Englishman with a red plume on his helmet, riding with the initial company, urged his horse closer and looked Anna up and down. "Princess Anna. It is a pleasure."

He took her hand and kissed the back of it. It was a gallant gesture, but completely out of place in this setting, and Anna was in no mood to be wooed. As his head came up, she pulled her hand away, and in the same motion, caught his jaw with her elbow. To her delight, her aim was perfect. His head jerked backwards, and he came within a hair's-breadth of falling off his horse.

The men around him laughed, a few in the back with utter abandon. By their dress, these were the Scots she'd heard speaking earlier. On another day, as fellow Celts, she would have viewed them as allies. But not today.

"Who are you? What do you want?" The words came out somewhat breathless because Anna was breathing hard with the effort she'd expended and wasn't able to modulate her tone. She didn't mind if the men thought she was afraid. She was afraid—but she was also able to stand outside that fear and evaluate her surroundings. If she was taken to a castle, and there were plenty within ten miles of this position, she could end up alone in a cell for a very long time. And worse, she could be used as leverage against Math or David or Papa. Or all of the above.

"Do you hear that, gentlemen? She doesn't know." The man whom she'd hit had recovered, though he rubbed his jaw as he looked at her, making her think that hitting him might have been a mistake. He wouldn't be underestimating her again. Still, he gestured expansively to his men. "Should we tell her?"

"What don't I know?" Anna's horse danced again, and she was pleasantly surprised by his energy. She'd raced him harder than he'd ever run in his life, and she'd assumed he'd be completely worn out. Perhaps, like a small child, the horse could sense the menace in the air, didn't like it, and it was keeping his adrenaline going.

The leader leaned forward. "Your brother is dead, along with your parents. They're dead on the floor of the great hall at Trim."

Anna stared at him. She could tell the man expected her to gasp or weep, but instead she felt herself on the verge of laughter at the absurdity of his claim. "When?"

"Yesterday. The day before. What does it matter?"

Anna's eyes narrowed. Ten seconds into being told one of the worst things a person could hear, she was torn between a gut-wrenching belief that he might be speaking the truth and mockery that he would tell her David and her parents were dead without knowing the particulars.

"I don't believe you," she said flatly. Anna found her stomach settling. She'd spoken the truth. She really didn't believe him.

"You should." A black-bearded Englishman, who'd come with the second contingent of riders, clenched his hand into a fist. "Soon the whole of Britain and Ireland will be in our hands."

"*Your* hands? And whose orders do you follow?" Still unsettled, Anna's horse turned in a full circle, prompting the men nearest to her to move farther away in order to give her horse more space. These soldiers were all medieval, of course, so they hadn't watched any movies and didn't know you should always secure your prisoner before answering questions or monologuing. Nobody had taken her reins either. It was a rare man who didn't underestimate women. For once, Anna preferred it that way.

"Are you saying you yourself will be king? Who has these delusions of grandeur?" Anna encouraged her horse to spin one more time, a move that allowed her another complete view of her surroundings. Her horse's dancing movements had put the man closest to her well out of reach, and while the way forward and back on the road remained completely blocked, nobody had moved to fill the space on her left or right.

The left-hand way involved a ditch and a thick wood and was the way Mair had gone. On Anna's right, a crumbling stone wall fronted an uneven grassy field.

"Who is it you serve?"

The red-plumed leader scoffed. "You'll see him soon enough."

"Why can't you tell me? Are you so ashamed of this allegiance you don't dare speak his name or wear his colors openly?"

Before the leader could answer, one of the Scots, who'd spoken earlier, shouted, "We don't fear to speak King John's name!"

The Englishman twisted in the saddle, anger in his face, though since he'd been boasting too, and several of the men with him were Scots, it didn't take a genius to put two and two together and come up with John Balliol, the King of Scots, being behind whatever was happening here. Why an English lord would support Balliol's plans wasn't yet clear, but Anna wasn't going to hang around to learn his name. At least if she survived this, she could tell Math about the Scots.

The thought of what awaited her if she escaped solidified her courage, and Anna took advantage of the leader's moment of distraction. Her horse wasn't one to gallop if he could help it, but he could jump, so she took a chance on the field. With a nudge, the horse surged forward, needing only a few steps to get his legs underneath him and leap.

He sailed over the wall, and in a few strides, had left the startled men behind.

The fog was thicker over the field, not surprising because that's how fog formed—when warm ground met colder air—and Anna could see virtually nothing in front of her. She wracked her brain for an image of what this area had looked like yesterday when she'd ridden past on her way to the birth, but she had no clear idea of where she was. In the fog, all fields and forests looked the same. Still, her horse's hooves pounded steadily on the turf, and though she hadn't yet escaped completely, she exulted. For the moment, she was free.

Behind her, the leader shouted directions to his men, sending some after her directly while the rest rode east and west in the hope of cutting her off.

"I see her!"

Anna prodded her horse to go faster. She'd gained a few yards in leaping the wall before her pursuers responded, but though her horse could jump, he hadn't become faster in the last ten minutes, and whatever adrenaline he'd been running on was fading. The rider behind her held a torch, but as sometimes happened in fog, it made it almost harder to see, since the light reflected off the water droplets in the air before her. But then the fog thinned, and she could make out the silhouettes of trees in front of her.

She'd reached the far side of the field. While she could turn left or right in an attempt to evade the riders, she'd heard the leader's directions to his men. Her best chance of escape was to ride straight ahead into the woods, which would slow her down, but also hinder her pursuers. If she was very lucky, she might be able to lose them entirely. So she urged her horse forward, and he cooperated with a burst of speed. He had to be exhausted, but he kept going, filled with the same fear and urgency she was.

He leapt the equally decrepit wall that bordered this end of the field, bounded between two birch trees, and trampled the scrubby undergrowth. He had barely recovered from the leap, however, before he was faced with a three-foot-high blackberry bramble, beyond which more fog, thicker even than over the field, blocked her vision. Behind her, the torchlight bounced, indicating the nearest rider had leapt the wall too and at any moment might be close enough to touch. There was no time to lose.

"Yah!" Anna snapped the reins, and the horse hitched its step and leapt. Unfortunately, though they sailed easily over the bramble, they didn't find themselves on another road, which would have been ideal, or in an adjacent field.

Instead, they leapt into nothingness—literally off the edge of an escarpment. Anna's heart caught in her throat—how could it not?—and she recalled again the story of King Alexander.

He hadn't been a time-traveling twenty-firster, however. Instead of falling to her death as the King of Scots had done, she felt the all-too-familiar blackness overtake her.

One, two, three ...

2

19 March 2022

Anna

The horse's hooves skated on the smooth surface of the floor, and he whinnied as he tried to arrest his motion. Despite the suddenness of her changed circumstances, Anna had the presence of mind to haul back on the horse's reins, even though what she really felt like doing was throwing up. It wasn't as if the blackness had come as a surprise, and she was very glad not to be dead at the bottom of that ravine, but she was terrified to the point of nausea at how close she'd come to dying. *Again.*

Any arrival in Avalon instead of death was a good thing, however, and at least she wasn't galloping down some twenty-first century freeway. The horse was less happy about his situation, and he skidded around and ended up facing the opposite direction from which they'd come in.

They were in an enormous hall, and one, amazingly, Anna recognized. The roof was supported by elaborate wooden archways and buttresses, the floor was gray tile, and the walls, which in the

Middle Ages were lined with tapestries, today had banners spaced every few yards celebrating the thousandth anniversary of the birth of Harold Godwinson, the King of England who'd been killed by William the Conqueror at the Battle of Hastings.

Long before the twenty-first century, Westminster had become the Parliamentary building, rather than where the King or Queen of England lived, and if she remembered properly the pictures she'd seen, in Avalon the hall itself was dwarfed by the size of the buildings that had grown up around it. There were banners in here because the hall was for show, rather than a place Parliament met or the king dined. Still, it was not the place she would have chosen to appear.

"Police! Put your hands where I can see them!"

Anna obeyed instantly, dropping the horse's reins and slowly turning in the saddle so she could see who was speaking to her. By the black and white uniform, the man was obviously a cop, *a bobby*, she supposed, since this was Westminster Palace and they were in modern England. He wore a white shirt, black pants, and a black protective vest as body armor, perhaps David's beloved Kevlar. He also had a gun pointed straight at her heart.

She had thought modern British policeman didn't carry guns, but as she was trespassing inside a national landmark with a horse, maybe the police were making an exception for her. Anna had been to Avalon fifteen months ago when her whole family had spent Christmas Eve at the chicken farm that was all that was left of Aber Castle, but it had been a lot longer than that since she'd spent any time here—really not since 2010, when she'd driven Aunt Elisa's minivan into medieval Wales. She would have given almost anything not to be here now.

"Hi," she said to open the conversation, not entirely sure how to talk to a cop under these conditions.

The policeman moved slowly in a wide circle around her until he reached a point where she didn't have to twist in the saddle to face him.

Anna had given upwards of a hundred talks over the last five years to people of all walks of life. She didn't have any trouble speaking to complete strangers or constructing an argument. But no amount of rationality was going to clarify for a modern cop how she'd ended up in Westminster Hall wearing full-blown medieval clothing and riding a horse—or make him look on her with anything but distrust.

Judging by his relatively unlined face and the lack of gray at his temples, the cop was in his late twenties or early thirties. His body armor indicated how concerned the authorities were about security, probably fearing terrorists more than thieves or normal criminals. They had good reason to be worried. At that Christmas fifteen months earlier, a terrorist had blown up Caernarfon Castle, and before that, his organization had destroyed the government buildings in Cardiff.

So the more she stared at the gun, the more concerned she became that the cop might actually use it. Anna had already faced down a company of enemy cavalry tonight, so a single man should have been easy, but it was not a good sign that his hands appeared to be shaking more than hers. She was far more concerned about *his* fear, in fact, than her own.

In her most calm voice, one she saved for speaking to particularly recalcitrant barons—or one of her children when he was being unreasonable—she said, "I have no weapon other than this dagger at my waist." She twisted a bit to show him the sheath. "You can put that gun away."

"Toss it over here."

Anna's hand went to the dagger's hilt, but it seemed she'd moved more quickly than the cop liked, because he barked, "Slowly!" He seemed very twitchy, for which she couldn't blame him, and he appeared to still be trying to encompass the horse.

"If you want me to get down, I'm going to have to use my hands."

"Stay where you are!" He took a step back, as if he was afraid Anna was going to launch herself at him rather than dismount. She could have dismounted like Christopher had taken to doing, by swinging one leg over the horse's head. But even were she that good, she was wearing a skirt, which probably would have hooked on his ears.

Very slowly, his eyes never leaving her face, the cop took one hand off his gun to press a button on a black device hooked to his collar and spoke to somebody only he could hear. Anna had thought everything would be wireless by now, but she was hardly in a position to question the cop's methods. It could be cell phone reception wasn't very good in these old buildings. From the short time she'd had a phone in Caernarfon, she'd seen it was hit or miss in north Wales.

Regardless, the cop told the person on the other end of the line that he needed backup. Anna resigned herself to the fact that she'd ended up in yet another situation she couldn't escape. The phrase *out of the frying pan and into the fire* could have been coined for just this situation. It seemed the best thing she could do was sit on the horse and wait for whoever else was coming, though to do so was annoyingly passive. While she would have preferred not to be in Avalon at all, and hated to find herself so far from Math and her boys, now that she was here, she had an agenda. The last thing she had time for was to cater to some cop's fears.

Then the horse made clear he had an agenda of his own, and it didn't include standing still. As he'd done on the road twenty minutes and seven centuries earlier, he started to dance and even buck a little. The men who'd captured her there lived and breathed horses, so they hadn't been surprised by her horse's movements, but the cop here was a different story.

He backed off, his voice and hands shaking. "Hold still!"

Anna was too focused on the horse to answer. His ears were rapidly swiveling, flicking back and forth, telling her he was anxious and stressed. As he bucked again, it was hopeless to think she could control him with just her knees. In a quest to keep her seat, she brought down her hands and scrabbled for the reins.

Discovering they'd fallen to the floor, she caught her fingers in the horse's mane.

But it wasn't enough. The horse danced again, his eyes rolling in fear.

"Hold still or I'll shoot!"

"I can't hold him!"

Already alarmed by the unfamiliar place, the shouting pushed the horse over the edge. Perhaps remembering in his tiny horse's brain what had saved them on the road, he gathered his feet under him and leapt in the direction of the door. Unfortunately, it was also in the direction of the cop, who finally fired his gun. The bullet hit the horse in the chest, stopping him cold, and he went down.

Anna had only a second to clear her feet from the stirrups. Though she managed that part in time, the karate roll that would have taken the weight of her fall on her shoulder didn't come off as well. The floor was concrete tile and very hard, and as she hit the ground, something snapped in her left wrist, and she screamed.

The cop was shouting incoherently, but Anna didn't care about him anymore. She curled up into a ball on the floor, gritting her teeth against the pain in her wrist, her eyes on her horse. It lay on its side on the floor, blood from its wound seeping between the tiles. The scene was beyond awful. She couldn't believe she'd escaped the men in Wales only to be almost killed by a cop. Things could have gone more badly only if the bullet had actually hit her.

The thought was instantly clarifying. The situation had been life-threatening, but apparently not enough to cause her to time travel back to her world.

And that meant she was here for a reason.

3

19 March 2022

Mark

Mark Jones's mobile buzzed for the second time in as many minutes, but he ignored it, knowing without looking that it was a routine notification of the daily backup, which always occurred at this hour.

Instead, he pushed the stack of paper on his desk towards his metal outbox. The papers weren't yet ready to go out, but in the back of his mind he hoped if he left them over there for a while, he'd be that much closer to completing them. It was three in the morning, and he'd been at work all night, trying to finish a report for his boss's boss, who'd left nine hours earlier.

It was a little hard to believe, here in 2022, that so much paper was still being generated by any office. You would think there'd be none, but actually, the reverse was true. There was *more* paper being used now than ever before. If the twenty-first century had taught the intelligence services anything, it was that every email, text, mobile phone call, and electronic device could be hacked. Listening devices were thinner than hairs, and they could project for miles. Mark's office was swept daily for foreign electronics, and still he never felt quite sure nobody else was listening.

So if a person wanted secure communication *and* an official record, they were back to paper. Tasks like this had taken over his life, now that he was the lead programmer of a much-beleaguered group of satellite software engineers, part of a subset of the Security Service which focused on processing the millions—billions—of bits of data Britain's surveillance systems took in every day.

The government's focus was on stopping acts before they started, as it should be, but this required earlier and earlier notification. Such was the workload that Mark rarely left his office, and many of his staff at times slept at their desks in their quest to stay abreast of hackers. His people were desperately needed but never loved, and always one step behind, since if an incident took place, it was clearly their fault for not having prevented whatever Trojan, virus, or malware a twelve-year-old from Chiswick—or foreign spies—had directed at Britain.

Thus, if a person so much as made a joke about a bomb or anything resembling an act of terrorism, he or she should have a file at MI-5. Mark's section was also merely backup to the much sexier GCHQ (Government Communications Headquarters), which had risen from the ashes after its complex had been blown up nearly three years ago.

In the intervening years, Britain's intelligence community had worked frenetically to rebuild itself and its infrastructure. Three years ago, Five had been uniquely placed to step into the gap the loss of GCHQ had created, having maintained their own redundant covert surveillance program all along. Once GCHQ was up and running again—and more secretive than ever—Five, instead of mothballing its program, had, naturally, expanded it. Mark was, in effect, a beneficiary of that decision.

For the most part, Mark believed in what he did, which might have surprised some of his peers who didn't work at Thames House, the main office of the Security Service in London. They viewed the government's surveillance program as a violation of civil liberties. Which, in truth, it was. But Mark was convinced that without the CCTV cameras, microphones, and electronic surveillance, criminals and terrorists would have had that much more of a free hand. They'd caused a great deal of damage in recent years as it was, and people said the most amazing and terrible things when they thought nobody but the person they were talking to was listening. Of course, it was also the same technology that had caused the overload of paper on his desk.

High heels tapped down the hallway beyond his half-open door, and the familiar tentative knock of Livia, his newest tech, three months now on the job, echoed into Mark's office. As usual, technology services were in the bowels of the building, though he did, for once, have a window located high up in one wall. If he stood on a chair and looked out, it gave him a view of a narrow car park.

"Mr. Evans? I may have something interesting here."

Mark didn't consider himself immodest, but he knew himself well enough by now to state a bold truth: he was one of the cleverest people at Five. That was just a fact. He'd discovered within five minutes of meeting Livia that she was well into his range, though completely out of his league in dating terms, even if dating a subordinate could ever be appropriate. She was taller than he was, model-thin, and blonde.

When Livia had been shuttled into his department three months ago, Mark had run her through her paces, wanting to know why his boss had given him someone so obviously overqualified. He hadn't had his questions answered, however, and he'd decided, admittedly based on no evidence whatsoever, that she was a plant, a spy within his department, and probably specifically tasked with keeping an eye on him. He'd grown all the more certain of it the more often she kept the same hours he did.

So he didn't look up from his computer. It was deliberately rude, but he wasn't going to make spying on him easy for her, and he merely grunted, "Come in," even as he waved at her to enter his office.

The door squeaked all the way open, but when Livia didn't say anything more, he realized she was hesitating in the doorway, precariously balanced on too-high heels the Director-General had decreed were the current dress code. While other institutions were dressing down, Thames House was a bastion of knee-length skirts and suits, high heels and wingtips. Mark's parents had given him a tie for his last birthday, a gift that would have sparked laughter a few years ago, but now actually made him grateful.

Just thinking about what Livia's feet must feel like at the end of the day made Mark tired. She was at most six years younger than he, but a year at Five was like seven in the outside world, making her vastly less experienced than he was.

Thus, he relented, and though he was still mostly focused on his computer, he took a moment to glance at her face. "What is it?"

Livia had been hired to do quality control on the software his section designed, and she was very good at her job. "I found something in the software I wanted you to see."

He found himself grunting again. The only way to uncover credible threats to the nation's security was to flag many that never panned out, so Mark didn't dismiss her immediately. Meanwhile his mobile buzzed again.

"Sir, I really think you should look at that."

"It's just the backup notification." Mark pressed send on the email he'd been writing.

"It is, and it isn't. That's what I wanted to speak to you about. There's a hidden program in the backup notification."

She had his full and undivided attention. Such was Livia's composure, however, that she stood her ground as he glowered at her. Probably she could see right through him and knew he was all bark and no bite.

"What are you talking about?" He reached for his mobile.

"I found a Trojan horse in the software, hidden inside the backup notification you just received and others like it. The Trojan was built into the code itself, and the encrypted notification piggybacks on the standard one. It is sent only to you, and the latest notice was sent ten minutes ago. Sir." The last word came out stiffly.

Mark stood abruptly, and his hand trembled around his mobile to the point that he almost dropped it. Because, of course, she was right. He had been the one to write the original software for the satellite tracking system without which Britain's entire system of surveillance wouldn't work. That Trojan she'd found did go directly to him, and the buzzing he'd ignored was telling him that someone had arrived.

Someone had arrived!

Mark's heart was pounding, and his breath caught in his throat, all of which he worked to hide from Livia while at the same time trying to decide what he was going to tell her.

But she had her own ideas. "Please let me show you."

Livia's office was two levels down in a true basement, which was unfortunate. Thames House was (unsurprisingly) on the River Thames, which meant despite near constant cleaning, the concrete always felt dank and borderline moldy, though the engineers and environmental techs swore it passed all the tests.

Mark himself sneezed every time he ventured down here, even though he'd never been allergic to mold before. Consequently, he flat out didn't believe them.

Livia truly had the worst office in the building, not dissimilar to Mark's first office in Cardiff, back when he worked for Callum. While the room was twenty feet long and fifteen feet wide and would have been spacious if carefully appointed, it was crammed floor to ceiling with old equipment nobody dared get rid of, since every gigabyte inside every device had once been classified. Everybody *knew* it was impossible to delete data.

Technically they weren't wrong. When data on a computer was deleted, the space on the hard drive was freed up to be used again, but until it was overwritten, the deleted data could be retrieved. GCHQ's software engineers had created a program that overwrote the empty spaces with randomly generated patterns until the data was no longer recoverable. The United States military had come up with something similar, but no matter how many times Mark said the material was safe, his request to surplus the equipment was always denied.

Livia ushered him into her office, checked the hallway for signs of life, and carefully closed the door. Mark, meanwhile, from his mobile, shut down the cameras and recording devices in the room. He should have done it before he'd left his own office, but Livia's discovery had flustered him.

"What exactly have you discovered?" Mark had had time merely to glance at the notification, but he knew England well enough—and London in particular—to know the coordinates he'd been sent were close by. He hadn't called up the map yet, however, because he almost didn't want to dig deeper. Once he did, his feet would be set on a path from which he wasn't going to be able to deviate until he'd seen it through to the end. That he'd escaped the encounter with Christopher, Gwenllian, and Arthur with his cover intact was nothing short of a miracle. Christopher had found Gwenllian and Arthur in Pennsylvania, however, not London, and in the last nine months MI-5 had grown only more suspicious of their own.

Livia went around her desk to her computer and tapped on the keyboard. "It's the time travel project, isn't it?"

Mark's head came up, and his stomach turned to a block of stone. Still, he tried to brazen out his response to her revelation anyway. "What are you talking about? What time travel project?"

"Either that, or you're a mole, but I don't think so. The incidents all match the records, and I know you designed the software, so you must have embedded the Trojan into the code from the very start." Her voice revealed how pleased she was with herself for discovering this.

"What records?" Even having turned off the cameras and listening devices, Mark still spoke in a low whisper. The rest of his staff had checked out of work, and he and Livia were the only ones on the floor, but paranoia was all-consuming and contagious, and the longer he worked for Five, the worse it got.

Of course, sometimes someone really was watching. And sometimes that person was him. While the techs swept this room as often as any other, Mark knew the location of each of his employees at all times because nothing went on at Five that wasn't logged and turned into data.

"You erased everything in the computer records, most thoroughly, I might add, but nothing is truly ever erased at Five." Livia went to one of the dozen filing cabinets in the room, pulled open the second drawer, and gestured like a quiz show hostess. "Files."

Mark moved to look, pulling out one folder, just to humor her, and then, when it proved to be a dossier on Callum, setting it aside and grabbing a stack out of the drawer. He swept aside some discarded equipment, half of it falling to the floor with a crash, and spread the folders across the table. "How are these here? I shredded everything!"

"As far as I can tell, everything nobody else wants ends up in this room. The other filing cabinets are full of all sorts of material. I've gone through most of it, but—"

"But these caught your interest." He bit his lip. "You've read them all, of course." It wasn't a question.

"Yes." The word came out slightly defiant.

"What made you connect the Trojan to the time travel initiative?"

Her expression brightened. "So it is real! The written reports go back farther than the satellite records, but the Trojan is there, every time. Did you design the software all the way back to when you worked for Director Callum?"

Mark pressed his lips together, not wanting to answer, but Livia gazed at him so earnestly—and already knew so much—it was pointless to shut her out. "Yes."

"So what is the message it's sending?"

"Surely you worked that out too. You just said you did."

"I know ... but I can't believe it."

He just gazed at her, although his mobile was burning a hole in his hand.

"It tells you when someone has arrived."

"Arrived from—" he prompted her.

"—from the Middle Ages. From the alternative universe."

Callum's file in his hand, Mark stepped close to Livia and spoke so low he could barely hear himself. "Tell me you haven't said anything about this to anyone."

She shook her head. "No. Nobody. I wouldn't."

He looked at her hard. "No boyfriend, no coworker, no casual conversation down at the pub after work?"

She pressed her lips together for a moment and then amended, "When I first found the files, I asked Veronica over in records if she knew anything about the time travel project. She rolled her eyes and asked if someone had said something to me about it."

"Did she mention me?"

"No, and I told her no, only that I'd heard some of the girls talking in the loo. She told me to ignore them. It was a discredited project that for all intents and purposes had never happened. She said everyone who'd worked on it had been let go."

Mark tapped a knuckle to his upper lip. "That's true."

"Except for you. How come they don't know you worked on it? You've been to the Middle Ages!"

"New life, new identity, new job," Mark said. "I worked out of the Cardiff office, and few knew me there, since I was in IT. Nobody notices anybody in IT."

Livia made a rueful face because she couldn't deny what he said was true. "So ... your name isn't really Gabe Evans?"

"No," he said shortly.

In politics, and thus at Five, a few months could be a lifetime. Even though it had been only fifteen months since Caernarfon Castle had blown up and Mark had returned to work, with a change in government came a change in directors and a reordering of priorities.

Turnover in the early years of the Security Service had been slow and measured. Now, they had a new Director-General every few years, and his appointment had become more and more political. Employees rose and fell like a lift going up and down. It was terrible for morale, but it had been good for Mark and had allowed Director Tate to slide him into his new job without fuss, before leaving himself to become the Ambassador to Finland. He had, in fact, urged Mark to come with him, but Mark had respectfully declined, knowing he could do more good for David from here.

This new Director-General had given no indication he even knew a time travel project had once existed. Mark had put out feelers in every direction, making friends in many sections, trying to determine where he stood. Tate had warned him upon his departure to keep his head down, and Mark had done all he could to remain inconspicuous. At times, he felt like a mole in his own agency, a spy working against his own country, except the foreign power he worked for was the King of England—David, in other words, and in an alternate universe.

"Are you going to tell me what your name really is?"

"Not until I have to." Mark decided he couldn't put off dealing with the message any longer, and he activated the screen on his mobile. The map appeared with a dot showing the location of the entry.

Livia's eyes were bright. "Who is it?"

"It doesn't tell me that." Mark zeroed in on the map, and then straightened in surprise at what it showed him. "Unfortunately, if whomever this is tries to contact Five to find me, I don't exist, so that means we have to go looking for them."

Completely focused on the matter at hand, and apparently unintimidated by the truth, Livia leaned in to look at his screen. "Westminster Palace?"

And for the first time since Livia had been assigned to his division, Mark saw her not as a possible enemy, but as a genuine person, a colleague, and a computer scientist not unlike himself, who'd somehow found herself working for Five as a low-grade tech instead of getting a different—and better paying—job in the corporate world.

"We have literally no time to lose." Mark patted down his pockets, making sure he had no electronic devices on him, including his mobile, which he left on Livia's desk. From now on, he needed to think one step ahead of everyone else, even MI-5. The moment he connected with whoever had arrived, he needed to become immediately untraceable. He headed for the door. His heart was in his throat, half-excited and half-terrified at what and who awaited him.

Livia hesitated, her own mobile in her hand. "We?"

Mark paused in the doorway. "Yes, *we*. Don't you want to come?"

4

19 March 2022

Ted

"Ted, it's Chad."

"Just a sec." With a glance at Elisa to make sure she was still asleep, Ted swung his legs out of bed. He'd left the phone on vibrate, as he always did, knowing the hum on his bedside table was too quiet to waken Elisa. He pushed his feet into his slippers and pulled his bathrobe from the hook on the back of the door.

Once down the stairs, he flipped on the kitchen light and pressed the *on* button for the coffee maker at the same time he said, "Okay, shoot."

"Someone's arrived."

Ted almost dropped the phone. "You're sure?" And then he amended. "Of course you're sure, or you wouldn't be calling me in the middle of the night. Can we go get him?"

Visions of David's arrival in Avalon when he was sixteen danced in Ted's head. He'd come home to find his nephew in full armor, sword and all, in his kitchen.

And then his heart skipped a beat at the thought that David could have returned with Christopher.

"My men were not as alert as they should have been, and they didn't tell me until just now. Believe me, heads will roll. But Mark was. He just drove out of Thames House. I have men following."

"Where's he going?"

"I don't know yet. The initial scan showed whoever's here arrived inside Westminster Palace. That place is a fortress, and I don't want to expose my involvement unless it's absolutely necessary. My men are watching and waiting. If Mark isn't successful in retrieving whoever this is, I'll send them in."

"What can I do?"

"*You* are going to sit tight. If I'm to persuade David to let me help him, I can't send my men in guns blazing. He'll never trust me, and I have no interest in getting on the wrong side of MI-5. Where's the phone Mark gave you?"

"In my briefcase." Ted strode into his office where he'd left his briefcase by the door.

For months he'd kept the phone Mark had given him in his pocket or on the bedside table next to his regular phone, hoping daily for a call telling him exactly the news Chad had just given him. That kind of vigilance was exhausting, however, and in the end he couldn't sustain it, though Elisa still kept her phone with her. At the moment, it was in her purse beside the bed. It had been a rocky moment when she'd found out he wasn't keeping his phone at his side 24/7 anymore. To her it was a kind of betrayal—a loss of faith.

But it hadn't been that. He'd put it away when he and Chad had come to an understanding, and with the technology of Treadman Global at his disposal, he'd told himself that he didn't have to carry the phone anymore. Now, he pulled it from his briefcase, his heart in his throat at the thought that Christopher had called and he hadn't answered. But there was no activity on the screen, and no voicemail.

Not that there could have been from Christopher directly. He didn't have this number. But Mark did, and Mark hadn't called.

"What time do you all head into London?" Chad asked.

"Seven." Back in the kitchen, Ted checked the clock on the coffee maker. "Everyone will be up by six."

"You're going to have to pretend everything is normal until you hear from me. If Mark calls or, God willing, David, you can't let on you know about his arrival already."

"I don't see why I can't tell him, Chad. It would be a lot easier to convince David to let you help if I was honest from the start. I need at least to tell Elisa."

"You can't! Nobody can know. *Not even Elisa.* I know it's hard to keep this from her, but we agreed." Then, at Ted's silence, Chad tsked through his teeth. "David trusts Mark, and you haven't told him about any of this because we need him to trust you, and we didn't want to spook him. If David's initial response to the idea of working outside MI-5 is negative, I don't want to lose everything we've worked so hard for or have him no longer trust you."

Ted sighed. "All right. We'll do it your way. But David is a smart man." He laughed. "As smart as you."

"And what if it isn't David? What if it's Meg or Anna? They're going to need something different. You also don't know why they're here. Maybe somebody is sick." Chad sounded almost hopeful. "Make sure they know I can get them the best care, privately, with no questions asked and no records kept."

"I know. I know. Whatever they need, we'll be there for them," Ted said. "But that means *you* have to trust *me* too. You may not want me to tell them the whole truth up front, but I will if I have to. It's the lives of my family members on the line."

"I do trust you." Chad drew in an audible breath. "I can't believe this is finally happening. Thank you, Ted. Thank you for trusting *me* with the truth."

"Well, we'll see soon enough how this plays out." Ted's heart was racing almost more than before at the thought. "No way am I going back to sleep."

"Are you kidding me? Who can sleep? We're going to do great things together!" Then Chad sobered. "I hope it's your son, Ted. Truly."

Ted drew in a breath and let it out before he had the wherewithal to answer, and nine months of heartache and grief were compressed into three simple words. "I do too."

5

Anna

Anna wasn't the type to pass out, which she was regretting at the moment since losing consciousness would have come as a relief. Her head hurt, her wrist hadn't improved in the last minute, and the floor of Westminster Hall was cold.

She lay still enough, however, that the cop came over to make sure she was alive. Anna watched his approach through eyes half-closed against the pain. He had his gun out and was pointing it at her, and she closed her eyes all the way to shut him out. He could do what he liked with her, but she wasn't going to watch the bullet come, if that's what he felt he needed to do. She wasn't a threat to him, and she didn't know what had scared him about her so much he needed his gun.

Then she felt him next to her, so close she could hear him breathe, and he touched her shoulder. She opened her eyes, telling herself not to be a coward, and looked into his face. Though his expression remained grim, he'd holstered his weapon. Another policeman stood behind him, which appeared to be making him feel safer.

Her poor horse lay unmoving on the ground six feet away. Even from here, there looked to be an awful lot of blood. It was a mess she was happy not to have to clean up, but unfortunately, it was a mess she was still going to have to explain.

The pain had filled her eyes with tears, but what she was feeling now wasn't fear or sadness so much as *anger*. She'd almost *died*—far from home, without Math or her boys, and with the threat of treachery still unresolved. "Did you really mean to kill the horse?"

"I acted appropriately," he said stiffly.

Anna had nothing to say to that, and whatever came next, she'd much rather meet on her feet, so she made a move to sit up.

"Stay where you are." The cop's voice was commanding. "An ambulance is on its way." Then he softened enough to peer at her. "Is it your arm?"

"My wrist, I think." Anna lay back down, though with reluctance.

There was no way she was going to fly under the radar now. Truthfully, that hope had died the moment she'd arrived in the hall. Under the principle that everything happened for a reason, as part of some grand plan she wasn't a party to, she had to assume the power that had saved her life yet again would continue to protect her. In her head that power was God, an acceptable concept back in the medieval world but a bit too TV evangelist to say out loud here. Regardless, whoever or whatever had brought her to Avalon wanted the full court press of police and medical services to scoop her up.

Which meant an anonymous entry would have been even worse. The thought had her shifting gears from concern that things were continuing to go badly awry to confidence that this disaster would result in something better. She began to look for a way out of her predicament, telling herself that, just like on the road from Heledd's house, an opportunity for escape would come if she could bide her time.

Then the door at the far end of the hall opened, and two more police officers entered, though they came to a halt ten feet away beside the second officer who was already present, gawking at the sight of the horse and Anna on the floor with their fellow officer hovering over her. One of the new arrivals appeared to be of higher rank, judging by the chevrons on his uniform, and he gestured to the other officers that they should quarter the room.

The original officer stood and saluted. "Sergeant."

"As you were, constable." The sergeant looked around. "Anyone else with her?"

"Not that I've seen," the first cop said.

"Nobody appears on the cameras either. But this—" the sergeant gestured helplessly to the horse, "—this is going to blow up in our faces if we don't keep a lid on it. I don't intend to become the laughing stock of the Met. You remember what happened to Daniels."

"Yes, sir."

Anna suddenly really wanted to know what had happened to Daniels, but the initial cop continued speaking: "What about the ambulance, sir? She's hurt."

"It's already outside. Any weapons on her?"

"Not now." He pointed to the other side of the horse where Anna had tossed her dagger. "She had that in a sheath."

The sergeant gestured to the younger cop to go get it, while he crouched three feet away from Anna. "How did you get in here?"

Anna felt awkward talking to him from the floor, but the first cop had told her to stay down, so she did. "It's a long story."

"It would have to be."

But then it didn't matter because the medics arrived, followed immediately by a half-dozen policemen in riot gear. "We've secured the perimeter, sir," one of them said to the sergeant.

He nodded. "I want a complete news shutdown. We're taking care of everything in-house. Is that clear? If the press gets wind of this before we've straightened it out, there will be hell to pay—not just from me!"

"Yes, sir!" The men in riot gear departed as quickly as they'd come. In Anna's opinion, the response was very fast for three in the morning, and she wondered what might have happened in the last fifteen months to warrant it. Christopher hadn't spoken of anything disastrous, but then, he'd been finishing his senior year in high school and might not have been paying close attention to what was happening in Britain. Admittedly, she'd arrived in Westminster Hall itself, behind locked gates and doors. The seat of Parliament was probably as heavily guarded as Buckingham Palace.

The sergeant moved out of the way to allow the medics to tend to her. Unfortunately, when they rolled her onto her back, one of them bumped Anna's arm, and she screamed as intense pain shot through her. Stars danced before her eyes, and while she didn't genuinely pass out, her uneven breathing prompted the medic to put a mask over her face to feed her oxygen.

Anna had been hoping for a way to avoid questions and to appear more helpless than she was in order to lull her captors into complacency, so she couldn't have asked for anything better. Nobody thinks a person wearing an oxygen mask can be a serious threat, and as soon as it settled on her face, the cops stopped trying to talk to her and started to behave in a much more business-like fashion. One of the medics stabilized her wrist in a splint, which she observed through eyes closed to mere slits. Then they loaded her onto a stretcher, wheeled her out of the hall, and lifted her into an ambulance parked inside Westminster's vast gates.

Once the ambulance doors closed, they transported her to a nearby hospital, located a stone's throw from Lambeth Palace and just across the river from Westminster. She allowed herself an inward grin of delight that it was the same hospital, if she was remembering correctly, that had ended up on the moon in Dr. Who. The night was unreal enough that if she'd ended up on the moon herself it would have seemed about par for the course.

She ended up in a little cubicle in the emergency room. The people around her transformed from cops to doctors and nurses, and an intern lowered a portable x-ray machine down from the ceiling to take a picture of her wrist right there in the bed. She hadn't known such a thing was possible.

With no policeman actually in her cubicle with her, she lifted off the oxygen mask and focused on the middle-aged man in a white coat who'd just pulled back her curtain. He wore a stethoscope around his neck and carried a computer tablet in his hand—a tablet like she'd seen Captain Picard use on Star Trek. Everyone here had one. David's hands would be itching to use one, but he'd probably be frustrated by them too, since he wouldn't know how to work one any more than Anna did.

The doctor put out his hand to shake. "Hello. I'm Doctor Jamison."

"Hi. I'm Anna."

The corner of the man's mouth quirked. "You're American."

She nodded.

Putting down his tablet, he washed his hands in the little sink next to the bed and pulled on a pair of medical gloves. "May I?"

She nodded again, and he examined her neck and head, which somewhere along the way had been stabilized in a brace. Maybe she genuinely had passed out at some point because she didn't remember anyone putting it on her.

"How do you feel?"

"My wrist hurts."

"The x-ray shows your wrist has a hairline fracture. In a moment, we're going to put a brace on it. How's the head?"

"It doesn't hurt."

"We're sending you up for an MRI just to be certain."

As Anna rested her head against the pillows, a nurse wiped at her left temple with a cloth in a gloved hand. The cloth came away with blood, so Anna put her own hand up to her head. "I don't remember hitting it." Probably that was the reason for the neck brace and for them to have found credible that she'd had trouble staying focused all this time.

Then a raincoated man stepped into the entrance to her cubicle. The doctor turned with a frown. "Who are you?"

He held up a badge. "Inspector Smithem, Scotland Yard. I need to ask her a few questions."

"Not right now." Doctor Jamison hastened towards him. "She's injured—" He moved the detective out of the way as someone in blue scrubs brushed past them carrying a plastic brace for Anna's wrist.

"I must question this woman."

"What's she charged with?" Doctor Jamison asked.

"Trespassing on government property."

The doctor snorted. "I will let you know when she's ready to be questioned. As I said, she is injured, and she needs an MRI before I'm going to allow anyone to talk to her."

Inspector Smithem was clearly frustrated by Dr. Jamison's dismissal. He tried to move into the cubicle, as if he intended to ignore the doctor's prohibition, but Dr. Jamison put a hand on his chest. The doctor was taller and burlier than the detective and seemed to grow larger as he filled the doorway. "I said no."

The detective gaped at him, seemingly shocked at being touched, and then he glared at Anna. Anna averted her eyes, recognizing that Dr. Jamison was something of an ally, and she would do well to continue to let him run interference for her. She preferred to look at her new brace, which was purple and warm, and she had no need to feign reluctance to answer the detective's questions.

Once the detective was backed out of the doorway, the medic explained to Anna how to adjust the brace and said she could take it off to shower if she wanted. It wasn't quite Star Trekian, but medical advances remained the best reason Anna could think of to return to Avalon. Of course, in this instance, she wouldn't have broken her wrist if she'd stayed at home.

Meanwhile, Dr. Jamison continued to refuse the detective's request to question Anna, and after a count of ten, Inspector Smithem gave a grunt of disgust. "Call me when she's ready or let the uniform on duty know."

He gave the doctor his card and then jerked his head at an officer standing outside the cubicle. She hadn't seen this cop before, and the number of people who knew about the manner of her arrival here appeared to be growing by the minute. It didn't look to Anna as if, despite the sergeant's wishes, what had happened in Westminster Hall was going to remain a secret for long.

Still, Anna was glad to see the detective leave and even more glad she wasn't handcuffed to the bed. She knew herself to be strong and capable. She'd married a medieval man, was raising two sons, and faced the everyday challenges associated with that world with a measure of equanimity. She'd *chosen* to stay there. But the manner of her arrival had thrown her off her game, and it was taking some time for her to get her bearings back.

It wasn't as if she, David, and Mom hadn't discussed their traveling many times. It was the three of them who were at risk for ending up alone in Avalon, which for all they'd been born there, wasn't home anymore. It was they who bore the brunt of the time travel quandary they found themselves in again and again.

They didn't know why they traveled, except that it happened to save their lives. And even then, it was about more than that: it was to save Wales first and foremost, but also to preserve the special world their arrival there had created. Lying here in this bed wasn't going to do that.

In some ways it would have been easier to face the detective if she really did time travel rather than shift between universes. None of the changes they'd made in the Middle Ages carried through to the modern day because they were dealing with two separate universes. As a result, she couldn't sit here and tell the good Inspector Smithem she was Princess Anna, one of the original time travelers, and hope to be believed. If she said anything at all about what she was really doing in Westminster Hall, she would end up in the psychiatric ward.

Anna might be a princess, but she wasn't a princess in a tower, waiting for Prince Charming to come rescue her. Nobody was coming, and she was going to have to do her own rescuing.

If David had been the one to come to Avalon under similar circumstances, perhaps he would have been able to talk himself out of captivity, though he hadn't managed it even with Callum at his side. Then her heart skipped a beat at the thought that David could be here too, if what that captain back on the road to Dinas Bran had said was true. He appeared to believe what he'd told her: David's life was in danger. And Mom's. Either one of them could be here even now and have no idea she was here too.

And that meant she had to get in touch with Mark. It was the reason he'd stayed behind after Caernarfon in the first place. But a great deal might have changed since then, and the moment she put in a call to the MI-5 switchboard, they were all going to be on the grid. She didn't want to do that to him if she could help it. Better to get out of here first and then make a more thorough assessment.

"Why don't you get yourself a coffee?" Dr. Jamison, who'd followed the detective out of Anna's line of sight, returned and spoke to the police officer left behind.

"I'm supposed to keep watch," he said stiffly.

"Only patients and staff are allowed in imaging. She'll be getting an MRI and won't be going anywhere on her own. Let us give her the medical attention she needs." Dr. Jamison smiled over at Anna.

Maybe he meant to be reassuring, but the cop gave Anna a startled look—even a frightened one. Anna blinked, wondering if in this world *medical attention* had become synonymous for something far more dastardly. The trend within governments and nations towards more authoritarianism and rule by fear had begun with 9/11, which Anna barely remembered. But by her experience so far, things hadn't improved in the years she'd been gone.

And why would they have? She herself had witnessed bombings both times she'd been in Avalon before today, and odds were, those weren't the only instances. In a way, she was lucky the instinct of the police officers back at Westminster Hall was to prevent the public from knowing about her. They could have called in an anti-terrorism unit, which might have hauled her off to MI-5 directly instead of the hospital. Then she would have been close to Mark, but he might not have been able to help her.

The cop continued to look dubious, but in the face of Dr. Jamison's evident authority, he gave way, though he did wait to leave until Anna and the orderly, who wheeled her stretcher to the elevator, were inside and the doors had closed.

Dr. Jamison had come as well, and he nodded at the orderly, a young woman approximately Anna's age wearing blue scrubs, similar to the man who'd set Anna's wrist. "Take care of her."

"I will, doctor."

Dr. Jamison departed one floor before Anna's. The orderly wheeled Anna around the corner and down a long, brightly lit hallway towards MRI imaging. But as they arrived at the doors, the woman frowned and came to a halt while still in the hall.

Anna craned her neck to look behind her. "What's wrong?"

"Dr. Jamison was told it was free." Still frowning, she pushed at one of the swinging doors, poked her head inside, and spoke to someone. Then she drew back to say to Anna, "I'll be just a tick." She disappeared into the imaging area, leaving Anna alone in the hallway.

It was the chance Anna had been waiting for, even if she felt bad about getting the orderly into trouble. Once she disappeared through the door, Anna swung her legs off the stretcher and headed at a quick walk for the stairwell.

She was inappropriately dressed to say the least, since she still wore the riding dress, boots, and cloak she'd had on when she'd arrived at Westminster. Because she had been attending a birth, she'd worn a work-day dress, which consisted of a long-sleeved brown underdress topped by a green overtunic belted at the waist, both in fine wool, as befitted her station as a princess. None of the police, doctors, or nurses had quite known what to make of what she was wearing, but they hadn't made her change out of it either just to address her broken wrist or sore head. They had cut off the tight sleeve on her left arm at the elbow, however, so her dress was looking a little strange, even to her.

No doubt she stuck out like a sore thumb, but as she passed a nurse hurrying in the opposite direction, she put up her hand in a little wave. The nurse glanced at Anna, her eyes going to her black sling and purple cast, and she smiled. She had no reason to think Anna wasn't where she was supposed to be, since in a hospital the cast was the next best thing to an ID. It helped that even though it had to be four in the morning by now, the nurses appeared to be run off their feet. Nobody had any interest in questioning someone who didn't cause trouble.

Anna made it to the stairwell door but decided, as she hesitated on the top step of the stairs, that walking straight out of the hospital might be a great way to get caught. If she'd had more time to think, she would have ducked into an office and acquired a doctor's white coat. In her haste to be out of sight by the time the orderly returned, she hadn't thought of it when she'd been on the floor.

Her next hope was to find a back way out through a side door or a basement parking garage. But she didn't know, with all the security, if the hospital even had a side door, and this close to the Thames, it might not have been possible to dig a basement either. She would just have to take her chances.

She ran down the stairs, making it two floors before a door below her banged open. She froze halfway down a flight of stairs, marshaling her courage to brazen out yet another encounter—or worse, figure out how to evade the cop who had to be coming up to meet her. But then Mark Jones trotted up the stairs towards her.

Anna had ducked behind a supporting column, so he hadn't noticed her at first, but when she realized it was he, she bent over the railing to speak to him. "Mark."

His head came up, and he gaped at her in a most satisfying way. "Anna!"

He hesitated, one foot a step higher than the other, and then he bounded up the remaining steps. He wasn't looking as fit as he'd been when she'd last seen him, indicating he'd gone back to his old habit of living at his desk. The lights in the hospital stairwell were yellow-white, which gave his skin something of an unhealthy pallor. His suit was rumpled, his tie was undone, and he had a scruffy beard and mustache that didn't suit him. But it was four in the morning, and Anna couldn't look much better.

Once he reached her, he actually went to hug her in a most un-English-like fashion, but at the sight of her cast, he arrested the movement. "Are you okay?"

"I have a broken wrist and maybe a broken head, though I didn't stick around long enough to find out. We need to go before the police discover I'm gone."

"Is it just you?" Mark spun on his heel and started down the stairs, his hand under Anna's right elbow to steady her. Since her left arm was in a sling, she had to hold her skirt in that same hand to keep from tripping on the hem on the way down.

"Yes." She paused. "Well me and a horse, though it's dead."

Mark shot her something of a wide-eyed look but only said, "I want to hear everything, but now isn't the time." He nodded towards the camera in the corner of the ceiling. "Once I knew you'd gone upstairs, I shut down surveillance in here, but the camera will reboot within five minutes. We have very little time."

Probably there were listening devices too, which hadn't occurred to Anna until now, and she found herself going over everything she'd said since she arrived, trying to remember if any of it was in any way incriminating. She would have thought doctor/patient confidentiality would have precluded surveillance at a hospital, but this was England in 2022, a place she didn't know anything about—a fact that was becoming more clear with every minute that passed.

"You should know I was arrested. There's an Inspector Smithem who wants to question me."

"I'm sure a whole flock of inspectors are going to want to question you, which is why we have to get you out of here. How did you get away?"

"I took the first chance I got."

"Well it was a good thing you did. I didn't have to flash my badge."

"How did you know where to find me?"

"We went to Westminster first, and I pretended to be a reporter. I have another badge for that." He grinned as they came out of the stairwell onto the main floor, which was precisely what Anna had felt she couldn't do alone.

They were near the emergency room, which was a hive of activity. Nothing could have been better for their purposes, and they walked purposefully for the exit, out the door, and turned left, heading down the sidewalk to a black SUV—the obligatory color and vehicle of MI-5. A young woman was waiting inside the car, and she got out as they approached.

Mark gestured to her. "This is Livia. She knows pretty much everything."

Livia lifted a hand in greeting. "Hello."

"Hi." Anna looked her up and down, instantly feeling frumpy and outmatched. Even having apparently not slept all night, Livia remained put together, with her blonde hair done up in an elegant chignon, a dark blue suit jacket and skirt, and heels. Anna's hair had come loose hours ago. She'd managed to pick out most of the hairpins between getting her brace and waiting to be wheeled up for the MRI, but she definitely felt disheveled in comparison.

Still, it was best to ignore what she couldn't change, since the only person whose opinion she really cared about was her husband's, and he wasn't here.

"Do you trust Livia?" Anna said in a low voice to Mark as he ushered her into the back seat of the car. She really needed his help now, since whatever painkillers the doctor had given her had started to kick in, and she was feeling woozy and disembodied. The upside was that her wrist hurt less.

"She discovered who I was—and who you are—on her own. I could shut her out, but what would be the point?"

Livia gestured to Mark. "The sooner we get moving, the sooner we can address the fact that you were here at all."

"That might not be so easy," Anna said.

Having shut Anna's door and gotten in the front passenger seat, Mark hesitated in the act of closing his own door, his expression questioning.

"Didn't you hear about it while you were pretending to be a reporter?" Anna felt a moment of hope that the sergeant's news blackout might actually have worked. "Remember that dead horse I mentioned? It was killed by a policeman in the middle of Westminster Hall."

6

19 March 1294

Math

Math wanted to thunder at Mair, but the poor girl's crime had merely been to ride with Anna tonight, so he reined in his temper, which was driven primarily by fear anyway. Mair had escaped the ambush, which was remarkable in and of itself, and she deserved to be commended, rather than condemned, for her quick thinking and action. Anna had ordered Mair to ride to him, and Mair had obeyed her mistress, which was absolutely the best thing she could have done.

"What was Anna doing when you saw her last, Mair?" Math said.

"She was riding away." Mair had been crying earlier, and now she wiped at the tears on her cheeks with the back of her hand.

"Anything you saw or remember could be of help." Bevyn spoke more gently than Math had ever heard him. "Think."

Cadi cowered, her eyes on Bevyn, whom she seemed to be more afraid of than Math, despite Bevyn's gentle voice. As most everyone, even Dafydd, cowered at times before Bevyn, Math couldn't blame her. It was just Bevyn's luck—good or bad, they would soon see—that he'd ridden to Dinas Bran to confer with Math for their first meeting since Christmas. On his way to Dinas Bran, Bevyn had also stopped at Aber Castle where Goronwy, King Llywelyn's oldest friend, resided. Goronwy didn't travel at all anymore—too much riding and fighting and sleeping on the ground in his youth. Math would feel himself blessed if such a fate one day became his.

Which it wouldn't if Math didn't find Anna and bring her home safely—since he would never rest until he found her.

"I don't know anything more. It all happened so fast. Because of the fog, they came upon us suddenly, and after that, all I could think of was escape."

Mair was twenty-five and one of Rachel's most promising students, needing to attend only two more births before she would be ready to deliver babies on her own, which was why she'd gone with Anna in the first place. Over the years, Anna herself had delivered or been party to the delivery of more than fifty babies, and between the advice of traditional midwives and schooling by Rachel and Rachel's father, Abraham, she'd learned everything that could be done to aid a newborn and his mother in this time.

Math put out a hand to the young woman. "It's all right. We're not blaming you." He shot a quelling look at Bevyn, whose mustache quivered for a moment, but then he looked down at his feet, freeing Mair from his glare.

"What were the men wearing? Was there anything remarkable or unusual about them at all?" Ieuan was the other person Math had woken after Hywel had come to him with the news that Mair had returned home without Anna. He hadn't even woken Bronwen and Lili. They would want to help and hated to be left out of any important discussion, but neither would be riding out of the castle to search for Anna or her abductors. They could sleep a little longer, since after Math woke them, there wouldn't be any more sleep for anyone for the rest of the night.

Hywel, however, was a different story. He was the stable boy who'd aided Anna and Heledd's escape from Castell y Bere that winter of 1283. In the years since, he'd risen to steward of Dinas Bran and was married with several children himself. Math had never before thought about the fact that both Heledd and Hywel, despite their lives' diverging paths, had stayed close to Anna, but tonight he drew comfort from it. She had many protectors, not just Math and Bevyn. God and all of Wales were also on her side. Nobody had yet speculated that she was dead, and Math refused to consider it. Those men had been sent to capture her, not kill her.

She was out there, somewhere. They just had to find her.

"Some of them were speaking with a thick accent, and others spoke in another language entirely that wasn't English or Welsh."

"Could they have been Irish?" Math asked.

Cadi lifted one shoulder in half-shrug. "I don't know any Irishmen, but now that I think about it, I've heard accents like those before. That ambassador, James Stewart, spoke the same way."

"Scots," Bevyn said gravely, his eyes going to Math, undoubtedly to see how he was taking this revelation. The answer was *not well.*

"But not all of them," Mair hastened to add. "Many were English."

Ieuan dismissed Mair with a gesture and a word of thanks and then began to pace before the fire. His head was down, and he was thinking as he walked. "As I see it, three things could have happened here."

Math glanced over at him. Despite his fear and anger, he found a spark of levity to say, "Only three?"

Ieuan gave him a wry look, but otherwise ignored the comment, instead ticking off the items on his fingers, like Dafydd might have done had he been here instead of in Ireland. "The first possibility is that Anna was, in fact, captured. It's the most likely option, Math, and you need to be prepared for it. According to Mair, all of the men you sent with her are dead, so she was completely on her own."

Math nodded, accepting Ieuan's words as truth. "If so, we will pursue them to the ends of the earth."

Ieuan gave Math a tight-lipped nod and continued, "Second, she escaped and will soon find her way back to us, but if so, she is alone in the middle of the night and might not know where she is."

Math pinched the bridge of his nose. "We must find her if she is here to be found. We also have a band of marauders, at least some of whom are Scottish, roaming the countryside. If they do have her, they won't be in Wales any longer. We have to find them before they get too far away and can't be tracked."

Bevyn grunted. "Whatever has happened, you have to believe Anna survived. She is brave, that girl."

Ieuan took in a breath. "Third, she has gone to Avalon." Having traveled there himself, Ieuan knew as well as Math the danger and the miracle involved. "I know you've already considered the possibility."

Math nodded, because he had thought of it, and had been trying *not* to think of it. It was both the worst and the best case scenario. They'd cultivated the legend that Avalon was a safe place, even a haven, but Math had been there and understood it for the threat it was. He would much rather find Anna amidst a company of men riding to a nearby castle, even if that castle was held by a rebel. He could help her then. He knew what to do then.

It was far more terrifying to think about her entirely on her own in that strange world, with its enormous machines, its powerful weapons, and its complete disregard for the souls of men. He was glad both Dafydd and Meg remained in Ireland. Mair might have feared telling him Anna was gone or taken captive, but that had nothing on what Dafydd's response would be if he returned before Math got her back.

"I can't say which is more terrifying," Math said. "That she did go or that she didn't."

"She may have thought it was the only course available to her." Bevyn helped himself to a cup of mead and a slice of warm bread Hywel had brought from the kitchen. Between bites, he added, "The danger to Anna aside—" here he made a gesture with the cup, "—not that I'm putting it aside, but what I want to say is I don't understand the move these men have made. Why Anna?"

"It must be for leverage," Ieuan said. "She is the king's sister."

Math gave a disgusted grunt, again acknowledging the truth of Ieuan's words. "Lili and the boys are too well protected." He looked away. "I should have protected Anna better."

"Maybe you should have." Bevyn put a hand on Math's shoulder. "But what's happened to Anna is not your fault. The blame lies entirely on the one who ordered this, whoever he may be."

Ieuan was still thinking out loud. "Only a madman would seek an all-out war with Dafydd or Llywelyn, and whoever has done this has brought that upon himself. How can that be his intent?"

Math had no answer. In the aftermath of Gilbert de Clare's treachery last year, the what-ifs and if-onlys had gnawed at Dafydd. But the truth was Gilbert de Clare had always cared most for his own advancement; he had fooled them all into thinking he'd settled for being a high ranking baron—if not the highest ranking baron—in Dafydd's kingdom, when all the while he'd intended to reach for the throne.

A knock came at the door, and Hywel poked in his head. "The men are marshalling in the courtyard, my lords."

Math moved immediately for the door, but Hywel put up a hand to stop him before he reached him. "Pardon me, my lords, I spoke with Mair, and she told me Scots are involved."

"May be involved," Ieuan amended.

Hywel made a noncommittal motion with his head. "If I may be so bold to suggest such a thing, we were here fifteen months ago. We know already who these men are. We need to look only as far as Fulk FitzWarin at Whittington Castle on one hand and Red Comyn on the other to find her."

"I appreciate what you're saying, Hywel," Math said, "but we can't assume just because Scots rode among the company that they were from Whittington or would have returned there."

"Fulk FitzWarin allowed himself to be used before," Ieuan said, "but he is not so much of a fool as to involve himself a second time in a plot against Dafydd when he knows his castle would be the first place we'd look."

Hywel's expression remained skeptical. "Perhaps Lady Cassie could send someone from Shrewsbury to take a look."

For the first time since Mair had returned to Dinas Bran, Math allowed himself a full breath. Here was something concrete to arrange and he nodded. "I will ask her."

Then Hywel continued. "May I also suggest we send word immediately to Sir Cadwallon? He was among the searchers for James Stewart last time and knows this area as well as any man. More so now, actually, than before."

Cadwallon had been among the youngest soldiers in Dafydd's retinue when he'd become the Prince of Wales. Subsequently, he had nearly died at the hands of Humphrey de Bohun but had eventually recovered, to be named captain of King Llywelyn's guard. He'd been left behind from the Ireland trip, not because he'd lost his lord's confidence but because his wife was due to give birth to their first child at any moment.

In the old Wales, a father's presence at his child's birth would have been something of little importance, but in the new Wales, where warfare was no longer a way of life, there were enough men Llywelyn trusted that he could leave this one behind. Besides, Dafydd had ordered that each lord bring only twenty men to Ireland, which meant they had capable men to spare.

Thus, Cadwallon was staying just on the other side of the border with England in Overton, a town guarding one of the few bridges across the Dee and one with a forest of yew trees renowned throughout Wales. Back when Wales and England had been perpetually at war, the town had sat at a vital and precarious position on the border. Though Cadwallon had been somewhat taken aback when Llywelyn had told him to stay behind, he'd accepted his fate. Dafydd had shown foresight in not taking every man of worth with him to Avalon fifteen months ago—and as usual he'd been right.

In the current crisis, Cadwallon's presence on the border was a godsend. Although being present at the birth of his children was one of the greatest honors of Math's life, immediately upon the arrival of the child, a father was surplus to requirements. Whatever misadventure Math had facing him, no matter how dangerous, Cadwallon would want to assist. It helped that he'd married an English girl and spoke the language as well as any of them.

So Math nodded. "We have enough men within ten miles of Dinas Bran to throw out a wide net."

"Give me any of your men who speak English and French, Math. I will ride northeast with them, collecting Cadwallon on the way." Ieuan himself was fluent in those languages, having been a close adviser to Dafydd since long before he'd become king. The bond had only become closer since Dafydd's marriage to Lili, Ieuan's sister.

"If you do that, Bevyn and I will ride southwest and retrace Anna's steps, after which I will know if I have to ride farther afield." Math grimaced. "I wish I had more information."

Ieuan gave a tsk. "We will make do with what we have."

"As we do." Math was glad Ieuan hadn't tried to persuade him to stay behind. If Anna did return, he wouldn't know, but there was no possible way Math was going back to bed, and what he needed more than anything else right now was to move.

"I'm not such a fool as to tell you everything's going to be okay," Ieuan said as they left Math's office together, "but I truly believe it will be."

"Even if a band of Scotsmen have her, they won't harm her," Bevyn said from just behind them.

Math took comfort in his companions' certainty. He wanted with every part of his being to believe their words, but he was careening wildly between optimism and utter despair. Few ballads except those written about Dafydd ended well, and it was in every Welshman's soul to assume the worst—because up until very recently, the worst always came, usually at the end of a Saxon sword. Math clenched his hands into fists. *But not tonight. By God, not tonight.*

It wouldn't be light for another hour, but the night was typical for March, cool and wet, though not raining. The damp seeped into everything, however, and Math took his leather jacket and double-thick wool cloak from the hooks in the anteroom. His gear was nearly as waterproof as the modern jackets they'd acquired at Abraham's house in Avalon.

And again, as he thought of those few days, Math's stomach clenched. Anna was a woman of his world now, and though she wouldn't be as lost as he would have been, she was still entirely on her own.

Then, as Math prepared to mount his horse, Lili and Bronwen appeared on the top step to the keep, wrapped in blankets with their long night braids trailing down one shoulder. Even though they were still in their nightdresses, they both wore boots. They had their arms wrapped around each other too, which told him they already knew the bad news. He tossed his horse's reins to a stable boy and walked over to them. "I apologize for not waking you myself."

"Why didn't you?" Lili said.

"I couldn't bear to."

Math's words revealed the full extent of his pain, and Lili heard it. "I'm so sorry, Math. Something like this happening to me or the boys is Dafydd's worst nightmare, just as his disappearances are mine."

Bronwen put out a hand to him too. "We are here for you, whatever you need."

"Keep an ear out for Cadell and Bran?" Math had always admired Bronwen's approach to everything, which was straightforward and no nonsense.

"Of course. Don't worry about anything to do with them. Where's Hywel?"

"He's waking the kitchen staff. We're going to have people to feed."

"We'll be waiting when you return, come what may," Lili said. "I can send word to Holyhead, to see if the radio is up and running in Dublin yet."

Math took in a breath. The pair of them were far more experienced with crises than he'd like them to be. Meg had left her twins here while she went to Ireland because she trusted nobody more. If decisions had to be made, Lili and Bronwen would make them, and they would be the right ones.

"Hywel said you spoke to Cassie," Bronwen said. "Who else?"

"Edmund Mortimer. If you could listen for any further messages on the radio, I'd be grateful. Anyone who calls knows to trust your voice."

Once Edmund's stewards had woken him and sleep had cleared from his mind, he'd promised to prepare his forces for a possible move north. His seat of Montgomery lay thirty miles to the south of Llangollen, and Math had asked him to relay what had transpired to Humphrey de Bohun at Hereford, thirty miles beyond that. Edmund had been cold to the suggestion, confirming the rumor Math had heard of the falling out between the former close friends. He'd mentioned his concerns to Dafydd, who'd dismissed the news out of hand as Bohun's midlife crisis. As Dafydd had spoken, however, Math had seen a shadow in his eyes, but other topics had been more pressing, and they'd never returned to the issue.

Neither Mortimer nor Bohun had ever been to Avalon, but its existence was common knowledge throughout Britain now, and Edmund had taken the news that Anna may have ended up there with equanimity. Math could have told him just about the possible abduction, but he wanted Edmund to be prepared if Anna returned unexpectedly. Last time it had been Christopher arriving in a car in the middle of Westminster Palace's courtyard. Before that, Math himself had returned with everyone on the Cardiff bus. It was best, if such a thing was going to happen again, to make sure his allies were aware of the possibilities.

Avalon itself had been spoken of with awe and wonder long before Dafydd's arrival in Wales, since stories of King Arthur were common throughout Christendom. Dafydd had hardly spent six months in Math's world before whispers that he was King Arthur returned had begun to follow him around. There was no denying it now, and to Dafydd's credit, he no longer tried.

Bronwen put her hand on Math's arm. "Anna is smart and capable. Wherever she is, she will keep her head and do her best to get back to you and the boys."

"I know." He took in a breath. "I have to believe that."

Math moved to mount his horse, and Ieuan took his place in order to kiss his wife goodbye. Then the door to the keep opened, and a woman dressed like a warrior came out.

Lili said to her brother, "Take Constance with you. You never know when having a woman along might come in handy."

Ieuan gave her a hard look, but Lili persisted. "Be thankful I'm not asking to go myself!"

Constance was a newcomer to Dafydd's inner circle, one of many since the devastation among the king's ranks caused by Gilbert de Clare's treachery. She had won the archery contest in the King's Tournament last summer at Windsor Castle, and Dafydd had decided she would be the first woman to officially join his army. Bevyn had been the most outspoken of Dafydd's advisers in his opposition to including women alongside fighting men—and with only slight provocation would enumerate a list of reasons why it was a bad idea.

Dafydd had gone ahead anyway. It helped that Constance wasn't a maiden, as she was already married to one of Dafydd's men-at-arms, a Welshman named Cador. And since Constance was an Englishwoman, that made the pair a mixed marriage, which was another vote in her favor in Dafydd's eyes.

What's more, Constance's behavior suited her name. She was faithful, and reliable, and Math had seen her shoot. Even Morgan, the captain of Dafydd's archers, had grudgingly admitted Constance would be an asset, provided the men she rode with could get over the fact that a woman was a better shot than they were.

Thinking about the composition of his men was better than thinking about Anna, and in the bustle to get on the road, Math had been focusing exclusively on what needed to be done and what lay immediately before him. Math had a teulu of twenty men-at-arms of his own to call upon from Dinas Bran, and Ieuan had ridden with an equal number, many of whom were, in fact, English because they were men of Dafydd's personal guard, whom he had not taken with him to Ireland.

Ieuan would ride east, leaving Bevyn, whom all of the soldiers knew, if only by reputation, to support Math. Over the years Bevyn had acquired an almost mythical status among soldiers in both England and Wales. Math himself had been at Dafydd's side in those early days at Castell y Bere, as well as after. Though Dafydd had never told him—or anyone, as far as he knew—what had precipitated the falling out between Bevyn and Dafydd at the start of Dafydd's reign, the two men had mended the rift, and Bevyn was once again a much trusted companion.

Then, in the last few moments before everyone was sorted, Cadell came barreling out the door from the keep. "Dad!"

Math swung around at the sound of his elder son's voice and was on the ground and moving to intercept him before he had come more than a few feet from the steps. He crouched and caught his son. "It's okay, Cadell."

"I heard-I heard you talking." He was breathing in big gulps. "Mom's been take-taken. That's what the servants are saying!"

Math clutched his son to him, trying to calm his own breathing in hopes of soothing his son's. "They are right that she didn't come home last night. Her company was attacked on the road." He leaned back to look into Cadell's face. "I won't pretty it up for you. It's bad, but maybe not as bad as all that."

"Wh-why?"

"Cadi got away, and it may be your mother did too." He cleared his throat. "Maybe even to Avalon. You know how she is."

Cadell took in a shuddering breath and managed a nod.

"I am leaving now to find her if she's here to be found. I need you to stay with your aunts and look after your brother and your cousins."

"Are we going to be attacked here?"

"The company comprised twenty men, more than enough to overcome the guard I sent with your mother, but not enough to hurt us here, and we have watchers on the walls and all around Llangollen. We'd know if an army was approaching."

"But they didn't see these men."

Math pressed his lips together. Cadell wasn't wrong. "We'll sort out the reason for that later. Son—" he had his hands at Cadell's waist, "—you need to be strong now, like your mother is strong."

Cadell's hands clenched into fists, and Math was glad to see it. Anger would carry him for a little while, long enough for Lili or Bronwen to get him fed and find a means to distract him. Bronwen approached from behind Cadell and put a hand on his shoulder. "Your dad has to go now."

Math hugged Cadell again. "I'll be fine. You know that, right?"

Cadell nodded as Math released him, though both were blinking back tears.

"After breakfast, I want you to take a tour of the defenses with the garrison captain. I'll tell him to expect you."

Finally, Cadell managed a deep breath, and when he let it out, it wasn't trembling. "Yes, Dad."

Math nodded and stood. His eyes met Bronwen's as she took Cadell's hand. "Go," she said. "We're okay here."

"I know it."

But as the company descended the road down from the castle to the village below, Math couldn't shake the memory of his son's face—despairing and determined at the same time. He was too young to look that way.

Bevyn had watched the whole scene, of course, and he put out a hand to Math. "Your son is going to grow up more than you like today; he will learn, as we all have had to, how to be brave. He has a good head on his shoulders."

"He and Anna were abducted when Cadell was only three. He was too young then to know to be truly afraid. He knows it now."

"He has his family to get him through it," Ieuan said from the other side. "He isn't alone."

Math found a Bevyn-like growl forming in his chest. "Anna is."

And then they were in Llangollen. While Math got a handle on his anger, Ieuan woke the mayor, who instantly sounded the alarm to rouse the rest of the town. Within fifteen minutes, Math's company swelled to nearly a hundred strong.

Llangollen was closer to a small city these days than the sleepy village it had been ten years earlier when Math and Anna had arrived to rebuild the castle. With the adjacent university, the town stretched along the River Dee and held the status of a Welsh market town. Like its English counterparts, it had the right to govern itself, though that wasn't to say that Math, as the ruler of eastern Gwynedd, didn't have sway, and Llywelyn remained king.

"I'm off, then." Ieuan had already delineated the ten men (and Constance) he would take with him to immediately ride east on a quest to pick up the trail of Anna's abductors. Only a few roads in and out of Wales were capable of accommodating the large company Mair described, particularly one needing to move fast. By contrast, Ieuan was keeping his numbers small. His intent was to track the interlopers, not to start a war. Not yet anyway. "If the Scots took Anna east, I will discover where they've hidden her."

Bevyn lifted a hand. "Godspeed."

Math would have said the same, but his throat closed over the words.

Perceptive as always, Bevyn didn't press him and set about organizing their volunteers, dividing them into small groups, the members of which could spread out around Llangollen. Many would ride the less well trodden paths, and some would run farther afield. If a few more enemy men skulked in the hills around them or, God forbid, an army, Math needed to know of it. He didn't expect some of the searchers to come back for several days. He even sent six men towards Scotland. It was a long way, but Math needed to know if more men had crossed Hadrian's Wall.

If the Scots were clever—and since they'd come this far without being detected, Math was disinclined to underestimate them—this operation was well-planned. It pissed Math off (to use words bequeathed to him by the twenty-firsters) to have been caught on the hop, and he took shelter within the anger. Rage was better than fear—and far better than the cold pit of despair that twisted his belly and closed his throat whenever he allowed himself to imagine what might have become of his wife.

He had let her down, but by God, he would get her back, even if he had to voyage to Avalon himself to do so.

7

19 March 2022

Anna

Mark sucked on his upper teeth. "One problem at a time. Let's get you safe before we worry about a dead horse." Then he laughed. "I can't believe I actually said that."

His laughter was good to hear. At this point, it was either laugh or cry.

"If I told the detective who I really was, what would he have done?"

Livia, who was driving, pulled off the curb and out into the road. She was sitting on the right side of the car and driving on the left side of the road, which Anna had known to expect, but as always, it was taking a bit of getting used to.

"After he finished laughing and deciding you were mad, you mean?" Mark said. "It would have been one way to get the attention of Five without you asking for me outright, I'll give you that. But you know the Time Travel Initiative has been dead since before we saw you last?"

"I know," Anna said. "I was hoping with what happened at Caernarfon, things had improved."

"They have not, *especially* with what happened at Caernarfon." From the front passenger seat, Mark looked over his shoulder, not at Anna, but beyond her to the back window. She presumed it was to make sure they weren't being followed.

Anna found herself unable to care. If she was being followed, there was nothing she herself could do about it, so there was no point in worrying. She relaxed against the back seat, cradling her wrist to her chest. Then she realized she wasn't buckled in, and belatedly reached for the seat belt and tried to buckle it one-handed. Seeing her difficulties, Mark reached back an arm in an attempt to help her. "I'm really sorry it happened this way this time. Nobody has ever been injured on the journey before, have they?'

"In the past, any problem we've had we've brought with us." She gave him a rueful smile. "I suppose this arrival was comparable to last time when we ended up going down a road in Wales the wrong way."

"Mmm. Maybe a little worse."

As Mark adjusted her seatbelt, Anna eyed him. This was a different man from the one they'd left behind—older and more cynical.

Once buckled, he looked her directly in the eye. "Do you need painkillers?"

"I'm feeling pretty loopy as it is, but sadly, the ache is back and cutting through everything."

"Probably they gave you opiates, though they're supposed to be cutting back on them." Livia glanced at Anna through the rearview mirror. "Those pills can do that." They were moving smoothly through traffic, which was remarkably busy for so early in the morning. The big SUV dwarfed the cars around it, but nonetheless found spaces between them Anna wouldn't have attempted to navigate. She looked away, out the window, because her right foot had been pressing on the seat in front of her, repeatedly searching for a nonexistent brake.

"I wouldn't know," Anna said. "I don't know that I've ever taken painkillers other than Advil, and that was years ago. Alcohol is the only painkiller we have, and I can't say it's a good one."

Livia shot Mark a speaking look, which Anna took to be saying, *can you believe she's really been living in the Middle Ages?*

"Everyone's an alcoholic there anyway." Mark turned back to face front. "I think you could make the argument that very little has changed in seven hundred and twenty-eight years."

Anna laughed, as she was meant to, though the sardonic look Mark sent her indicated he both meant to be funny and had been perfectly serious at the same time. Then he pulled out a device with a large rectangular screen. It was too small for a tablet but far larger than any cell phone Anna had ever seen. Soon he was hunched over it, tapping rapidly on the screen. It was his usual position, and his desire to return to it had been one of the main reasons he hadn't stayed in the Middle Ages. Since Anna had arrived in Avalon, she'd seen dozens of devices like his of varying sizes, and she finally leaned forward to ask, "What is that, exactly?"

Mark glanced back at her. "It's a mobile phone. A smartphone. I know you've used them before."

"I suppose." Anna wet her lips and sat back, feeling like an idiot. She knew phones, but none like that one. At the Wal-Mart in Oregon three years ago, Callum had bought a touchscreen phone for her. It had been an impressive upgrade from the flip phone she'd owned at seventeen, and she hadn't seen a single one of those so far. Maybe they didn't exist anymore in favor of these massive things that were longer than the length of her hand.

Still looking at his phone, Mark said, "We're going to get you safe, Anna. After the bridge we want Kensington High Street."

Anna blinked in confusion before she realized Mark was giving directions to Livia, who replied, "If you tell me where we're going, I can set the program."

"Better not use the automatic pilot," Mark said. "Not today."

Livia gave a quick nod. "Of course."

It took a second for Anna to realize they were talking about the car. "It drives itself?"

"It can," Mark said.

Anna almost didn't know what to make of that. She had arrived with a clear list of specific items to acquire—a list that had been created months ago—but the fact that cars drove themselves made it clear to her how many things about this world she no longer understood. Rather than giving Mark the list her family had come up with, she might do better by telling him what they were looking to accomplish and letting him tell her what he could acquire to do the job.

Mark turned to look back at her. "You and I both know that you came here for a reason. Do you know what it is?"

Anna groaned inwardly. What he was asking was what she'd been thinking herself before the medics arrived. "I haven't a clue, except we know it can't be about *me*. As always, it has to have something to do with David."

"Agreed," Mark said, though his casual dismissal of Anna's importance raised her hackles for no reason, since she'd been the one to state it in the first place. "And why did you come to London? Why not Pennsylvania? Or Cardiff?"

Anna looked down at her sling, in which her broken wrist rested. "I don't know that yet either. I figured it was because you're here."

"Yeah, okay." Mark pursed his lips. "I don't know if I'm pleased to be so important or terrified. Both, probably." He let out a burst of air. "But it isn't just me who's here. Your aunt and uncle and Elen are too."

Of all the surprises since she'd arrived, and pretty much everything around her had been a constant surprise, that news topped them all. "Here? In London? How do you know?"

"Because we've worked together since Christopher left. How is he, by the way?"

Anna hesitated. "Last I knew, he was good, but he went to Ireland with David." As succinctly as possible, she told him about being chased by a company of soldiers, some of whom were Scottish, concluding, "And the captain of the men who tried to abduct me believed them all to be dead."

Mark stared at her. All the same things that had gone through her head had to be going through his. He finally said, "What do you think?"

"Of course he isn't dead."

Mark let out a breath. "That's what I feel too."

"Could he be here?"

"No. Nobody but you came through. I would know."

Anna heaved a sigh and relaxed—and then she laughed, realizing what good news that was: she was here alone, which meant David's life and their mom's life hadn't been in so much danger in Ireland that they'd traveled; she'd found Mark within two hours of her arrival; and while MI-5 was chasing her, what else was new? It wouldn't have been the same adventure without them.

"I have to tell you I'm torn between what I need to do here and what awaits me at home. While Math's men are well-trained, and he would never be complacent about my disappearance, he might not even realize yet that I'm gone.

"Even more, if Mair didn't make it safely to Dinas Bran, he won't have any information about who made the attempt on my life. David doesn't know about the treachery in England, and Math doesn't know about what's going on in Ireland. The longer I stay here, the worse it could be getting in both places. I'm the only one who has any inkling of what they're up against, and I'm stuck in Avalon."

"I'm afraid you'll have to be stuck for a while longer." Mark's lips twitched. "I'm glad to see you, Anna." Then he laughed as well, as if he were completely unfazed by what was happening.

"I'm glad to see you too." Anna put a hand to her forehead. The bandage on her left temple itched a bit. Before they'd left the hospital, she should have asked how long she was supposed to leave it on, or if she could just remove it.

Meanwhile, Mark went back to his phone as if he couldn't stay away from it. He could still talk, though. "So what's up with the Scots? Why are they rebelling now?"

"David has never trusted John Balliol and would much rather have had Grampa Bruce on the throne of Scotland. Things have been a bit more tense all the way around since Gilbert de Clare turned traitor last year—"

She stopped as Mark jerked his head around, a horrified expression on his face.

"He did what?"

"Obviously, that's a long story too. Christopher killed him with his car when he came in." The rest of the story tumbled out of her. "That was at Westminster, now that I think about it."

While Anna and Mark had been talking, Livia had kept driving, though her eyes flicked every so often to look through the rearview mirror—and while she had to be checking for cars following them, she was also looking at Anna.

But now Livia's chin came up as she looked in the mirror again. "Could that be significant?"

"I have no idea. We were together at Dinas Bran this morning, not Westminster." Anna found her throat closing and fought for control. She needed to keep it together. Up until now, she'd kept her anxiety about what was happening back at Dinas Bran or in Ireland at bay by focusing on what was directly in front of her, but she didn't know how much longer she could juggle all these little bits of worry without falling apart. "Math is going to have no idea what has happened to me."

"He'll have a pretty good idea, once you don't return straight away," Mark said matter-of-factly. "You don't die. You time travel."

"But I've been captured before. Last time it was because someone wanted something from me."

"Roger Mortimer, wasn't it?" Mark said.

She nodded. "I assume *he* at least would have learned his lesson." She paused. "Mark, where are you taking me? Where is safe?"

"Callum has a flat here in London, did you know?"

"He mentioned it, sure," Anna said. "We never went there."

"Well, we're going there now." Mark put away his phone. "His financial adviser is very good. You might mention that fact to him when next you see him. Even if anything were to happen to me or his adviser, the succession plan is in place and the accounts will continue to accrue."

"I—I'll tell him." A bit flummoxed, Anna sat back in her seat and stared out the window as the city flashed past. Then she closed her eyes, feeling dizzy from the lights and too many things to look at moving too quickly. It should have been Christopher who was here, so he could see his parents again. Or Cassie.

The tears she'd so far refused to shed were pressing on her eyes, and several managed to escape and roll down her cheeks. She wiped them away with her good hand, uncaring if Mark or Livia saw. She was never more vulnerable than when she came to Avalon, though you would think it would be the other way around.

And while she appreciated Mark's assistance—more than she could say, really—he wasn't Callum. He wasn't David. Here in 2022 London, she was exposed and out of her depth in a way she didn't remember being before, even when she and her mother fell from the tower at Rhuddlan three years ago. They'd made a good team, and it had been comforting to know that whatever they had to do to get back to the medieval world, they would do together.

But Anna was nobody here, ghostlike almost. In such an interconnected world, her lack of connectedness meant she didn't exist. She had no papers, no money, no standing whatsoever, and even if Mark was hoping to protect her, Anna herself needed to accept the fact that at some point on this trip she was going to be sitting before a panel of hostile men defending her existence. She'd seen it every time she'd come here, and heard about it from David whenever he came here without her. Somewhere in the basement of MI-5 was a cell with her name on it.

When the time came, she would be facing that alone. Mark might go to bat for her, he might even put his life on the line for her, but MI-5 didn't let you share the room with anyone. For the first time, it occurred to her that maybe it was a good thing she was here instead of David.

The thought woke her up a bit—and shook her up a bit because it wasn't like her to wallow in self-pity or denigrate herself, even to herself. She'd been thrown off her stride by the suddenness of the transition from one universe to the next, but she was no longer the seventeen-year-old girl who'd had trouble reading a map and driven her aunt's minivan into medieval Wales. While on the whole she'd prefer not to be by herself, right now she was responsible only for herself.

And as a result, what happened next was up to her.

8

19 March 2022

Mark

Finding Anna here alone had Mark's head spinning, a fact he was trying to cover up by getting them to Callum's safe house with as little fuss as possible. He was regretting including Livia, not for his sake so much as her own. But given Livia's foraging among the files and the fact she appeared to know most everything about Anna and her family—and him—already, it seemed pointless to shut her out. That wasn't to say, however, that he didn't have some serious reservations about exposing Callum's safeguards to her. Once he led her to Callum's flat, Livia was in the inner circle, full stop.

Unfortunately, as had become clear to him months ago, he was at a significant disadvantage in trying to manage everything on his own. His lack of allies was the reason he'd been forced to ask his friend in the FBI for help nine months ago when Arthur and Gwenllian had arrived in Pennsylvania, a request that had almost killed his friend. With Tate gone as well, Mark had nobody to trust. Nobody at all.

Not even Livia, though that was less because he thought she was spying on him than because the truth about what was really going on could put her in even more danger. Mark had lied to Anna when he'd told her the Time Travel Initiative was dead. It wasn't. It had gone to ground. He'd uncovered that much in the nine months since he'd changed his name and transferred to London. Mark had been petrified when Livia had mentioned the Initiative—not because it might expose Mark, but because it might expose *her*.

Since Tate had transferred him from Cardiff immediately afterwards, Mark had never learned exactly what had transpired in Pennsylvania, only that it had been government sanctioned but outside the purview of the FBI. That meant CIA involvement. It confirmed Mark's suspicion that not only had remnants of the Time Travel Initiative survived at the CIA, but they'd thrived. Livia so far had been calm and steadfast, but she didn't know the Americans like Mark did. If the CIA had again reached out to Five, then men in dark suits driving black SUVs wouldn't be far behind.

Livia pulled over. It was still early in the morning, so there was plenty of parking on the street near Kensington Palace. "We're close, aren't we?"

"Somewhat." In fact, they were closer to Callum's flat than Mark should have allowed her to drive, but he was torn between his concern about the GPS in the vehicle tracking their movements and his fear of being out on the street for more than a minute or two on foot. "Why did you stop?"

"Anna and you should get out here." She put the vehicle in park and twisted in her seat to look at him. "You shouldn't tell me anything more, and you certainly shouldn't show me where you're staying. Not unless it becomes absolutely necessary."

Mark studied her. "Don't you want to know?"

"Of course I want to know! But Callum doesn't know me, and now we're in his territory. You can't expose him to anyone whom he hasn't specifically designated. Not even me. Not unless you have no other choice." She shrugged. "Besides, the coming day may rain hellfire down on both of us, and the less I know about what you're doing and where you've gone, the better."

"So you can say you were only obeying orders?" Anna leaned forward from the backseat. Mark was pleased to see that her chin was up again, and she seemed to have acquired a second wind.

Livia looked at her. "So I can protect you. I can't reveal what I don't know." She canted her head. "And yes, to protect me too. Gabe—" she cleared her throat, "—Mark is my boss. If he asks me to drive him to the hospital to pick someone up, who am I to argue?"

Mark gave a low laugh. "Sell me out. Absolutely sell me out. It helps that tonight was the first conversation we've had about any of this, and you've never met Anna before. You obeyed your orders. Good." He nodded. "Unfortunately, it's a Monday, which means everybody is going to be on top of this." Impressed and pleased with Livia's reasoning, Mark reached into his knapsack and pulled out a mobile phone. It was one of a dozen burner mobiles he carried in his go bag, because he never knew how many he'd need at any one time or to whom he might be giving them. "From now on, unless we're on official business, ring me only on this. My burner mobile number is programmed into it."

Livia took the phone. "How much good is this going to do now that every burner phone bought has to be reported to the authorities?"

"These were bought before the law was passed," Mark said. "Thank you for your help. You're thinking more clearly than I am. I do trust you, or I wouldn't have had you come with me to meet Anna. You're right, however. I need you back at Thames House with plausible deniability." He opened his door.

Livia slipped the phone into her purse. "Where should I tell them you've gone?" She shot a grin at Anna. "That dead horse isn't going away any time soon."

"The GPS in the vehicle will tell them you dropped us here, in Kensington. That's all they'll know, and hopefully they will think I'm more clever than I am, and I had you drop me here because my destination is nowhere close."

Livia eyed him as he got out of the SUV. "Good luck, boss."

Mark's expression cleared. "You too. Thank you, Livia. You're a godsend."

She laughed. "We'll see if you're thanking me by the end of the day."

"What will they do to you?" Anna said.

"They'll question me, maybe for hours, but I have nothing to tell them, and regardless of what you might see in the cinema, we don't torture people. On second thought—" She reached into her bag, took out the phone, and handed it back to Mark, who still stood in the doorway of the SUV. "I don't want them to find a second phone on me or in my desk. What's the number of your new mobile?"

Mark rattled off the number, which Livia appeared to memorize instantly.

"I'll contact you. Don't worry—if and when I do, it will be clean. I know how this works." She looked at Anna. "If I don't see you again, it was an honor to meet you. Good luck."

Anna looked confused, or maybe that was the drugs making her cross-eyed, so Mark took another moment to explain while he opened the back door to let her out, "MI-5 tracks every ping off every cell tower in Britain. If any unregistered phone is being used within MI-5, it will eventually be noted. Once her new number appears in the record, all the calls on it can be traced, and it will link back to mine."

"But then won't any phone she uses be linked to yours?" Anna said.

"Yes, if I used a phone," Livia said.

Anna blinked, clearly not understanding, but they needed to move now, and he had no more time to explain. "Surveillance is fine until you want to do something which the authorities would not approve of." Mark took Anna's arm and moved her onto the sidewalk. Then he leaned in the window to speak to Livia. "Thanks again."

As Livia drove away, for a second he and Anna simply stood on the sidewalk and looked at each other. Then Mark put a hand on Anna's good shoulder, like Callum used to do when he wanted to be supportive. One of the hallmarks of the Middle Ages was the way a single person could effect change. David, a fourteen-year-old American kid, had transformed an entire country. Admittedly, he was the son of the Prince of Wales, and events had time and again conspired to put him in the right place at the right time, but each time he'd done what needed doing. David was so damn righteous, as Callum had said more than once, but he was also the man everybody's money was on. For good reason.

Because she was a woman and not Llywelyn's natural daughter (though by now everybody assumed she was anyway), Anna hadn't transformed the political landscape in the same way as David, but the impact of her presence was no less abiding and deep. At the very least, from the start she'd provided David with the grounding he needed, and given voice to her opinions without regard to his elevated station.

It had been she, as well, who'd pulled Gwenllian out of Castell y Bere in a no less noble or heroic act than what David himself had undertaken. And it was she who was responsible for bringing Edmund Mortimer into David's fold. She was an American woman misplaced in time, and by her example, women in the Middle Ages had opportunities that history wouldn't have afforded them for hundreds of years.

As they started down the sidewalk, he could tell Anna was favoring her wrist more and more. "I'm worried I took you out of the hospital when you still needed to be in it."

"We had no choice." There was definite hollowness to her voice. "I admit I don't feel great."

"None of us have slept, and you've just time traveled from medieval Wales. Don't worry about anything right now. It will all look better after a nap."

Anna shot him a skeptical look. "You know better than that. Bruises are always worse the second day."

"It's going to be okay. We'll be there in just a tick, and you can rest."

Anna's morose expression didn't change. "I would never have intended for you to be hung out to dry. That wasn't what Callum meant to happen when we left you here."

"That may not be what he wanted, but it's what we've got."

"Can you tell me what happened to Jon, Christopher's friend? Christopher has been worried."

"*That* was a mess, though not one solved by me. Director Tate intervened with the FBI." Mark paused. "I don't want you to worry. You have enough on your plate to be going on with. Just be glad I was here for Arthur when he came with Gwenllian and landed in Christopher's lap, and I'm here for you. That may be as good as it gets."

Most of the time, Mark didn't think too hard about what he'd been caught up in. He kept his head down and did the job. But the magic surrounding Anna was a part of him now too. Earlier, he'd declared, as she had, that whatever was happening here was about David. But on consideration, he didn't believe that was entirely true. It was about Anna too. And Meg. And Callum and all the rest of the time travelers without whom David could never have saved Wales, never mind become King of England.

And it had been Anna who'd been driving the day they'd saved Llywelyn from his English attackers. It was important not to forget it.

Mark led Anna down an alley and through the side door of a five-story building comprised of high-end flats, each taking up one floor of the building. Callum had established safeguards upon safeguards, as he would, but Mark had the key and the keycode and the proper thumbprint and eyeball, and ten minutes later, he was closing the door of the expensive flat behind them.

It looked just like he'd left it when he'd come by here last week to stock the refrigerator. For fifteen months he'd done it every week, on his own time, taking multiple forms of transport and avoiding cameras, all the while telling himself the day Meg showed up and needed cream in her coffee, he'd have it on hand. He didn't know if Anna drank coffee, but he was ready if she did. "Not everyone knows what to look for in a safe house, and not every flat you might think is safe really is.

"What you need is a place on the third floor of a large building with multiple entrances. Ideally, it would have its own parking garage with more entrances, but Callum chose this spot because the building is full of part-time tenants, many of them international, so long absences aren't remarked upon. The building has excellent security but no attendants, which is rarer than you think, and it's near a tube station and multiple bus stops. We'll be safe here."

"I believe you." Anna came to a halt at the kitchen island, part of a large great room. The window was framed by the deep blue curtains and opened onto a garden, beyond which were beautiful buildings. They were a stone's throw from Kensington Palace and Hyde Park.

Because ... Callum.

It wasn't just David who'd had destiny thrust upon him. Callum had done his best in the modern world, but it hadn't been until he'd traveled to the medieval world that he'd come into his own. David had made him the Earl of Shrewsbury, and Mark was pretty sure *that* was his real identity, not the mild mannered MI-5 agent he'd been in Avalon.

Anna walked forward. Mark hadn't yet turned on the lights in the flat because the moment he did, the two of them would be visible to anyone outside. The outside lights were bright enough to lift the room's shadows, however, shining in from faux-Victorian lamp posts lining the road. Anna leaned her forehead against the pane to look down at the garden. "What am I doing here, Mark?"

"We'll figure it out." Mark resisted the urge to move her away from the window and draw the curtains. For now, nobody knew they were here, and she'd had a really long day. She deserved a moment of peace. "We'll get you home again."

It was on the tip of his tongue to promise it to her, but she wasn't a child who needed those kinds of promises. She knew nearly as well as he did the obstacles facing her. 'Controlled chaos' was a kind way to put what she, Meg, and David experienced every time they returned to Avalon. There was no reason to think this time would be any different. It already wasn't.

But he was surely going to try to make it so. "Let me get you settled, Anna. I have work to do, but you're knackered and in pain. You need sleep."

Anna acted like she hadn't heard him and continued to stare through the glass, though after a moment, Mark detected a hint of a nod.

"How are you going to cover this up?" Anna still hadn't left the window. "I rode a horse into Westminster Palace. I had contact with upwards of fifty people in two hours, including that detective."

"Let me worry about that," Mark said.

"Too late."

Mark smirked. Back at Caernarfon, Mark had not-so-nobly volunteered to stay in the twenty-first century in order to be David's eyes and ears in Avalon. He'd been totally up front that he was doing it as much for himself as for Callum or David, and neither of them accused him of being selfish or judged him for not wanting to stay in the Middle Ages. But as the months had gone by, he'd been forced to acknowledge how little he really could do for them.

Mark had promised he'd protect their interests in this world, and so far he'd gone above and beyond to do exactly that, even to the point of contacting Anna's family outside of normal channels to arrange a way to communicate that wouldn't be monitored. He had guarded the safe house. He'd bought disposable mobiles. He'd wiped every mention from the internet of anything to do with their time travel and helped deep six the Time Travel Initiative. The real question now, and he had a nervous curl in his stomach just thinking about it, was whether or not it had been enough.

He took in a deep breath through his nose. He really did have work to do, not the least of which was covering their trail, and for that he was going to need Livia's help. She should have reached Thames House by now and returned the vehicle. He was a little embarrassed, in fact, that her tradecraft was better than his. He thought he'd learned enough in the months he'd been here alone, but at heart he was a computer hacker, not a spy.

A half-hour later, having showered and changed into pajamas he'd bought and left in a drawer in one of the bedrooms for exactly this purpose, Anna was asleep. Ten seconds later, after opening his laptop, Mark's mobile rang. It was Livia.

"How are you calling me?"

"I'm using an old computer and routing the signal through thirty-two countries. I'm not completely ignorant, you know."

"I'm just being cautious. How's it going?"

"Fortunately, the rotation for the parking garage ends at four in the morning, so the same guard wasn't on duty. I waved my badge and entered."

"What about the GPS tracker?" Mark fingers itched to access the server remotely, but he knew it was a bad idea even before Livia gave a low laugh.

"You know we can't fix that. I could corrupt all the data since the backup at two, but GCHQ has forensics that can trace the source of any meddling."

"And we can't have that, because then they might find my Trojan in the satellite software—and then I'd be truly screwed." Mark took in a breath and spoke into the pause that followed, "Thank you for all you've done. I'm still hoping you can be protected."

"We'll see," she said. "How's Anna?"

Mark allowed Livia to drop the subject. He'd brought her in—or allowed her to force her way in—because he needed help, and here she was, helping. He had no right to complain. "I gave her a pain pill and a sleeping pill from the medicine cabinet. By the time she was out of the shower, the drugs kicked in. She didn't have a chance."

Livia's breathing hitched. "She's not a child, Mark."

"I didn't treat her like one. It's what I'd do if she were an agent coming in from the cold, isn't it? I'm impressed she was getting out of the hospital by herself, and even without us I think she would have managed that part just fine. But that's why we need her fresh and thinking in the morning. God knows we aren't going to be."

"How do you know what you'd do if she were an agent?"

"You've never met Callum, Livia, but he was the best, the very best, and he trained me. Just because I never ran agents doesn't mean I don't know how to." He got to his feet and went to the kitchen to get himself a coffee. He pressed the button and was momentarily mesmerized by the gurgling of the water. "And you ... there's more to you than in your file, isn't there?"

Through the phone he could hear her start up another one of the computers in her office—or his. "What do you mean?" She sounded very wary.

"Your file says this is your first posting, but it isn't."

The pause before Livia spoke was longer this time. "Yes, it is."

Mark scoffed. "If you want me to trust you any further, you're going to have to come clean on this. I've guessed some things, but I want to hear the rest." Livia drew in a breath, but when she still didn't answer, Mark added, "You aren't the only one who knows how to read between the lines, and you are far too competent an agent to be a lowly tech in my division. Which means you were sent either to spy on me or as punishment for something you did. I have been assuming the former, but after today I'm thinking it's the latter."

"I'm not here to spy on you." Livia's response was immediate. "I was part of a team for a year and a half in the Balkans office. I was the technology specialist."

"How old were you then—twenty-three?"

Livia voice was steady. "Twenty-two."

Mark couldn't help but laugh. She was so young. "What happened?"

"An operation went bad. I was blamed for failures that weren't mine, but I was expendable, so they fell to me."

"Why weren't you fired?"

"Because it wasn't my fault, and my supervisor knew it."

Mark laughed with actual humor. "So they sent you to the Island of Misfit Toys."

Her silence was telling. "You're not angry?"

"Of course I'm angry, just not at you. Is anything in your file true?"

"I did graduate from Cambridge."

"That's to be expected if you were recruited by Five." He went back to the lounge and sat in front of his laptop. "What was your impression of Anna?"

"It really isn't appropriate to say after such a short interaction." But then she proceeded to modify her initial demurral. "She was very subdued in the car, which could have been a product of drugs and pain. I saw a tear or two, but otherwise she conveyed a quiet acceptance of what has befallen her. You spoke of returning her to the Middle Ages, and her jaw firmed, just for a second. She's determined. But if she's distressed inside, she's doing a good job of keeping a lid on it."

"She is distressed, but she's always been good in a crisis."

"So I understand, but she's not a soldier, and we can't expect her to be one."

"I'm not a soldier either. That's why I'm here instead of there." Mark stared at the wall for a moment. "Again, unlike you, perhaps?"

"I've had the usual training for someone who spends any time in the field."

"I bet." He bobbed his head in a nod, though of course she couldn't see it. "Good to know." He checked his watch. "I should let you go. We don't want any one call to last more than a few minutes."

"I appreciate you trying to protect me, but really, you shouldn't bother. I have this end covered. I'm far more concerned about what's going to happen to you."

"I was serious about selling me out, Livia. If the choice is between you and me, choose yourself. I'm the one who put a Trojan in the software. I went to the hospital. You were just along as a driver."

Livia was silent for a moment. "I've been too busy to think very far ahead, but how are you going to come back from this?"

Mark paused before speaking, because saying out loud what needed to be said made it real, and he hadn't been ready to do that. "I don't know, Livia. All this time, I've been hoping to skate under the radar, but I can't do that any longer. Anna and her family are real people. After this, there will be no more hiding."

9

19 March 1294

Bevyn

Dawn did not bring Anna home nor offer any resolution to the problems that faced them. Before dawn, they'd ridden to Heledd's house, but when Anna did not appear along the way, and the rider Bevyn sent back to Dinas Bran returned with no news, they were forced to accept that what they were doing was tracking Anna rather than finding her. And with that thought, Math reached the conclusion that in the dark they might trample over evidence of Anna's passing. So they rested at Heledd's cottage until first light and then left again with the intent of retracing Anna's exact steps.

If Anna had been a regular midwife and not a princess—and hadn't promised her young son she would try to be at home when he awakened—she might have spent the entire night at Heledd's house. Fortunately, mother and baby were doing well, though Heledd immediately expressed guilt that her child's birth had exposed Anna to danger. Math told her they all felt guilt. As Anna's husband, her welfare ultimately rested on his shoulders, however, and it made no sense for anyone else to take on the responsibility that was his.

Bevyn, in truth, didn't disagree. Anna's welfare *was* Math's responsibility, even if her loss wasn't his *fault*. That lay resolutely on the shoulders of the one who'd ordered her abduction.

With the coming of day, the fog lifted, and the sun shone weakly through a low cloud cover. "Here. This is where I veered off the road." Mair pointed to the spot and then turned in the saddle to look in the other direction. "Princess Anna kept going back the way we'd come."

Bevyn trotted his horse along the road, his eyes on the ditch to the southeast of the road and the trees beyond it. A crumbling stone wall lined the road on the other side. Because Math was in no condition to do so, Bevyn made a mental note to discover what farmer claimed these fields and why he'd allowed the wall to crumble. There were no sheep or cattle in the field, but it was far less costly to maintain what was already built than to tear down an existing wall and rebuild it. Just because the field wasn't in use today didn't mean it never would be again.

He turned back to Mair. "Where are the bodies of Anna's guard? You said they fell in the onslaught."

"They did." Mair dismounted and paced out the steps. "It was dark, so I'm not certain of all the particulars, but they came around the bend and ran into us."

Bevyn and Math's company had come through here on their way to Heledd's, but in the dark, Mair hadn't been as sure of the terrain as she appeared to be now.

Bevyn dismounted too and walked with her to the curve in the road where the assault first began. The earth had been churned up by many horses' hooves, and the tracks crisscrossed one another to the point that it was impossible to tell which were the result of alien hooves and which were theirs.

Then Bevyn stepped to the edge of the road where bits of grass grew. Sections were flattened, and as he looked closely, he could see boot prints. He followed the tracks into the trees. Here, the soil was less soft, but once Bevyn knew what he was looking for, the prints were evident.

"What do you see?" Still mounted, Math called after Bevyn from the road.

"We have two bodies." Twenty yards into the woods, Bevyn crouched beside the corpses. The marauders had hastily shoved them underneath a blackberry bramble. In the dark, they might have seemed well hidden, but as it was March, the bramble was hardly more than a tangle of prickly sticks, with no leaves or fruit. The blue jacket one of the men wore stood out clearly against the green grass and brown bush, along with Math's crest, a red dragon rampant on a field of yellow.

Math walked to where Bevyn crouched. He didn't curse, just gazed silently at the bodies. Then he gestured to three other men to come closer. "Get them out. There should be three more about somewhere."

"Over here!" The shout came from the direction of the road.

Bevyn caught Math's arm before he could respond. "No remains we find will be Anna's."

"I know. They wouldn't have gone to this much trouble to cover up what they'd done if they meant to harm her. That's why they hid the bodies. If not for Mair, they might have slipped away without anyone seeing them, and we would have been truly lost as to why she never came home. Because Anna was seeing to a birth, if she took longer, I wouldn't have worried, and I wouldn't have realized until sometime today that anything was amiss."

Bevyn's frown was permanently affixed to his face. "Does this mean we have a spy in Llangollen?"

"She rides to the university most days," Math said. "Everyone knows her habits, so a stranger at the tavern could have asked around. It's only because Lili and Bronwen are here, and then the birth, that Anna's routine was disrupted."

Bevyn took in a sharp breath through his nose, understanding Math's meaning. "Whoever took her was stalking her, awaiting their chance."

"Though if that's supposed to make me feel better, it doesn't." Math glowered. "I was complacent with her safety. I thought five men were enough to protect her from any threat she might face."

"It would have been enough—except they brought a company of twenty." Bevyn's earlier anger at what he perceived as Math's carelessness was gone. "This was well planned. It's impossible to protect anyone in that situation."

"More guards would have evened the odds."

Bevyn shrugged. It was pointless to argue. "Come on. We're not done. She didn't leave the road here."

They returned to the road but didn't mount their horses again, instead walking back along it away from the bend. If Anna had escaped capture it would be because she had found a way off the road, as Mair had done.

"Here, my lord!" Rhys, Math's best tracker (other than Bevyn himself), waved from a spot ahead of them where the broken down stone wall that lined the road was particularly destroyed.

Bevyn bent to put a hand to the impressions of horses' hooves in the dirt and then climbed over the wall to find similar tracks on the other side. He nodded at Math. "Several horses leapt the wall here."

"If one was ridden by Anna—" Math's face was white as he scrambled after Bevyn.

"We know for certain she was being chased, and it stands to reason she would have looked for a way out." Rhys gestured to the mass of hoofprints that had torn up the turf in the field. "This early in the spring, the grass is still only a few inches tall, and it's rained every day this week, so the ground is soft and muddy. The impressions are impossible to miss."

Math studied the ground and said with clear regret, "Her horse was not built for galloping, and she's never taken to riding, even though she worked hard to learn."

"There are so many other things she's good at," Bevyn said.

Math shook his head. "I didn't see the need to press her on becoming a better horsewoman than the minimum she needed to be."

"Again, this is not your fault, Math," Bevyn said. "I know you're angry, but the only man to blame for Anna's abduction is the one who ordered it."

Math sighed and turned on his heel, trudging across the field in a northerly direction with Bevyn, both of them careful to skirt the hoofprints they were following. Rhys loped ahead of them and came eventually to a halt before a stand of trees that prevented them from seeing the land on the other side. In the dark last night, Anna would have found them even more impenetrable, but it seemed she'd entered them anyway because that's where the tracks led.

Rhys didn't continue into the woods until Math and Bevyn had caught up.

"I hear water." Math swiveled his head this way and that, trying to orient himself.

"The stream below us is running fast," Rhys said. "I haven't stood in this exact spot before, but I know the area. The invaders chose their place for an ambush well. It is hemmed in on one side by the slope of the hill, and on this side by a ravine." He frowned. "But it's too steep; it isn't possible to cross at this location."

"The tracks tell us she did." Bevyn shoved his shoulder between two bushes, breaking and bending many branches in the process. The horse would have leapt the lower branches, and Bevyn could see more broken at head height.

"But she couldn't have." Rhys hustled after him. "At least two horses galloped through here, but they had nowhere to go."

As Rhys came abreast, Bevyn caught his arm, and the young man realized the danger at the same moment, grasping the trunk of a white birch tree clinging to the edge of a steep ravine, at the bottom of which the stream was running high. The landscape in this area was riddled with streams such as this, rising and falling depending upon the season and sometimes disappearing altogether.

Below them, a man and horse, both unmoving, lay half-submerged in the water.

Math reached Bevyn's other side and stared down at the body. "He has to be dead."

"Indeed."

Neither man was a stranger to death, but this was not the morning they'd envisioned having when Bevyn had arrived yesterday to confer. Bevyn turned to command several men to make their way down to the stream, though at this time of year, it was more akin to a river, flowing high with spring rains. They'd have to use ropes to descend if they themselves didn't want to end up with broken necks.

Math let out a breath. "No Anna, thank the saints."

"You realize what this means, don't you?" Bevyn gestured to the dead man and horse. "Anna isn't here, so we don't have to worry about looking for her anymore. She's gone to Avalon, my lord."

The tension eased out of Math's posture. "We'll keep looking anyway, but you're right: our priority now is to discover where the rest of the soldiers went and who they were working for. Even if they don't have her, they still invaded Wales."

"I'll get the men organized. What do *you* want to do now?"

Math looked off into the distance. "What do I want? To be in Avalon with her. I hate that she's there all by herself." He clenched his hands into fists. Bevyn recognized the signs of a man who wanted to punch something. Anything. But Math wasn't a sixteen-year-old youth, and he was wise enough to know breaking his knuckle on a tree trunk wouldn't help his wife—or his boys, who were missing their mother.

Bevyn nodded encouragingly. "We will do what we must and more. They had twenty riders; it shouldn't be hard for Ieuan— for me—to pick up their trail."

"Don't ask me to stay home for this."

Bevyn scoffed. "Ieuan didn't, and I won't overrule him. You have every right to remain in the thick of things. Dafydd would." The two men exchanged a glance, acknowledging that only Dafydd truly had the power to go after Anna. It was the one thing he could do that they could not. Bevyn had never been to Avalon, but he'd heard enough stories by now to know it was a world of miracles and mysteries. According to Dafydd, it also had ten times as many people as they did here. Were Dafydd to go after her, he could end up an ocean away, and then they would have two people stuck in Avalon instead of one. Better to solve the mystery before Dafydd even learned she was missing.

It came to Bevyn, however, that he wouldn't be the one to find Anna. He'd been less than twenty years old when Meg had come to King Llywelyn and in his early thirties when Dafydd had arrived in Wales to save his father. Now he was past forty, and most of the men with whom Bevyn had trained as a youth were dead. Many had died in battle, the rest from sickness and disease, and at times he felt as if he'd achieved his position in life not from his skill with a sword or his acumen but simply because he was the last man standing.

When Dafydd had sent him away after being crowned King of England, it had been a dark time in Bevyn's life, only brightened by his new wife and growing family back on Anglesey. Now that he was returned to the fold, so to speak, he was damned if he was going to allow some Scottish plot to upend his well-ordered life. Given that Bevyn *was* the last man standing, he had the experience to do the job that needed doing, even if it was the last thing he wanted: "It is I who will stay home, my lord."

Math swung around to look at him. "You?"

"What if these men didn't try to abduct Anna for the reasons we think? What if the point is to send you into a frenzy?"

Math stared at him. "To what end?"

Bevyn pointed towards the castle. With the morning growing older, the clouds were higher above the earth, and they could see Dinas Bran perched on its mountain top. "With all of us gone, who's guarding the heir to the throne of England?"

Math's eyes darkened. He could see the implications as well as Bevyn. So all he did was nod. "I suppose *you* are."

10

Elen leaned forward from the backseat of the car as the not-so-dulcet tones of Attica's new hit song, *My Baby Shakes It,* blared out from the recesses of Elisa's purse. "That's a new ringtone, Mom. I'm impressed."

"I wanted to make sure I could hear it when it rang." Elisa's hands shook as she rummaged in her purse for the phone. She'd allowed it to fall to the bottom, rather than keeping it in the cell phone pocket, because every time she came upon it, she cried. She'd been weary of crying.

Ted, who was driving, kept his attention on the road ahead of him, but she could see his eyes flicking towards her every few seconds. "What—are you saying that's *the* phone?"

"Watch the road, Ted. I've got this." Elisa finally came up with the phone. Brushing some eyeliner dust off the screen—or maybe that was ancient crayon that had been crushed inside her purse long ago—she pressed *talk* and then put the phone to her ear. "Hello?"

"Aunt Elisa?"

"Anna! Oh, thank God! Please tell me you aren't in Pennsylvania."

"No. London."

Elisa put her hand over the receiver. "She's in London!"

The moment Elisa said Anna's name, Ted pulled to the side of the road in a gravel turnout. "Put her on speaker." It was raining, and once Ted turned off the windshield wipers, Elisa couldn't see much through the windows. Nobody seemed to be around them, but now that she had Anna actually on the phone, she found herself instantly paranoid that MI-5 or some other secret agency was going to descend on them and whisk them off before she could see Christopher.

"Hi, Anna!" Elen was bouncing up and down on the back seat. She had grown a great deal in the nine months Christopher had been gone to the Middle Ages, but she was still only twelve, and Elisa was pleased she had yet to acquire that Teflon coating many kids wore from being hurt too many times. She was just as eager and cheerful as ever—especially any time her time traveling cousins were mentioned. Somehow six months in an English school hadn't dampened her enthusiasm any. Elen appeared to have the ability to win over even schoolyard bullies.

Anna laughed. "Hi, Elen. I'm so happy to hear your voice."

In Elisa's head, Anna would always be seventeen, but she reminded herself what she was hearing now was the exhausted voice of a twenty-eight-year-old woman who'd just time traveled to the modern world from the Middle Ages.

"Are you alone? Did anyone else come with you?"

"No. I'm sorry. Christopher is with David in Ireland."

Ted coughed and laughed at the same time, though as Elisa glanced over at him, he had tears streaming unselfconsciously down his cheeks. That was Ted. He was the most honest and stable man you could ever hope to meet. He was her rock. And yet he cried to hear his niece's voice.

Now he leaned closer to the phone, and when he spoke, if Elisa hadn't been looking at him, she wouldn't have known he was crying. "We decided we needed to be here, Anna. We—" He glanced at Elisa, and she knew he was wondering how much he should say over the phone. Ultimately, he simply added, "We haven't been idle any more than Mark has."

There was silence on the other end before Anna said, "I don't know what that means, but I can't wait to find out. Where exactly are you?"

"We rented a house in Kent."

"You did what?"

Elisa stepped in. "We have a house—listen, Anna. I know Mark has all sorts of safeguards in place, and it would be better if we could talk in person rather than doing it over the phone."

"I know. Just a sec." They could hear walking, and then the phone being set on a table. "I've put you on speaker. Here's Mark."

"When did she arrive, Mark?" Ted said.

"Two in the morning. I would have called then, but I wanted to get as much as I could sorted before I did."

"We planned for this, Mark," Ted said.

"I know—" Mark paused, and Elisa had the sense he'd wearily wiped his brow. "But I didn't foresee her arriving on horseback in the middle of Westminster Hall."

There was total silence in the car. "Did he say she brought a horse?" Elen said.

From the background, Anna said, "It wasn't my fault! I was being chased by Scots!"

Ted laughed, and Elisa suddenly found her shoulders shaking too, though whether from laughter or tears she wasn't entirely sure. She had lived daily with a tension in her shoulders and stomach at what Christopher had to be going through in that faraway world, and though he hadn't returned with Anna, to know he was alive and well—and the rest of her family was too—had her breathing normally for the first time in nine months.

She hadn't lied to herself either that a great portion of that tension derived from guilt. Her last conversation with Christopher had been a fight, and she knew in her heart that part of the reason he had wanted to go to the Middle Ages in the first place was because she'd been holding on too tightly to her almost-grown-up son. At the time, she believed she couldn't help it—and told herself it was for his own good.

But the nine months without him had torn her apart and remade her in ways she never would have expected. Though the tension and fear of losing him forever had never left her, she'd learned to live with it and without him—and without knowing what had happened to him.

That he'd gone to the Middle Ages had been pretty clear once things had gotten sorted, as Mark would say. Mark himself had known only some of the story, and he'd reached out to Ted as soon as he could no longer contact Christopher. Time travel had been the first assumption they'd made, since Christopher had told his father the straightforward truth the evening before about who he was with and what had happened so far.

And that was another source of guilt, because of course she'd had calls from Christopher on her phone all morning. Normally she might have left her meeting to answer them, but she hadn't. And by the time she chose to answer them, he had ditched his phone. She hadn't even been able to hug Arthur, her own great-nephew, because of her stubbornness.

From the deaths of her father and mother, she was well acquainted with the five stages of grief: denial, anger, bargaining, depression, and acceptance. The grief she'd felt at Christopher's loss had been genuine, but it was the grief at her own culpability that kept her up at night. She'd gone through all the stages: angrily denying she'd done anything wrong or that it was her fault; promising God or fate or the powers-that-be that she would do *anything* if only they would make things right; utter despair that she was a terrible mother and incapable of change; and then acceptance.

And it was the acceptance that had lit a fire under her—and changed the course of their lives. Christopher's expressed desire to find a career that could one day help David had made both her and Ted think that's what they needed to do too.

"Unfortunately, as usual, things got out of hand fairly quickly." Mark had come back on the phone. He sighed heavily. "A police officer arrived in the hall right after Anna did. He panicked and shot the horse."

"Who else knows Anna is here?" Ted said.

"The policemen who found her in Westminster Hall, the doctors and nurses who treated her, and the inspector who briefly interviewed her before I arrived." Mark reeled off the list. "And that's only the ones we know about. I have no idea if anyone else has been paying attention recently and tracked the flash as she came in. We have to assume it."

"So too many to squash," Elisa said. "What are we going to do?"

"No idea," Mark said.

"We have to come up with an explanation as to what she was doing there," Ted said.

"And why Five took it over?" Mark said. "We're working on that."

A new voice came on the line, causing Elisa to almost drop the phone.

"Anna's best bet, for the time being, is to lay low."

"This is Livia, my—" Mark paused, "—she works with me, and she knows pretty much everything. She's patched in from Thames House on another untraceable line."

Elisa and Ted exchanged a look, but then they both shrugged. If Mark trusted her, they had to too.

"My first concern is if someone is watching us right now," Ted said. "We've been stopped here a while. Nobody else has pulled over that I can see."

"Your mobile is secure, which is why Mark gave it to you," Livia said, "but if someone is tracking your regular mobiles, they could start pinging cell towers for all mobiles in use near you. If you've been sitting a while, it's time to move and get somewhere where there are more people and more electronic activity."

Elisa looked around. In fact, they were currently the only ones on the little road they'd taken from their house in the countryside. Having lived all her life in Pennsylvania, she was used to rain and green landscapes. Kent never experienced much of a winter, however, and it didn't rain so much as drizzle all winter long. "I'm due at the embassy at ten. We were going to have breakfast and then drop Elen off at school." They'd learned through much trial and error to leave a long lead time with everything they did that involved London. As a rule, they parked on the outskirts and took the train into the city together, since they all worked near Hyde Park.

"Have breakfast with us, and we'll hammer out the game plan," Mark said.

"But leave your normal mobiles in the vehicle," Livia said. "We have to assume they are being tracked."

Elisa gritted her teeth, knowing Livia was right. But now that it was time to implement some kind of plan, she was frozen in her seat.

Fortunately, Ted was not. "This is why we moved here, isn't it?"

Elisa nodded. And truthfully, she'd been more afraid at other times. If she could handle the disappearance of members of her family for years at a time, MI-5 or the CIA or whoever was tracking them couldn't be worse than that. The most awful moment had been at Caernarfon when they'd feared David and Llywelyn had been blown up in the bombing. Mark had tracked Elisa and Ted down there too and told them their bodies weren't among the dead. They hadn't *known* all was well, however, until Gwenllian had told Christopher.

"If anyone at the embassy knows about what's happened, I will find out." Elisa had worked for twenty years at a marketing firm in Philadelphia, and through a series of fortuitous events, just before Christopher had disappeared, the firm had acquired the contract for the United States embassy in London. Before she'd started looking into how to get to Britain, she'd had no idea the embassy had any interest in marketing.

But of course it did. The diplomats handled the crises, and the marketing department made them look good. Her own firm had been delighted to have someone with her experience volunteer to uproot to the UK, and there'd been so much upheaval in the State Department in the last five or six years, they'd been desperate for anyone who could mitigate anti-American sentiment in Britain, even a little.

Ted, meanwhile, had taken his financial acumen into the very heart of Treadman Global, which last year had bought out the powerful military-industrial behemoth, CMI (Conflict Management Industries). Once called The Dunland Group, its representatives had pursued David in hopes of tapping into his ability to time travel. They'd been thwarted by Callum and Cassie. Purportedly, the company's initiative had died after their failure to retrieve him and after the shake up in the CIA and MI-5.

In the six months Ted had been working for them, however, he had grown close to Chad Treadman, the owner, who shortly after he bought the company had divested himself of all military operations. Subsequently, Ted had risen to the point where he was now the Chief Financial Officer (CFO). Ted had even been considering approaching Chad with the story of their family and the now-defunct Time Travel Initiative. But he'd been waiting for someone to come through before he did so, because if he went behind David's back, there was no telling how David might respond.

It was Mark who'd had the most difficult job, treading a fine line between serving his country, as he always had, and spying on it. After the departure of Director Tate and Mark's relocation, MI-5 had been resolutely anti-time travel. It was as if they had their hands over their ears and their eyes closed, shouting all the time, "We're not listening!"

In more ways than one, the move to London had been the logical culmination of what began with Meg's disappearance twenty-five years earlier. It seemed—and at this point Elisa didn't bother to spend any time thinking about it—that the Middle Ages was the family business. It had been long past time Elisa herself joined the company.

11

19 March 2022

Anna

The first thing Elisa needed after she, Ted, and Elen arrived at Callum's flat, immediately after she hugged Anna, was a rundown of everything Christopher had been doing since he'd gone to live in the alternate universe.

Anna hadn't seen much of him herself, since he was David's squire, not Math's, but she knew enough—and she didn't pull any punches. He was the Hero of Westminster, he was a soldier, and the sooner his parents understood that, the sooner they would be able to accept the man he'd become. She also had to tell them she didn't know his exact current situation and about the rebellion overtaking her world.

Elisa, Ted, and Elen listened to her narrative with fixed attention, a few moans, and otherwise wide eyes. For years now, they'd heard about Anna's life in the medieval world. They'd witnessed arrivals and disappearances, but Anna was a mother herself, and she had a pretty clear understanding of what they were going through in missing Christopher.

Anna hadn't yet figured out how she was going to return to Math and her boys, but she knew how she felt to have them there and her here; she knew how different it would be to have her own son caught up in something so crazy. She herself had disappeared from her own mother's life in the exact same way Christopher had disappeared from Elisa's. It was a loss that simply wasn't possible to recover from and an ache that wouldn't let go. Elisa had lived with it for nine months. She'd lived with something similar, in fact, for years, what with losing Anna's mom, David, and Anna herself.

Christopher had told Anna a little about the circumstances of his leaving and his regret that he not only hadn't been able to say goodbye, but he'd parted from his mother on poor terms. Elisa's reaction now, however, was a far cry from what Anna would have expected, given how Elisa had behaved to Christopher in Caernarfon: she didn't blame Anna for Christopher's loss, feelings which wouldn't have been entirely illogical; she didn't rage around the room. Instead, she took what Anna had to tell her with a white face, but otherwise just nodded.

And when Anna finished, Elisa drew in a breath. "It's what we talked about, Ted."

Uncle Ted put his arm around his wife's shoulders and squeezed. Then he turned to Anna in order to explain: "We met David again when he was sixteen, you'll remember. He was a soldier and the Prince of Wales. We saw then what was in Christopher's head, and we hoped he'd grow out of it, but he never forgot seeing David and listening to him speak about the world he'd gone to. Christopher never stopped wanting to stand at David's side."

"So him living there wasn't what we worried about most," Elisa said.

Ted nodded. "What we feared was that he and the children had run into trouble immediately upon their arrival, what with the car and everything. Once he connected with any of you, we told ourselves he'd be fine."

"As fine as any soldier in a war zone can be," Elisa said with a bit of tart in her voice, more her former self. But then she gave a sad smile and put out her hand to cover Anna's where it lay next to her teacup. "I don't blame you. I don't blame anyone for what has happened."

Anna decided that since Aunt Elisa was speaking the truth, it was best if she did too. "I know at one time you did blame Mom. And David. In Caernarfon, you were really angry at the thought of Christopher going with us."

"That was then. I might as well be angry at the weather." She wrinkled her nose. "What good does it do to rail against God or the fates or the powers-that-be? For whatever reason, your universe-shifting, as Ted insists we call it, is in your blood. You can't help it, so we might as well accept it and work with it. From what I understand, every time you shift, it's because your life is in danger. That means you'd be dead if you didn't. How could I possibly prefer that?"

Anna squeezed Elisa's hand, pleased her aunt was talking to her as an adult, maybe for the first time. "I have been angry at times too. David, Mom, and I—and now Arthur too, it seems—are thrown around like ping-pong balls. On one hand, it's nice not to die, so there's that. But arriving in Westminster Hall on a horse wasn't easy either."

"I'm a forty-five-year-old woman," Elisa said. "You're twenty-eight and far more mature than I was at your age. At some point we all have to accept the cards we've been dealt."

"Breakfast!" Mark raised his spatula in the air to gain their attention.

He'd concocted a full breakfast, with eggs, ham (though the British called it bacon), sausage, fried mushrooms and tomatoes, and crumpets. There was also plenty of cream and sugar for Anna's coffee, which she didn't normally drink but today took like Bronwen. It was real food, and it was nice to know people in Avalon were still eating it. She said as much to Mark.

Uncle Ted snorted under his breath. "Not everyone eats this well, believe me. We've had some scary food shortages." He eyed Mark. "You know anything about that?"

"No more than you." Mark shrugged. "Crops fail. You have to expect bad years every now and again."

While everyone ate, Uncle Ted and Aunt Elisa related what they'd been doing over the last fifteen months since Anna had seen them—and particularly the last nine months since Christopher had disappeared with Gwenllian and Arthur. Uncle Ted confessed he'd been eyeing his current job since that trip to Caernarfon and had been struggling for months with how to tell his family what he wanted to do and why. He'd eagerly made the leap once Aunt Elisa got on board after Christopher left.

Finally, Uncle Ted pushed back his plate, having eaten everything on it. "So what I think we need now is a game changer."

"A what?" Anna raised her head. She'd been hungrier than she'd thought and was eyeing her third crumpet, but her difficulty in buttering it herself with her left arm in a sling was holding her back. When she was distracted with food, her wrist ached less—or maybe that was this morning's painkillers finally kicking in. If she wasn't careful, she might doze off right at the table.

"A game changer," Uncle Ted repeated. "You all have done a great deal of good for the Middle Ages, at least from a modern perspective. Have you considered how some of that good could be undertaken in this world too?"

Anna put down her knife with the butter still unspread. In fact, several more utensils clattered on plates as their owners stared at Ted.

"What exactly do you mean by that?" Mark said.

Ted eyed his wife, who had a little frown between her brows. Either she hadn't heard this before or she would prefer he didn't talk about it right now. Ted hurried on. "As you know, when all this first came to light for the authorities, certain entities like the CIA or MI-5 focused on the *how* of your universe-shifting. CMI too. But inquiries in that direction proved fruitless, and ultimately pointless, so they dropped them. And, because they were incapable of thinking outside the box, they closed down operations. I propose we stop worrying so much about the *how* in favor of looking at the *why*."

"We know why." Elen's nonchalance indicated she, at least, had heard this before. "To save Wales." She reached for Anna's crumpet, buttered it, and returned it without comment.

Ted mock-glared across the table at his daughter. "Yes, that's true, but there has to be more to it. David talks openly about your universe-shifting, and he believes—I think we all believe—that you shift between worlds for a reason that's more than simply to save your lives. That reason was initially to save Wales. Now it's to transform England and maybe the whole of Europe, moving it towards modernization at a far faster pace than we experienced in our history in this world."

Anna nodded. "What we now call Avalon." This was bread and butter to them. They didn't even talk about it anymore, it was so self-evident. "We need a better name to call our alternate universe too, since the Middle Ages doesn't really make sense. We aren't time traveling, and that world is its own thing."

"We'll work on that." Ted waved a hand dismissively. "What I'm interested in are the big questions, the biggest of all, to me, being: *what if the ultimate point isn't to make the Middle Ages a better place, but to make* this *world better?*"

From the expression on Mark's face, Ted had talked to him about this too. Now Anna really wished David or her mom were here because one of them would definitely have had something to say right about now, but all Anna managed was, "How?" spoken around the bit of crumpet.

"You all *choose* to stay there, right?" At another nod from Anna, he continued. "That right there should tell us something about the Middle Ages we're missing here. How could anyone in her right mind, a person raised with every material possession, *choose* to give them up and live for the rest of her life without them?"

Anna almost rolled her eyes, the question was so easy. "Because those material things don't make life worth living."

Ted snapped his fingers. "Exactly. How many modern people know that?"

"Surely lots," Anna said. "It's hardly news."

"Nor is it news you might want to put others before yourself or family comes first," Elisa said. "Ted's saying the Middle Ages has proved to be a training ground for greatness."

"You want David to permanently return? He'll never agree to it."

"Then let other people learn its lessons and return. Like Mark here."

Mark blinked. "Me?" He waved his hands. "Leave me out of it."

"Come on, Mark," Ted said. "What were you doing before you started working for Callum?"

Mark narrowed his eyes. "I was a computer tech in Cardiff for the Security Service."

"And now what are you?"

"The head of his section," Anna answered for him. "In charge of software for satellites."

Ted leaned in, more earnest than Anna had ever seen him, which was saying something because he had the ability at times to put David to shame. Being King of England, in fact, had given David a harder edge than what she saw now on Ted's face. "Don't you think you owe the modern world something? You've traveled back and forth from an alternate universe. The scientific advances alone such knowledge could bring are beyond reckoning!"

Anna watched her uncle over the top of the coffee cup she'd brought to her lips but hadn't drunk from. "You really mean this, don't you?"

"We do." Elisa nodded, having warmed to the conversation herself. "The way this world has treated you has made you stop thinking or caring about it—" Anna made to protest, but Elisa lifted a hand. "Let me finish. I'm not saying you don't care at all, only that you care far more about the medieval world." She stopped and looked at her husband. "We really do need a better name for it, especially if we're going to go there ourselves."

Anna blinked. "What did you say?"

Ted was sitting next to Elisa, and he took her hand. "We need you to take us with you when you go."

"What about Elen?"

Elen was ready with her answer. "Me too."

"You can't be serious." Anna set her cup in its saucer. "You realize that's crazy, right?"

Elisa looked around at her family. "We've talked about it, and we are agreed."

"Why is it crazy for us to go but not you?" Ted said.

Anna had to laugh. "Because I didn't have a choice the first time, and then my whole family was there."

"My whole family is there. You just told us that Christopher's life may be in danger." Elisa gazed at Anna. Her jaw was really tight, and she spoke around it. "I need. To see. My son."

And that was the one thing, of all the things Elisa could have said, with which Anna couldn't argue.

12

19 March 1294

Ieuan

At one time, the sight of a Welsh band riding openly through England would have prompted an armed response, but Ieuan had spent most of the last five years at Dafydd's side, and the whole world knew England and Wales were at peace. Besides, three-quarters of the men with Ieuan were English or half-English. Ieuan was just sorry they didn't have any Scotsmen among them, but James Stewart, Robbie Bruce, and their men had gone to Ireland with Dafydd.

Ieuan's company had left Llangollen before dawn, heading east following the River Dee. At every farm and hamlet, they'd woken the household to ask if they'd heard a company ride by. Nobody had. As the hours wore on, Ieuan began to fear they were on the completely wrong track. Then morning came, and with it, a growing anger that burned in his stomach and closed his throat over words best not spoken.

When they reached the confluence of the Dee and the Ceiriog, he turned more north, though how a foreign company could have traveled from south of the Dee to north of it without encountering anyone, he couldn't guess.

As Math had promised, he'd sent a rider to Overton ahead of Ieuan, one riding fast and direct. An industrious farmer, through whose lands the river ran, had established an inn at the Overton Bridge. By the time Ieuan's company arrived there, it was late morning, and the farmstead was bustling with activity. As they'd been riding for hours already, it was as good a time as any to rest the horses, and even with the urgency of their mission, a bite to eat wouldn't go amiss. To Ieuan's relief, Cadwallon himself met them.

Ieuan ordered a halt and dismounted in order to clasp Cadwallon's hand. Though Cadwallon's smile was wide, he was looking a bit haggard and unkempt.

"How's the baby?" Ieuan said.

Cadwallon grinned. "A strapping boy." Then he sobered. "He cries every time I hold him. And all night long last night."

"They can do that." Ieuan himself was the father of two. He tipped his head toward the inn. "Introduce me?"

Cadwallon was built like a soldier at above average height with shoulders and arms designed for wielding a sword. His only flaw was that at thirty, he was prematurely balding. Rather than lamenting the loss, he simply shaved his head, making him look like a particularly robust monk.

The two men entered the inn just as a middle-aged woman with slate gray hair was adding wood to the fire. It hadn't rained on their journey from Llangollen, which was a blessing, but the warmth was pleasant, and Ieuan approached with his hands out to the fire.

"Good day to you, madam."

The woman curtseyed, eyes on Cadwallon, whom she appeared to recognize. "Are you here for breakfast, my lords? Cook is laying it out now in the kitchen. We don't usually have guests at this hour."

"There's twenty of us, and we can pay." Cadwallon put his hand to his right hip where his purse lay. "Did a company of men cross the bridge this morning?"

The woman's eyes widened, and Ieuan had his first spark of hope.

"I'll be wondering first who's asking. You or—" She looked at Ieuan. "Him?"

"I am Welsh like Sir Cadwallon, but we mean you no harm." Ieuan put a hand to his breastbone. "I am Lord Ieuan, servant of King Dafydd."

The woman glared and shook her finger at Ieuan, making him think at first she was angry, but then she said, "I've heard of you, haven't I? *Servant of the King.*" She scoffed. "Brother-in-law more like. Saved our good King David's life a dozen times, haven't you?"

Cadwallon grinned. "Indeed he has, madam. I'm sure he'd be happy to tell you a tale or two over breakfast, but first we'd be grateful if you would speak of what you heard this morning."

"I heard 'em." She nodded. "Thundering through here. Disturbing my chickens. It was twenty men. I would have said they were highwaymen because they showed no colors, but they rode like soldiers and wore swords. We've known some august companies to pass through here, but not usually in the early hours of the morning like they did."

"Was a woman among them?" Ieuan tried to keep the urgency out of his voice, but the way the woman whipped her head around to look at him told him he'd failed.

"A woman? Not that I could see, but it was dark, and I was focused on collecting the toll, not counting their number." Then the woman frowned. "I did notice one thing, my lords. Several were dressed funny, not like I've seen before."

"Dressed funny how?" Cadwallon asked.

"They wore no cloaks and instead were wrapped in blankets. I've never seen men-at-arms wrapped in blankets before. How do they fight like that?"

"The blankets are called a *brat*," Cadwallon said. "It means they're Scots, and they don't wear them to fight."

Ieuan raised his eyebrows. "How did you know that?"

"I've spoken with James Stewart. He dresses like a Norman, but many of his companions are Highlanders."

"Highlanders in Wrexham?" The woman gaped at them. "Well, I never."

"Did you see where they were headed?" Ieuan cut through her astonishment.

"East."

"Not north?" Cadwallon said.

"If they were going north, they wouldn't have crossed the Dee." She nodded firmly. "They were definitely heading east."

Cadwallon looked at Ieuan. "Where are they going if not to Scotland?"

"Be grateful we found them, my friend." Ieuan found his features hardening into grim lines. "We are close. I can feel it. And they can't run forever."

13

19 March 2022

Anna

Before, when it was just herself she had to think about, Anna hadn't seen the need for an actual plan to get home that was any more complicated than climbing up to the roof and jumping off. Given this genuinely lovely apartment building near Hyde Park, the opportunity to leave was constantly available.

But now she was deeply concerned not only about her family's desire to return with her, but also Ted's enthusiasm with what to her was a very personal thing, and a twist in her stomach had her actually thinking maybe Ted wasn't the ally he had always been. It wouldn't be because he had gone over to the dark side, but rather because he was naive, and he was still predisposed to trust where he shouldn't. Back when MI-5 were the bad guys, Mom and Goronwy had come to Avalon to save Papa's life. In the fallout from that event, Ted had given Mom the keys to his rental car, but he'd also worked afterwards with MI-5. He didn't have a fundamental distrust of modern authority, which by now was hard earned in Anna.

But she didn't say anything to her family, just said goodbye and hugged them to speed them on their way. There was enough for them to think and worry about without her adding to their burdens.

Elisa, however, was a mother herself, and thus half-psychic. Before she had walked four paces down the corridor, she turned back to Anna. "Don't you dare go jumping off any roofs without us."

Anna blinked. "I won't."

Elisa moved back to her. "Promise me." She took Anna's arms. "You have to promise me you won't leave without us."

Anna took in a breath and managed a smile. "I promise."

Elisa looked into Anna's eyes for a few seconds, and then she nodded. "Okay." She pulled her into a hug. "I love you. We'll be back tonight."

There wasn't anything Anna could do after that but stand dully in the doorway of the apartment, watching them walk away.

Mark stepped beside her. "She's right you know." He took her arm and guided her back inside.

As Mark shut the door, Anna moved towards one of Callum's couches, both of which were incredibly soft and squishy. Though Anna had slept for a few hours, she was still exhausted, and her wrist was hurting again. Heedless of propriety, she lay down full length on the cushions, while Mark sat in a chair opposite.

"I know." She relaxed and closed her eyes. "I'd be fooling myself to think I can go anywhere until I have what I need."

"And what's that?" Mark was only paying half-attention as usual, since he was again on his phone.

She didn't answer because what she needed most was him. The problem was how to tell him.

So instead, Anna said, "With all those precautions Callum took, are you comfortable with Ted and Elisa knowing about this safe house?"

Mark didn't answer at first, and Anna opened her eyes. He had actually looked up from his device. "Aren't you?"

Anna grabbed a throw pillow to put under her head and turned onto her side. "I don't know."

"Nobody knows about this place but us. You need to rest and heal up a bit."

"I don't feel safe."

Mark grumbled but set his phone aside. "Nobody followed us."

"Someone could have followed Ted and Elisa, and Ted seems to have thought an awful lot about how the time traveling works and what it means." Anna found herself torn in two. On one hand, it had paid in the past to be cautious, but on the other hand she couldn't fundamentally distrust her uncle. She knew he loved her and wanted what was best for her, and the man didn't have a deceitful bone in his body.

"He would have if he was planning to take his family with you."

"That's just it. I'm not comfortable doing that. David would kill me."

Mark leaned back in his seat. "As you may recall, a few years ago, you took an entire busload of people to the Middle Ages, including me!"

"That was an accident. This would be on purpose." She eyed him. It was on the tip of her tongue to say what she was wanted from him—what she, in fact, needed.

Mark rubbed his chin. "You made things right in the end by bringing them back. You have to admit the traveling has become a bit more like a revolving door than a one-way ticket."

"I'm glad to hear you say that." Anna swung her legs back to the floor, no longer feeling as tired.

"Are you? Why?"

Anna let out a breath and took the plunge. "We need you to come back with me." And then before he could make any reply, she put out a hand. "Just for a little while."

"A little while? You think you can promise that?"

She gestured around her. "Can't I? Didn't you just say that our time traveling has become a revolving door?"

Mark scoffed and rose to his feet. "Putting me aside for the moment, let me show you what I have for you, and we can talk about what else you might need." Mark went to the entryway closet, from which he pulled a mid-sized army-green backpack and set it on the floor. "The bag I brought from MI-5 is only the tip of the iceberg. I'm ready for you to leave at a moment's notice. I've been ready." He unzipped the bag and laid out a myriad of electronic items, most of which Anna couldn't identify. Before she could object to the obvious problem—that they all needed charging—he pulled out a flat packet, which he unfolded into a series of small squares and triangles, hinged together, with a little stand. "The *piece de resistance!*"

At her questioning look, he added, "It's a solar charger."

He placed his hand on a leather case he'd put next to it. "This is a tablet with every resource I could think of loaded on to it. Schematics, plans, designs, maps, books, books, books." He gestured to the bag. "I have a dozen more, plus more solar panels. Your kids will be able to *read*, Anna."

Anna put a hand to her heart. "Thank you." She paused. "You haven't said no."

He laughed, but without humor. "Of course the answer's no." He canted his head. "I do want to hear why you're asking."

Anna let out the breath she'd been holding. "A year ago, we saw how foreign Avalon's technology was to us, and even though I've been here half a day, I can see that the gap between our knowledge and what we need to know has only gotten larger. You can send this with me, and we're delighted to have it, but there's no guarantee we'll be able to work any of it, and what we already have we don't know how to repair. If we are to survive with one foot here and one there, we need your expertise. At the very least, we need you to teach someone else to do what you do." She paused again. "You have *no idea* how much we need you."

As she'd been speaking, Mark had started packing up the solar charger. All the while, he kept his eyes on the electronics rather than on her and didn't answer.

She drew in a breath. "And we've missed you. That's not a reason to come with me, I know, because you have a family and a life here, but you need to know that part too."

Still avoiding her eyes, Mark started putting everything back into the bag. "I can show you how all this works before you go." He hefted the bag with one hand. "Is this too heavy for you to carry?"

Anna took the pack in her good hand, and awkwardly slung it over her right shoulder. She guessed it weighed thirty pounds. "I could carry it for a while. If I took off the sling, I could put both arms through the straps, which would make it easier."

"Good, because I have a second one that's heavier." Mark reached again into the closet and pulled out a bag larger than hers.

She stared at it and him. "So you are coming with me?"

He snorted. "I'm carrying it for now. Vehicles have been working for you, so I'll load one up with everything you need before you crash it. I don't see how else to get your family and all this stuff there in one piece."

Mark helped her adjust the straps so her back and shoulders were more comfortable, and as Anna didn't bring up the subject of him traveling again, she saw him become more businesslike and relaxed. For Anna's part, she could bide her time. Mark was adamant about staying in Avalon now, but he might not always be. At the very least, she'd planted the seed. It was better too that she had been the one to ask. On one hand, Mark could say no to her more easily, but on the other, if she eventually got a yes, it would be genuine. David wanted a yes—no matter what—but today that wasn't his call to make.

Then a knock came at the door. Mark put a hand on her shoulder in a brief gesture of reassurance and walked on quiet feet to the foyer, making sure as he did so that he stayed to the left of the door instead of walking directly to it. Long ago when Anna had watched cop shows, she'd seen police take that precaution so they wouldn't be shot through the door.

Before opening the door, Mark checked the security camera monitor, which was a small flat device on the wall—another tablet it seemed. Like cell phones, they were everywhere.

"Who is it?" Anna whispered.

"Ted." Mark checked the security camera feed again, to make sure nobody else was with him, and pulled the door wide. Uncle Ted stood on the threshold, just raising his hand to knock again.

"Hi." Mark didn't step back. "Did you forget something?"

"You were leaving?" Ted looked past Mark to where Anna stood, appearing for all intents and purposes as if she was prepared to walk out the door.

"Just practicing." Anna wished Mark hadn't put her sling back on because she was stuck with the pack on her back. Uncle Ted was looking at her with such disappointment, as if it had just occurred to him that she would leave the safe house—and ultimately Avalon—without telling him. But Anna had promised Elisa, and she probably couldn't have justified leaving even if she didn't need Mark's help to carry all this stuff.

He turned back to Mark. "Great minds think alike, I guess. I've had second thoughts about leaving you here, and it seems you've had second thoughts about staying. I can't shake the feeling we were followed this morning, and there was a vehicle that looked suspicious outside the building as we came out."

"What kind of vehicle?" Mark took the tablet off the wall and showed Ted how he could access cameras set up all around the building. As with Mark's big phone, now proven to be an entire computer the size of her hand, his fingers flew effortlessly across the screen.

"It was a repair van with no windows. A plumber." Ted went to the window and looked out. "I took Elen to school, and Elisa set off on foot for the embassy, trying to draw anyone away from you and not wanting to look anything but normal, but I don't feel good about any of this." He looked at Anna again. "Other than seeing you, of course."

"Can't we come to Avalon *one time* without being chased all across the planet?" she said.

"Apparently not." Ted looked again at Mark. "Is there a back way out? Maybe I'm wrong. I hope I'm wrong, but I think I have a better place for Anna to stay than here."

"It's hard to imagine better," Anna said.

"Where is it?" Mark had been focused on the tablet, swiping between images, but now he looked up.

"It's a private house owned by a friend of mine. He's got tons of security. There'd be no reason to suspect you would go there, and it's a big enough estate that nobody will stumble upon you by accident."

"Who's the friend?" Mark said.

Ted swallowed. "Chad Treadman."

Anna gaped at her uncle. "Your boss at Treadman Global?"

Ted nodded. "He has invited Elisa, Elen, and me up to his house a dozen times since we moved here." He reached into his pocket and pulled out a keycard. "See. I have access any time I want."

"I didn't realize you were so close," Anna said.

"I'm the CFO of his company, Anna. We'd better be close."

Uncle Ted was so earnest and nice, it was amazing to Anna that he was such a star in his field. You'd think he'd have at least one cutthroat bone in his body, but she'd never seen it.

Mark had gone back to his tablet. "I don't see the van now, but it doesn't mean it wasn't there. If someone was following you,

Ted, he'll know you entered the building again. We need a vehicle to get to Treadman's house."

"I can call for a car from the fleet. I work just down the street."

Now Mark turned to Anna. "It's your call. This isn't a decision I can make for you, even if Callum would."

Anna actually managed a bit of a laugh. Callum would have made the decision, and she would have trusted him implicitly to do so. She trusted Mark too, but he was right that the decision had to be hers. "Do you agree that we are no longer safe here?"

He drew in a breath. "I don't know. This building is a fortress, but—" He checked his watch. "You arrived less than twelve hours ago. If we can get you out of London—" He glanced at Ted. "That's what we're doing, right?"

"Right," Ted said.

Anna gave a jerky nod, making up her mind. "It could be that a private car belonging to Treadman Global is the safe passage I need."

Mark nodded too. "Even if Livia was able to make my role more innocent than it is, there were cameras at the hospital and the parking garage. Realistically, she and I were seen. Once Five begins to focus on me, they'll eventually get to you—and then Ted—and the truth will come out."

Anna sighed. "Sorry about all this. I'm sorry you may lose your job over this."

"Oh—I could lose a lot more than my job." Mark laughed. "But this is what I signed up for. We'll use the back stairs."

"How can you be sure we won't be followed now?" Anna twitched the pack higher on her shoulders. Standing with it on her back for the last ten minutes had shown it to be heavier than she'd thought, and she hoped she wasn't going to have to carry it very far. While she never had to carry anything of her own—ever—in the medieval world, because she had servants to do that, she did carry Bran, and she'd even been known to heft eight-year-old Cadell now and again on her back. She told herself he weighed more than thirty pounds and not to be a wimp.

"We will be careful," Mark said.

Ted started dialing, and Anna hoped it was a burner phone he was using. Mark had given her one too, and though she'd tucked it into the side pocket of the sweater she was wearing, since then she hadn't given it a second thought. Everyone else was constantly pulling out their phones and poking at the shiny screens. At breakfast, everyone had left their phone on the table beside their plate, and Elisa had been carrying hers as she'd walked away. Even Elen, who was only twelve, had one.

Mark had filled the closets with clothing, and Anna had chosen clothes she remembered her mother wearing when she traveled: tan slacks, white button-up shirt, and red sweater. While Anna wore tight-fitting pants all the time to keep warm, it was extremely odd not to be wearing a dress over them. She'd left her medieval clothing folded neatly on a chair in her bedroom, and while Ted arranged for a car, she headed down the hall to get it.

"Anna, what are you doing—" Mark swung around the doorframe of the bedroom to see her with her arms full of clothing. "Right." He turned Anna around so he could get to her pack, pulled open the top, and stuffed her clothing on top of whatever else was in there. "Can't forget that."

Anna could still hear Ted talking by the door, so she took a moment to whisper to Mark. "Are we good?"

"I hope so. I have more reason to believe he might have been followed than I've told you so far."

Anna swallowed hard, wanting to know more but acknowledging that this moment wasn't the time. "Can we trust this Treadman guy?"

"A year ago I wouldn't have said so, but since he bought CMI, he's pulled a Tony Stark and divested his company of all its military and mercenary operations. It's purely a tech company now. Maybe Ted had something to do with that."

"Okay," Anna said, "but let's hope he's not a wolf in sheep's clothing."

Mark put a hand on her arm. "Ted would never turn you over to a wolf, you know that."

"He can be naive."

"We were all naive once." He shrugged. "Whatever happens, I'll be with you every step of the way."

Anna's breath hitched. "Will you, Mark?"

His face took on a determined look. "It isn't fair for you to ask this of me."

"I know. I'm sorry." And Anna was, though not so much for asking as for the genuine need. "I won't mention it again."

Ted had hung up and was peering at them from fifteen feet away, but Mark remained in the darkened hallway, and Anna waited beside him, though without knowing what was keeping him.

Then Mark let out a long breath. "I can hardly deny what I myself experienced, and Ted isn't wrong that what you have in that world is special. It's worth sacrificing for, as you and your family have done time and again. I can't live there—or at least I don't want to—but I can do my best to ensure your ability to do so."

Anna bowed her head, as she might have done had they still been in her hall at Dinas Bran. "Thank you."

"What happens to you is magic." He gave her a rueful smile. "It's like touching God, and I say that even though I don't believe." He paused again. "But I do believe in this."

14

19 March 1294

Bevyn

Math and Bevyn didn't part right away, since it seemed important to gather all the information they could on the troop they were chasing, and to do that, they needed to retrieve the dead man. With the help of ropes and a number of men pulling, they managed to get him all the way up the bank and ultimately laid him out in the field. The horse was a different story. To remove it from its watery grave, the best option was to build a raft and float the corpse downstream. Bevyn was pleased to leave that to those who knew what they were doing.

It was gruesome to have the man lying in the grass in the spring sunshine, which was rare enough to be celebrated. The dead man had been of average height and wore full armor but no tunic. He could have been asleep. As it was, his face was white with death, and he hadn't drowned but appeared to have broken his neck in the fall.

"We also retrieved his saddle bag, my lord." One of Math's men laid the leather pack on the ground beside the body. Bevyn crouched to go through it, believing the detail work of the investigation should fall to him rather than to Math. At first, he didn't seen anything unusual: a few provisions, a spare cloak, and a money bag with five small coins. The dead man hadn't been wealthy, but to possess any coins at all put a man a cut above most of his peers. Nor was Bevyn surprised the man had brought the purse on a raid. Most men-at-arms took all their wealth with them wherever they went.

The last item in the bag was a wad of cloth tucked at the bottom of the pack. With a feeling of grim satisfaction, Bevyn shook out a warrior's tunic and held it up to Math and the small group of men who surrounded them. They'd been right to wait to leave, because this told them what they needed to know.

Math grunted, immediately recognizing, as Bevyn had, the red chevrons and stripes on yellow background as the FitzWalter crest. "FitzWalter's first wife was niece to John Balliol, the King of Scots."

"That's our Scottish connection," Bevyn said. "I must point out, however, that his second wife is the niece of Humphrey de Bohun. I've never trusted the man."

"Are you genuinely suggesting Humphrey has turned traitor after all this time—after what happened to Gilbert de Clare?"

"Something's going on with him."

"I pressed Dafydd on the matter before he left, but he refused to tell me anything, though he did me the courtesy of not lying." Math grimaced. "I can say too that Edmund is not much pleased with his friend—or perhaps former friend by now."

"I've even heard that Bohun has been seen several times this year in the company of Roger Mortimer," Bevyn said.

One of the soldiers nearby looked horrified. "Not at court, surely?"

"If it were at King Dafydd's court, I'd be less concerned than if they are meeting privately." Math took in a breath. "And yet, for all that my first instinct is never to trust a Marcher lord, Bohun's son is with Dafydd. The Bohun family hitched its cart to Dafydd's horse long ago, and they have never wavered in their loyalty and allegiance, even when given every opportunity to do so. Humphrey de Bohun is not Gilbert de Clare."

"But FitzWalter might be," Bevyn said.

Robert FitzWalter had acquired Beeston Castle as part of a deal worked out when John Balliol took the throne of Scotland. To appease the Bruces, who felt themselves much the injured party, Balliol had given them land in Scotland. In turn, so Balliol could feel good about doing anything nice for his sworn enemies, Dafydd had granted Beeston to Balliol's niece, who happened to be FitzWalter's wife, now deceased.

"I met FitzWalter when he came to offer his fealty to Dafydd. Even had I been disposed to like him, I couldn't miss his sharp beak of a nose and flinty eyes," Bevyn said. "Nicholas de Carew spoke of him as though they were not friends."

"Carew is a Lord of the March and the Earl of Pembroke and Oxford. Before his marriage, FitzWalter was a mere knight. Likely, Carew hardly knew the man existed before Dafydd made his deal."

"Well he knows it now." Bevyn said. "FitzWalter is nothing if not a climber."

"With this, he has gone far beyond mere climbing. Abduction and rebellion." Math's eyes were narrowed slits. "He won't be working alone either. If, God forbid, it is Humphrey behind FitzWalter's actions, we will stop him."

An anger that matched Math's stirred within Bevyn. He loved Anna like she was his own blood, but he would have felt the same had it been Lili missing. Or Gwenllian. His only consolation was that if Anna had fallen into FitzWalter's hands, he'd find himself with more than he bargained for. Welsh women were not known for their acceptance of being caged, and Anna less than most.

"FitzWalter's men chose a narrow place in the road for their ambush," said Rhys, who'd remained close by. "There are water courses and ravines all along this route which gave less chance for Princess Anna to escape another way. Too bad for them they didn't believe the legends."

The men around them nodded, revealing how far they'd come in the last ten years that the men of this land would not only accept that Anna and her family had the ability to travel to another world, but be glad of it.

Math nudged the body with the toe of his boot. "He shouldn't have brought the tunic."

"On the contrary, they're probably wearing them even now while riding through England," Bevyn said. "There would have been no reason not to and very good reasons to do so. A company of men showing the colors of their lord is something to remark upon but not something to fear. If all you'd done was hear of twenty of FitzWalter's men riding through England it would have been far less alarming than men showing no colors at all."

"Had they stayed in England, I wouldn't have marshalled men to investigate," Math said, "which is why they waited until dark to enter Wales. We do not countenance masterless men here."

"Nor in Dafydd's England," Bevyn said.

Rhys put up a hand, wanting to speak again. Like Dafydd, and Bevyn himself these days, Math valued men who thought for themselves, so he didn't discourage Rhys. "Could it be he brought the tunic as a means to deceive us into accusing an innocent lord?"

"That is an interesting line of thinking, but if true, he would have been wearing it openly," Bevyn said.

"We will keep that alternative in mind, but I think we should continue with the idea he was FitzWalter's man and not read more into this than needful. Not unless we acquire evidence that causes doubt." Math turned to another one of the men. "Pedr, do you have your paper and charcoal?"

"Yes, my lord." The young man in question had been standing a few paces back from the body, awaiting orders. He wasn't even twenty, but his eyes were thoughtful, and he knew how to represent a man's likeness on paper.

"Draw his likeness." As Pedr set to work, Math handed the tunic to Rhys. "Keep this for me until we have cause to bring it out."

"We ride to Beeston, my lord?" Rhys asked.

"We do." Math's face was set in grim lines. "I'd say FitzWalter owes me an explanation."

15

19 March 2022

Anna

They came down the stairs, but instead of crossing the beautifully appointed lobby and leaving by the main door, Mark led them to the back of the building. He poked his head out of the rear entrance, which opened into an alley between Callum's building and an adjacent one. As this was about as upscale a neighborhood—posh, as Mark would say—as it was possible to find, the alley was free of debris.

"Aren't you worried we'll be spotted?" Anna asked from behind him.

"There are easily a dozen embassies in this neighborhood, many of them for Middle Eastern countries. Because they don't like CCTV cameras, there are none in this alley."

Ted smirked. "Money and politics are the lifeblood of London."

That was as cynical a statement as Anna had ever heard from Ted, and she reconsidered her assumption that he was naive.

It could be he assumed the best in people even though he knew they didn't actually deserve it.

"It's the lifeblood of everywhere. That's our problem." Mark entered the alley just as a bus pulled up to a bus stop on the other side of the main street to which the alley connected. "Run!"

Anna took off after Mark, the backpack slapping awkwardly on her back. The sight of the three of them hurtling from the alleyway was enough to stop people on the sidewalk. Anna had to slow down to edge between the parked cars and then dashed across the street. Mark swung around the front door of the bus and ran up the steps. London buses no longer took cash, apparently, but Mark was ready with a card, which he swiped three times, once each for him, Anna, and Ted.

"You didn't have to pay for me," Ted said a little stiffly. "I have my own."

"Which you probably bought with a credit card," Mark said over his shoulder as he squeezed past commuters in the aisle heading towards the back of the bus.

"Yes, I did." Ted let out a heavy breath. "If someone was watching, they're following now."

"I do this for a living, Ted. Let me do my job."

They found space to stand at the back. Mark had spoken sharply to Ted twice, but he didn't appear offended and instead asked, "What do I do?"

"Call your people." Mark ducked his head to look out the rear window. Traffic was backed up behind the bus, which had stopped twice more since they'd gotten on.

"And tell them what?"

"To meet us outside the Natural History Museum on Cromwell Road."

They rode for a few minutes with several more stops. Then the bus stopped again. "Get off now." Mark grabbed Anna's arm and drew her out the back door, Ted on their heels. Their feet hit the sidewalk and a second later they were running along a narrow road between buildings, and then under them, as walkways passed above their heads.

"Where are we?" Anna was nearly gasping. The pack was heavy and slowing her steps, even as it made her heart and lungs work harder.

"Imperial College, London." Mark pulled out another key card, which he held in his hand until he was able to swipe it on a device next to a door. It unlocked, and Mark herded her and Ted inside the building.

"Why do you have a keycard for here?" Anna said between breaths.

Mark gave her a sidelong look. "MI-5, remember?" Then he pointed at the phone Ted still held in his hand. "That's the burner I gave you, yeah?"

"Yeah."

Mark snapped his fingers. "Give it here."

Ted obeyed, and at the next junction of two hallways, Mark stopped, took out the battery, and dropped the pieces of the phone into the garbage. "Yours too, Anna."

Anna gave up her phone, which she'd barely looked at anyway. Mark had been working constantly on his various devices, all with a touch of a finger, but she hadn't yet figured out where the keyboard was on hers. Regardless, her phone was followed into the trashcan by Mark's. It seemed a painful waste, but she accepted that it was necessary. Then, from his satchel, which Mark carried in addition to the giant backpack, he pulled out three more phones, tossing one each to Ted and Anna. "Call your people back, Ted. Have them track that phone so they'll be ready when we come out of the museum."

A far doorway banged, and feet pounded in the corridor. Stowing her phone without turning it on—which she hadn't yet figured out how to do either—she did the one thing she appeared to be good at: fleeing. "Come on!"

At that moment, as it was a school day, a bell rang, and the hall filled with people.

"Good." Mark hustled after her towards another doorway that took them outside again. "More students. We can blend in better."

"Did you see anyone following us?"

"An unmarked van was behind us as we got on the bus. We moved quickly into the college, but I would have preferred a shopping mall." Mark took a right, entered another building, left it, then crossed a street to enter another building, which he again led them through. Finally, he looked up. "Ah. The museum."

They went inside and immediately a young man with blonde spiked-up hair stopped them, wanting to check their bags. Mark flashed his MI-5 badge, but so quickly that it would have been next to impossible for the man to actually read his name. "Security Service. We were never here."

"Yes, sir!"

"Let us in the back, will you?"

"Of course, sir." The man had what Anna thought might be a cockney accent. He opened an employees' only door, which led to a maze of corridors that ultimately dumped them back out onto a sidewalk.

And the second they appeared, an SUV with dark tinted windows slid next to the curb on their side of the road. Anna couldn't see the driver because of the tint, and she felt Mark hesitate beside her. But Ted was already holding the rear door open for Anna, and because they were trying to be quick and not seen, she threw caution to the winds and got in.

Mark still hesitated. "You're sure about this, Ted?"

Ted pulled open the front passenger door. "I'm sure, Mark. It's okay. And we have no better option right now. We have to get off the street!"

Another car pulled up and parked on the curb behind the one Anna was in. A man in a tailored dark suit got out and approached Mark. "George Hanson, Mr. Treadman's deputy." He spoke with a flat American accent exactly like Anna's own.

Mark shook the man's hand. "Thanks for picking us up."

"No problem." He bent to look into the SUV at Anna. "It is a pleasure to meet you, ma'am."

Anna almost laughed at being called ma'am by someone so close in age to her. His brown hair was cut close to his head, so she had an inkling he might be former military. That caused her stomach to twist, since The Dunland Group turned CMI turned Treadman Global had been a mercenary outfit.

George gestured to the seat beside Anna. "If you'll just get in, sir, we'll be on our way. The cameras won't be down on this block for long." He looked around, unbuttoning his suit jacket as he did so. Anna saw the flash of a holster on his right hip, and then he was urging Mark into the vehicle. George closed the door, the driver of Anna's vehicle waited a beat for George to return to his car, and then he pulled smoothly out into traffic.

Once they were on their way, Ted turned around to look at them. "Isn't this great?"

Anna shook her head at her uncle. "I don't know, Uncle Ted. Is it? It feels an awful lot like I'm being taken to a black site."

"Oh no! Don't think that." Ted was twisted around in his seat, and he made a move to put a hand on her arm, but then he adjusted his motion because of her broken left wrist. "This is all going to work out just fine. You'll see."

The driver, who up until now had said nothing, looked at Anna in his rearview mirror. He was a black man with distinguished gray hair, likely older than any of them. He also had George's same military bearing, though when he opened his mouth, he proved to be English. "We're going to take good care of you, miss. Our mandate is to keep you safe."

"That is good to hear." Anna hoped she kept the sarcasm out of her voice.

Ted gestured to the driver. "This is Andre."

Anna bobbed her head. "It's nice to meet you." But then she turned again to Mark and spoke in an undertone, "You okay with this?"

"For now." He leaned forward and directed his next words at Ted. "I'm realizing that you have told Mr. Treadman far more about Anna—and me—than you previously let on."

Ted's expression turned grave. "Like I said back at Callum's apartment, we—and by that I mean everyone from David and Anna to MI-5 to Elisa and me—have been doing the same thing over and over again. Don't you think it's time for a change?"

Then Ted's phone rang, and he answered. "Yes, she's here." Pause. "Yes, we were followed." He dropped the phone slightly and spoke to the driver. "Are we being followed now?"

"I would have let you know if we were." He pressed his finger to his ear and spoke to someone who wasn't there, perhaps George in the follow car, "How are we doing?" He nodded to a response only he could hear, and then he said, louder, to everyone in the car, "We took care of the cameras on the street, but with so many buildings and tourists, dozens of people could have seen you get into this vehicle. That said, we hope to be well away from London before those chasing you realize you've left the city."

Mark studied the man for a count of three before saying, "You're not just a chauffeur, are you?"

Andre laughed. "Hardly."

Ted looked embarrassed. "Andre is head of Mr. Treadman's security. He insisted on driving you today. We don't want any mistakes."

Andre nodded. "I've just heard from some of my men. They've collected Elisa and Elen."

"Good." Ted relaxed a little more.

Mark looked at his phone to read a message that had just come in. "The horse has made the news."

Anna gaped at a video—on Mark's phone!—of the dead horse being wheeled out of Westminster and levered into a large animal van. The newscaster said, "No word yet on how the horse found itself *inside* Westminster Hall." It showed an image of the police sergeant Anna had met talking to a man in a suit within the gates of Westminster. "Authorities report it was a prank gone wrong, as the horse went wild once confined to the hall and had to be put down."

"So do we know who was following us?" Anna said, though her eyes were still on the video.

"Not yet." Andre's eyes flashed once again to the rearview mirror, and he and Mark exchanged a long look that Anna couldn't interpret.

"It had to be Westminster Palace, didn't it?" she said.

Mark leaned his head back against the rest. "Apparently so."

By contrast, Ted was the opposite of despondent. "You are going to be safe and protected, though Mark—" his expression sobered, "—you may never go back to MI-5."

Mark made a rueful face. "I think we can assume that." Then he patted her thigh. "Regardless, Anna, you have nothing to fear. You aren't in danger. You're the goose that lays the golden egg."

While Anna didn't like the sound of that, it was true that the one laying the golden egg is the one with the power. Maybe right now wasn't the time to exert it, not without a plan to do so, but it was food for thought and maybe something to plan for in the future. This time around she was set back on her heels, but maybe next time, between her, Mom, and David, they didn't need to be.

16

19 March 1294

Ieuan

"Why Scots?" Cadwallon said. "Why is Balliol stirring?"

"I hate to speculate." Ieuan stood in the clearing in front of the inn, studying the landscape. His eyes had taken a turn for the worse in his late twenties, and he didn't see distance as well as he once had, but he had spectacles in his pack if he needed them. For now, he pulled out a pair of binoculars, another gift from Dafydd. At this point, it was trite to say Dafydd and his family had transformed the world and the people around them, but that didn't make it any less true.

"Do you think they're riding all the way to Scotland?"

"Not tonight, they're not," Ieuan said. "It's too far. Besides, according to the innkeeper, only a few of the men were Scots. The rest are English, they speak English, and that means they must come from an English lord."

Cadwallon bit his lip, and his eyes went to the east too. "But who?"

"If we keep riding in the same direction they went, we will eventually find out." Ieuan turned and whistled through his teeth, calling the men together, and they gathered around him.

England and Wales had been at peace for ten years. There had been battles, mostly one-offs, and nothing large scale. So while Dafydd had taken the most experienced of his men-at-arms to Ireland, Ieuan still had plenty of capable men at his disposal. Nothing else was acceptable in Dafydd's train.

And yet, as Ieuan looked into their faces, he saw them as so *young*, and he was reminded again how the world had changed since he'd hunted in the woods outside his uncle's house, pretending Humphrey de Bohun was William de Braose and he was Cadwallon the Brave. In those days, war with England had been a way of life, and he'd never questioned that it always would be.

Today, the men (and woman) who looked at him were Welsh and English both, and many of them had been children when King Edward had died and the world had changed. They didn't know another way to be, and Ieuan was more determined than ever that they never would. They were *not* going back to the bad old days when parents died and children grew up too fast.

Without war, however, his men weren't exactly seasoned, though they would be gaining experience by the hour today. "We will continue on the trail of the company. They came through here and should be easier to track from now on." He looked darkly all around. "I'm feeling more confident that Princess Anna wasn't with them, but we still don't know for certain. The innkeeper did confirm Scotsmen were included in this company, but it was not led by a Scot. I don't know where they are going any more than you do, but as we have been doing since we left Dinas Bran, we will stop at every croft and village and trace this company's movements across England. Any questions?"

That was something Ieuan would never have asked his men once upon a time, but Dafydd's open-mindedness had influenced him, and Ieuan had chosen these men in part because they weren't simple soldiers. They might be young, but they were thinkers, and that's what he needed today. It was what Dafydd had needed when he'd elevated Ieuan himself to captain ten years ago.

One young man of twenty raised his hand. "I don't know this land well, but Venny does." He pointed to the man standing next to him. And really, the pair couldn't have been more different. Mathew was English, son of a London wheelwright, but smart as a whip and built like a boar. Dafydd routinely went into the London academies and chose the best and brightest for his service, and Mathew was one of the finest examples of that. He rode beside the sons of noblemen, whose predecessors would have insisted Mathew wasn't good enough to do anything more than polish their boots—or build the wheels of their carriages. Dafydd didn't tolerate such attitudes, however, and any nobleman who expressed them—or even thought them in Dafydd's presence—was soon deprived of Dafydd's favor.

Venny, by contrast, was really named William Venables. His ancestors were Norman, and he was heir to a barony that had risen just high enough to be exactly the kind of nobleman who, in the past, would have stepped on Mathew in order to emphasize his own greatness. But instead, he had accepted his place in Dafydd's new order.

Being slender and short of stature, Venny didn't look very much like a soldier. What an outsider wouldn't know was that he didn't have a thimbleful of fat on him, and his slender body was a powerhouse of energy. Ieuan had personally witnessed him jump four feet straight up and land on a wall with no running start. He could out-wrestle men twice his size, and when he threw a knife, it hit the bullseye every time. Before he'd gone to Ireland, Dafydd had asked Ieuan to assess the candidates for captaincy of his personal guard, and Ieuan was eyeing Venny as his first choice— which at one time would have made him laugh out loud to think he might admire a man of Norman descent enough to recommend him for promotion.

At the same time, he suspected somewhere beneath that long Norman nose and pointed chin lay some Welsh blood: Venny had a sense of humor that was right on the edge at times of getting him into trouble—and he could sing.

Now Venny nodded. "My father is Baron of Kinderton, east of Chester. No Scots have settled in the region, and nobody has ties to Scots except for—" he paused, and his face twisted into a grimace.

"Except for whom?" Cadwallon prompted.

"My lords!"

They turned as a rider approached from the north. His horse was lathered, and he himself was breathing hard.

"Thank the saints, I found you." The man dismounted in front of Ieuan. "I am Harold of Lyons Castle. My lord Warenne learned from a rider sent by Lord Mathonwy what has befallen Princess Anna. He sent me to find you."

"John de Warenne?" Cadwallon said. "Why?"

"He would like to assist in the search for her, requests you come to Lyons Castle to confer, and even offers it to you as a base."

Ieuan took in a breath. This was help from a not entirely unexpected source, but one he would never take for granted.

For all that he'd lived these past years in England at Dafydd's side, Ieuan cared not a whit for politics and the jostling among barons for power and land. He'd become a knight because he was a lord's son, and he'd been well rewarded for his skill and loyalty. He'd never thought beyond becoming Dafydd's captain, much less commanding all of his men throughout the whole of England.

These Normans were a different story. They lived and breathed politics and intrigue. Not only had Warenne's daughter been John Balliol's first wife, making Warenne the grandfather of the heir to the throne of Scotland, but his son had married a daughter of Robert de Vere, who, along with Roger Mortimer and Roger Bigod, had opposed Dafydd's rise to power in England. This castle of Warenne's lay some eight miles north of Overton on the Welsh side of the Dee. Like Nicholas de Carew, back in 1285, Warenne had been faced with a choice of bowing to Llywelyn or giving up the castle.

But like most Marcher lords, he had more love for his own power than for King Edward, who was dead by then anyway. Warenne had also been among those who'd sided with Simon de Montfort (and by extension Llywelyn and Gilbert de Clare) against the English throne thirty years earlier. Though he'd switched back to the royal side before the end, that animosity towards authority remained.

Once Llywelyn had been crowned king, Warenne had chosen to bend a knee to him. And then again to Dafydd, to pay homage for the rest of his lands, which remained in England. He hadn't even rebelled with William de Valence, his wife's brother, when Valence had tried to overthrow Dafydd. Ieuan knew Math had deliberately wooed the man, and they had remained on good terms throughout the years. Math had even offered him a radio, though Warenne had respectfully declined. Not everyone was ready for the new age Dafydd was ushering in. Warenne had heard the news of Anna's abduction the old-fashioned way.

Thus, even though Ieuan had a momentary pang of suspicion, he took Harold at his word. If Warenne hadn't betrayed Dafydd by allying with Valence, FitzWarin, or Clare, it would have been an odd play to be opposing him now, even if Balliol, his son-in-law, had come calling and offered great reward. Warenne had enough wealth and land to refuse, and his only son had died in a tournament in 1286. Admittedly, he had grandchildren, one of whom was Balliol's heir. Another was Henry Percy, an upstanding young man and a follower of Dafydd, though not so close he'd gone to Ireland with him.

"How did you know where to find us?" Cadwallon asked, inherently suspicious of an offer of help from anyone other than a Welshman, even though he himself had married an Englishwoman.

"The rider who reached us said you had left at the same time he did and explained what you intended. Again, Lord Warenne has resources and men waiting for your command."

"Please thank him for his offer and tell him we may see him before the day is out."

Harold hesitated, obviously unhappy they weren't coming with him, but after a moment, he bowed. "I will, my lord." He went to his horse and mounted. At a much slower pace, he headed back the way he'd come.

After watching him go, Ieuan turned to Venny, "Who were you going to suggest?"

"Warenne." Venny shrugged. "But that idea is obviously wrong. Are we taking him up on his offer to coordinate?"

Ieuan pursed his lips as he thought. "No. Not yet. I appreciate Warenne's desire to help, but the trail of our quarry calls me onward. Until I know for certain Anna wasn't with these riders, I don't dare stray from it."

17

19 March 1294

Bronwen

"I don't like this any more than you do." Bevyn's growl was in fine form as he paced back and forth in front of Bronwen and Lili. "Though unlike you two, staying behind was my idea."

"And we are grateful you made the sacrifice to protect us," Bronwen assured him. "It's just frustrating to find yet another plot against David by someone he thought was faithful."

"Men want to be rewarded for their loyalty, but the cynical handing out of favors isn't something Dafydd likes to do—or is good at." Lili moved to sit in a regal chair set up in the university's main hall. "In fact, he did do it for FitzWalter and look where it got him."

They'd located their command center here so that, when the exhausted men returned from their scouting missions, they wouldn't have to ride all the way up to the castle to report their findings. Plus, the university was designed to feed and house large numbers of people at one time, and nearly the entire population of the town had turned out to help with the search for Anna in one way or another.

It was strange not to see Constance at Lili's side, as she'd been for the last six months. Similar to Lili, Constance had been a child no older than Cadell when her father had taken her to shoot with her first cut-down-to-size bow. King Edward had been alive then and had started enforcing the law that all Englishmen equip themselves with bow and arrows.

Becoming an archer couldn't be accomplished overnight, however, and just because a man owned a bow didn't mean he had the skill to use it. The Welsh started training their boys—and some girls—to shoot practically from birth, but the bow had never been part of English society the way it was in Wales. That made the English very late to the game, and before David had ascended the throne, the only real archers in Britain had been Welsh.

While David's elite force of two hundred archers were made up exclusively of Welshmen, the years he'd been on the throne and actually enforced the archery laws had started to bear fruit. Despite years of practice at Constance's side, her father still couldn't hit the broad side of a barn door, but Constance had learned to, and so had the rest of the Englishmen in her company. Constance's husband, Cador, was their captain, but though he called himself a Welshman, his grandmother had been English, and he spoke her language fluently, which was why Ieuan had included him on the mission too, rather than leaving him in Wales with the rest of the Welshmen.

Despite the number of people absent, or maybe because of it, Lili and Bronwen were trying to keep everything as normal as possible for the children. Thus, the older kids were at their lessons with their tutors, among them Aaron, Meg's friend and Samuel's father, who had retired from active medical practice to teach at Llangollen. Gwenllian, the eldest of the cousins at almost twelve, had declared her desire to attend university rather than marry at sixteen, so she was hard at work writing up a physics experiment Bronwen would rather not know anything about, since she'd gone into anthropology so she'd never have to do math again.

Next oldest was Anna's son, Cadell, who'd be nine this summer and was having the most difficult time of any of the children. He was old enough to understand exactly what had happened to his mother, and equally old enough to worry about it. Latin declensions were the last thing he wanted to do today, and Bronwen was considering letting him off early for archery practice instead. Though, again, he would be without Constance. Not only had Cadell's shooting improved dramatically under her tutelage, but the two had formed a bond.

Then came Arthur, Elisa and Padrig, Catrin, and Bran, all four and five-year-olds. Their lessons were not extensive and usually took no more than an hour out of their days, but Catrin and Arthur, in particular, were on their way to reading well. Simple math and French were also on the menu in one of the classrooms down the hall from where Bronwen, Lili, and Bevyn were considering their options.

That left the two youngest, Bronwen's Cadwaladr and Lili's Alexander, who were currently playing with blocks and toy cars at Lili's feet. The cars were precious commodities, having come in the backpack of one of the bus passengers, Shane, whom they'd returned to Avalon because he was sick. He'd left the toys behind as a parting gift. Fortunately, he'd carried a whole sack of them on the bus that day in Cardiff, so there were enough for both boys to be content, and there was currently no squawking between them.

"I am most concerned that the attack on Anna wasn't an isolated incident and is part of a much larger plan," Bevyn said.

"That's why we called in Edmund Mortimer," Bronwen said. "I'm hoping we will hear from him soon."

"Tell me the truth, Bevyn," Lili said. "Are we safe here?"

"It is as Math told Cadell. Men are posted in the watchtower on the escarpment. We will know if anyone marches into the valley long before they arrive here. We will certainly have enough warning to retreat to the castle."

"I feel so useless." Lili kicked her heels against the foot of the chair.

"Dafydd would not thank me if I let you ride out with your brother," Bevyn said. "He is free to do what he does because you and Bronwen are safe here. You sent Constance as your representative, and that's enough."

"What I want most is to hear from—" Bronwen cut herself off as Dinas Bran's pigeon keeper approached with a vibrant expression on his face. She'd been about to say she wanted to hear from David.

The man bowed, his Einstein-like white hair sticking up in a fluffy halo around his head. "My ladies. My lord." He straightened and held out a trembling hand. "News."

Lili was on her feet in an instant. "When did it come in?"

David always traveled with a dozen messenger pigeons, since the radio wouldn't work across the Irish Sea. Though most were homed to London where Nicholas de Carew was holding the fort, a few were homed to Dinas Bran. David had sent one when he'd arrived in Dublin three weeks ago, and they hadn't known if he wasn't sending more because he was dead or because he was saving them for great need.

"Just now, my lady."

Lili took the paper, and Bronwen came close to her side so she could read the message over Lili's shoulder. Bronwen's hands would have been shaking like Lili's if she'd been the one to open it. Like all messages sent by pigeon, this one was short and to the point.

Tara 3/18. We are alive/well. Rebellion among Irish/Norman barons. Scot involvement. Beware. Love D.

David's wording was at the same time both horribly specific and frustratingly cryptic. Bronwen was grateful the first words David had written told them the family was alive, but the rest was cause for true alarm. David would have known that, of course, and thus he'd written the note himself, despite his terrible handwriting. He could have designated someone else to write it for him, but he knew the sight of his hand would be a comfort to Lili.

And if the handwriting didn't make it clear enough that the message was from David, the use of many slashes and the American dating system *3/18* would have given it away. The English, even in the Middle Ages, put the day before the month.

Lili's face was white as she handed the piece of paper to Bevyn. "Scots again."

Bronwen glanced at the pigeon keeper, who was doing his best not to look at any of them, as no doubt he could tell the news could have been better. Hardly one to punish the messenger, she merely commented to him, "It says he wrote this yesterday."

"Yes, my lady. It's only a hundred and fifty miles to Dublin from here. Perhaps the weather delayed the bird."

Bronwen still struggled with the concept of a bird that could fly forty or fifty miles an hour and keep it up for a day.

Bevyn finished reading the note. "It can be no coincidence we have Scots in Ireland and Scots here. The two rebellions have to be coordinated.

"Who has the power?" Bronwen said. "Is it really Balliol?"

Bevyn shook his head. "I don't know. But I have to think FitzWalter moved last night because he knows Dafydd is otherwise occupied."

"They could even think him dead," Bronwen said.

"But he lives." Lili pressed the paper, which Bevyn had returned to her, to her heart. "We know something they don't."

"We should send messengers to Ieuan and Math," Bevyn said. "They need to know we received word from Dafydd."

Bronwen shook her head. "No, we shouldn't."

Both Bevyn and Lili turned to look at her, and Lili said, "Why is that?"

"As you implied a moment ago, we have information our enemies do not. They are moving because they think David is besieged—"

"Or dead," Bevyn amended.

"Or dead," Bronwen agreed. "That is why they have shown their hand. We don't want them to stop or go to ground. With Anna safe in Avalon, we *want* them to move, and we can't risk this information falling into the wrong hands."

"You have become very Welsh, my dear." Bevyn's growl this time was admiring. "How did we hold off the English for so many years? It wasn't by confronting them in open battle. It was by waiting, biding our time, and then when the enemy was most exposed, when they'd fully committed to the fight—" he pounded his right fist into the palm of his left hand, "—we pounced."

18

19 March 2022

Anna

It took them an hour just to get out of London, though they ultimately managed it without any untoward events, ending up in a countryside that at least had the benefit of looking more familiar to Anna. At first she thought they were following the Thames, but then she realized they were heading more north, maybe even following the old Roman road that in her day (meaning in the medieval world) would eventually take them to Chester—and with a slight detour, to Dinas Bran.

Unfortunately, to reach Math she would have to not only traverse that road but seven hundred years and another universe. She had a vision of Math searching for her, much as Papa had searched for Mom and Anna herself when they'd disappeared from his life before David was born. He would be desperate, made all the more so by not knowing if she'd been captured or if she'd come to Avalon.

And that's if Mair managed to escape and tell him what had happened. Without her testimony, all Math would know was she'd disappeared off the face of the earth somewhere between Heledd's house and Llangollen.

Feeling worse by the second, Anna looked out the window, tinted, of course, which meant the cameras couldn't see inside. She was upset for Mark, though he was taking his possible unemployment in stride. As always, he could not be parted from some electronic device. He had his new phone on his thigh, showing a map of England, with a little blue dot that was their vehicle, moving along a road.

Cassie had navigated that way when she'd driven them around Caernarfon, but Anna hadn't been involved, and she was reminded again how out of place she felt here. More than any of the other times she'd returned to Avalon, she felt as if she'd time traveled to the future.

Still, she leaned in to get a closer look. "Where are we?"

"Approaching Chalfont St. Giles," Ted said, answering for Mark.

"Of course we are," Anna said under her breath, suppressing the urge to laugh at the typically English name, which could have come straight out of one of the Harry Potter books. "Okay. Why are we in Chalfont St. Giles?"

"Because that is where Mr. Treadman lives when he's in the UK," Mark said, this time answering for Ted.

Andre glanced at Anna in the rearview mirror. "No need to worry, miss. We are almost there." He clearly meant to be reassuring, and he obviously knew where he was going, but Anna was wound so tightly her shoulders were starting to ache more than her wrist.

Cradling her left forearm in her right hand, she closed her eyes and leaned back against the seat. After three deep breaths, through which she forced herself to relax, she opened her eyes and looked again at Mark. So far, he'd been much calmer than Anna thought he had any right to be, and he'd abdicated his leadership role in taking care of her very easily. It was almost as if he welcomed the idea of being rid of her.

"Why aren't you worried, Mark?" Anna said.

Ted was back to talking on his phone, and she kept her voice low so he couldn't hear.

"If I was, would it help?"

She tsked through her teeth. "Treadman Global bought out CMI. Why don't we think this is a trap?"

"Because I have met Chad Treadman, and when your uncle started working for him, I did a vetting so complete I know the brand of fitted trunks his assistant buys for him. MI-5 has a dossier on him an inch thick. He's unconventional and a genius, but he isn't a traitor or a killer."

Anna felt a little better. "So you think this is for real?"

"Like your uncle, Treadman is eager, not evil."

Ted hung up his call and turned to look at Mark and Anna. "If I hadn't been worried about being tailed, I would have left all this for tomorrow. But I want you to know before we arrive that I truly believe Chad Treadman can be an ally in this."

"And what is *this* exactly?" Anna said.

"In coming to terms with the time traveling."

"So we're not just here because it's safe," Anna said. "Chad Treadman—"

"—is a visionary. I think he can help us." Ted gestured expansively. "I wouldn't have brought you here if I didn't trust him."

"Maybe he is trustworthy," Anna shifted the pack on the floor so it rested more comfortably between her feet, "but enlisting the aid of an outsider makes me very uncomfortable. He's an entrepreneur, not the government, but that doesn't mean he isn't going to want something from me."

"The government wants to control you," Ted said. "Chad doesn't care about power that way."

"Then he's going to want to make money off the Middle Ages," Anna said. "We've been down this road before—with the same corporation!"

"It isn't the same company anymore." Ted made a motion with his head. "This isn't like it was before. He's not like anyone you've ever met."

Anna didn't bother with a rebuttal. She wasn't in a position to give one anyway, or get away, since she was hardly going to throw herself from a moving vehicle. Talking to Mark had made her feel momentarily better, but she was feeling again as if her uncle had betrayed her.

The feeling only got worse when Ted added, "Anyway, Chad already knew you were here." He twisted further in his seat and caught her good hand. "He didn't come to get you at the hospital because he doesn't work that way."

"How did he know?"

Ted tipped his chin to Mark, who said, "Because he owns a dozen satellites he put into the sky himself."

Ted nodded. "He would never have abducted you. He only intervened at my request when MI-5 appeared to be close to taking you."

"So you have told him everything." Outrage was giving way to resignation.

"I didn't tell you because I didn't want to spook you," Ted said.

"Is that supposed to make me feel better?" Anna was growing irate at their complacency. And she was really tired of sitting in this car. All of a sudden, the passivity was intolerable—as was the helplessness. "Whose side are you on, Mark? David's going to *kill* me when he finds out about this."

Mark put out a soothing hand. "I'm on your side, Anna. Always." He took in a breath. "But I haven't told you everything either. MI-5 can never be the ally it once was. The Time Travel Initiative in its original form is dead, but I have reason to believe certain elements in Five—with the help of the CIA—have resurrected parts of it. You need my help, and I've given it, but it's at a cost."

Anna's anger was gone in an instant. "I'm sorry."

"This just came in from Livia." He turned his phone so she could see the text. *They arrived at the hospital right after we did. They know what we did.*

Anna leaned in to see Mark text back, *Who's they?*

Five.

How did they know?

I don't know. I've shredded all the records I found.

Do they know who I really am?

I don't think so. But they seem very thorough. I fear they will soon.

A cold feeling swept over Anna. "She needs to run."

Mark snorted. "Run where? She works for MI-5. She knows how impossible it is to truly disappear."

"Isn't that what we're trying to do?" Anna said.

The three men in the car sat silent for a count of five. And then Andre said, "We're buying you time. That's all."

"And that was before Livia texted me," Mark said.

She looked from one man to the other. "I should have gone straight up to the roof this morning and jumped off."

Uncle Ted shook his head. "You have a broken wrist. What would you have done if you arrived in a similar situation to here?"

"I wouldn't have had a horse," Anna said tartly, "and there are no guns where I'm going."

"You could have fallen into a river, or tumbled down an embankment," Uncle Ted said. "If you hurt your wrist more, what then?"

"I'm not hiding in Chad Treadman's house for six weeks until my wrist is healed!"

Ted made a calming motion with his hand. "Nobody is saying you should."

"Besides which, you don't have six weeks. I'm hoping for six hours." Mark's expression was very serious. "They know you're here, and they know you're with me. I do believe some of my security measures have worked. They don't have Callum's flat, and they don't have our phones. If they knew where we were, they would have stopped us. Still, the hunt is on. It's only a matter of time before they put the pieces together."

"Ted is right that you'll lose your job?"

Mark and Ted exchanged a quick look, and then Mark met her eyes. "It is worse than that. They are coming after you now, and they are going to keep coming. If you'd arrived on Hampstead Heath, the satellites would have caught it, so Five would know, but they would have had no grounds to chase you. Your arrival on a horse inside Westminster makes you a terrorist. Five will pursue you with every means at their disposal."

"But why?" The sound came out almost a wail.

Andre answered this time, which made sense since he was the security expert. "This is the era of stopping acts before they start. That's the Holy Grail, and you don't get there with anything less than total commitment."

"Chad Treadman can help," Ted said.

"How?" Anna still felt belligerent, but with the government breathing down her neck, her choices were diminishing, if they hadn't disappeared entirely.

"I'll let him tell you himself," Ted said, "because here we are."

All the while they'd been talking, Andre had continued driving. With a spin of the wheel, he pulled the car smoothly off the road to arrive at what could only be described as a gatehouse. It even had a portcullis, though at a wave from the driver, the metal barrier slid quietly upwards, rather than being winched up by hand. The driveway wound its way up a hill through an oak and birch forest that extended from both sides of the road, before the car came out ultimately on a high plateau.

Before them sat a castle, though like the gatehouse, it was completely modern. No detail had been spared on its external appearance, however, and it was as if every aspect of the medieval castle had been taken to its logical conclusion. There were towers and battlements, wall-walks, and an inner gatehouse, all built in stone, but the guard at this second gatehouse wore Kevlar and an ear piece, was heavily armed, and kept checking his tablet. He waved the car through with a flick of his hand.

Andre drove the car underneath this second gatehouse tower, around a circular driveway, and parked in front of a great square keep.

19

19 March 1294

Ieuan

Math spoke low in Ieuan's ear. "You, my friend, are very good at what you do."

It was late afternoon by now, and the search parties had converged on Beeston Castle—Ieuan because he'd followed the trail of the company, and Math because he could apparently read minds.

Ieuan didn't take his eyes off Beeston's battlements, which he was studying through his binoculars. He'd found a spot on the top of a hill three-quarters of a mile to the south. It was the closest his company could get without calling undue attention to themselves. "I take little credit. Once we learned the riders crossed the Dee at Overton, the way was plain. What about you?"

"One of FitzWalter's soldiers died falling into a ravine. He had a tunic with the FitzWalter crest in his saddle bag." Math proceeded to relate all that had transpired in the hours since Ieuan had last seen him.

"I'm glad Anna is safe in Avalon." Ieuan gripped his friend's upper arm. His chest tightened to think about how it could as easily have been Bronwen these men had targeted—and she didn't have the ability to time travel. "Anyone else would have been dead."

Math shot him an aggrieved look. "I don't know that *safe* is the correct word."

"Better than being here. It was only a matter of time before the Scots grew restless, but that they've allied with English barons makes me very nervous."

"FitzWalter looks to be a very busy man." Math held out his hand for the binoculars. The sun was well down in the west by now, the light glinting off the glass in the keep's windows.

"The traffic in and out of the gatehouse has been nearly constant in the last hour since we arrived," Ieuan said, his hand itching to take the binoculars back.

Beeston Castle was a mighty fortress built on a rock five hundred feet above the Cheshire plain. From the castle, the garrison could see for thirty miles in every direction, which was why Ieuan had ordered his men to approach cautiously, as Math had done. It was a fine thing to have a compatriot so completely trustworthy.

Math put a hand on Ieuan's shoulder. "We need to regroup."

"We found an abandoned barn at the bottom of the hill."

"I know. We're there too."

Ieuan laughed and followed his friend down the trail to the barn. It was large enough to hold all thirty of the men they'd brought between the two companies.

In their leaders' absence, Math's men and Ieuan's men had brought each other up to date, even to the point that Rhys, Math's tracker, had pulled the tunic in question from his saddle bag. Everyone stopped talking as soon as Math and Ieuan entered, and Math stepped to the center of the barn floor. "I am satisfied the company we are tracking is even now inside Beeston. The question before us is what we are going to do about it."

Venny was the first to speak. "Thirty men isn't enough for a siege, my lord."

"Are we agreed the princess isn't in there?" Cadwallon said. "We dare not do anything to endanger her."

"She's in Avalon," Math said, "I'm sure of it. But regardless, we need to think carefully about our next steps."

Venny raised a hand to speak again. "Once night falls, we can get closer; perhaps one or two of us could infiltrate the castle as peasants. With all those extra men, they need supplies like any other castle and hands to do the work."

"Send me, my lord," Constance said. "I can dress as a woman, and it might disarm them into letting us pass."

They all turned at the high voice, some of Math's men clearly not remembering that Constance had ridden with Ieuan. Bevyn thought letting women be soldiers was a runaway carriage he would have halted immediately if Dafydd had been willing to listen. Fortunately for Constance, Bevyn didn't have a say, and most of the time, Constance served as Lili's bodyguard. Ieuan had chosen her to come with him today for the same reason he'd chosen the men: because she was needed, and maybe for exactly this reason, though it hadn't been at the forefront of his mind at the time.

Cadwallon frowned. "Entering the castle aside, my lord, I don't know that all of us can stay here for very long without arousing suspicion, especially those of us who are Welsh. We can't risk FitzWalter getting wind of our presence."

Ieuan nodded, acknowledging that five years was not enough time to dissipate the hundreds of years of distrust between English and Welsh. "Venny, as a lord of Kinderton, you would be known to FitzWalter, wouldn't you?"

"Yes, my lord."

"You know the politics up there better than I. Do you think you could get us into the castle?"

Venny took in a breath, but he nodded.

Math put a hand on Ieuan's arm. "You know it can't be you, right? You and I shouldn't even stay here. We are both known to many in this region."

Ieuan grimaced. It was one of the very few downsides of having spent the last ten years at Dafydd's side. So he turned to his small company. "Lord Mathonwy and I will ride to Lyons Castle and reconnoiter with Warenne as he asked hours ago. Cadwallon, you will stay with those who remain behind here overnight, as support for Venny, and we will regroup in the morning. We need a complete accounting of everyone and everything that goes in and out of that castle."

"What if an army marches tonight?" Cadwallon said. "We don't know how close FitzWalter may be to implementing whatever he's planned."

"Then follow it, but you must send word to me as well," Ieuan said. "Most importantly, we cannot let FitzWalter know we are on to him."

"That means we should wait until dark to enter the castle," Constance said.

Ieuan looked at Venny. "I won't order you to lead the mission, but I am asking you to."

Venny took in another breath and let it out, a little shakily, but his expression remained determined. "How many men should I bring with me?"

"Constance and Cador, Mathew—"

"And me!" Rhys put up a hand. "I'll do it."

Ieuan nodded. "God willing, we'll see you in the morning."

With the decision made, the men began preparing for what came next. Venny punched Mathew in the upper arm. "The women of this region are very pretty. Maybe you'll get lucky at last and find one who favors you."

Mathew snorted. "It's a wonder Lord Ieuan chose you to lead us. One look at you and the guard will know you've never done a day's work in your life."

The two men walked away towards their horses, their bantering continuing out of earshot. Ieuan said to Math, who'd overheard as well, "It's good they still have a sense of humor."

Math nodded. "With the darkness that faces us, they're going to need it."

20

19 March 2022

Anna

Uncle Ted was so excited he was practically bouncing up and down. "We're here!" He pushed open the car door.

Andre graciously opened Anna's door for her, but when she got out, unlike Ted, she didn't feel like celebrating.

They were greeted by an Englishwoman dressed in jeans and a silk blouse and speaking with a BBC British accent. "Welcome to Treadman Castle. I'm Sophie Price, but please call me Sophie. We're very informal here." The follow car had also arrived, pulling up smoothly behind them. George and two other security men joined Andre and Sophie around Anna, Ted, and Mark. Nobody took Anna's elbow or did anything threatening. It was more like they were intending to be protective.

Anna summoned a smile. She'd been a princess for long enough to be able to fake happiness when she needed to. In fact, she had a huge well of experience in smiling when she didn't want to and being polite when she would have much rather expressed her real opinion. In those cases, rather than an uncomfortable encounter with an American tech genius, she would be required to make small talk with a Norman lord who thought Welshmen—and all women—were inferior to him.

She'd learned, however, in the last ten years, that changing people's hearts was possible, and by being polite and keeping all but a fraction of her true thoughts to herself, often she and Math could nudge a man in the proper direction and even make him think an idea was his own. Was he resisting opening a school in one of his villages? It was often a matter of laying out all the ways an educated populace was going to bring more wealth to him. Was he dismissive of advances in agriculture or to planting potatoes? They could enumerate the more stable (and larger) yields other lords were experiencing. No lord liked being told his neighbor was doing better than he was.

So Anna could be gracious—and at the first opportunity, she could find her way to the topmost tower and jump off.

Then she laughed, which at least made Ted happy, though he wouldn't be smiling if he knew what had amused her. In another woman, the idea of jumping off a tower would have sent friends and family running for a psychologist, thinking she had a death wish. But really, all Anna wanted to do was go home. It wasn't only to escape what was happening here, either. She'd left her boys for a few days at a time in the past, even to come to Avalon, but that didn't mean the ache in her heart at their absence was any less. Heaven forbid she ever had to get used to it.

For all that the outside was a near perfect replica of a medieval castle, the interior was decorated like a modern hotel with medieval leanings. Like Dinas Bran, the high ceiling was painted white, which nicely set off the varnished wooden beams supporting the floors above. Tapestries and oil paintings decorated the walls, and the floors and walls were made of stone. But the stone had to be a façade, hiding vents, pipes, and conduit, because the entryway was warm and well-lit. It was a castle with central heating and track lighting.

Andre had carried in Anna's pack, and she thanked him, adding, "The castle is beautiful."

Sophie made a deprecatory gesture. "I'm sure it's nothing like you're used to—" she cleared her throat, "—there."

She was telling Anna she knew where she was from, prompting a genuine laugh from Anna. "No, it isn't. I love Dinas Bran, but there's something special about being truly warm in winter."

Sophie continued to smile, though it became somewhat fixed, and her eyes were a little too wide. Perhaps the reality of meeting someone from the Middle Ages was a bit different from the theory. Still, she led them to an elevator, which took them up two floors. Anna didn't bother to comment that they didn't have elevators at Dinas Bran either.

But Uncle Ted was thinking of it. He rocked back and forth on the balls of his feet. "When was the last time you were in an elevator, Anna?"

"I don't remember, honestly. They're ... uh ... low on our priority list, though really, they're just a matter of winches and levers."

Ted laughed. "I want to see one in the next castle David builds." Then he paused and said more thoughtfully. "Or I'll tell him myself when I see him."

Mark, meanwhile, had brought out his phone and was working furiously on it, his fingers flying across the screen. Sophie's eyes kept flicking to him, and finally she said, "The password is *Cilmeri82* with exclamation marks for the I's. You don't have to hack into our network."

Mark looked up. "Oh, I wasn't. I was checking in with someone."

Anna looked at his screen, though he had it dimmed down so low she couldn't make anything out. "How are things?"

He gave her a baleful look. "They don't appear to know where we are, and they're frantic about it."

"That's good, right?" Uncle Ted said.

As the doors to the elevator opened, Mark gave him a wry smile. "Inquiries are being made. They're trolling through records for flats in Kensington, pulling footage from CCTV cameras, and tracking cell phone pings. Livia has been questioned and her office scanned, though not yet searched." He cleared his throat. "They have my real name."

Anna stopped in the middle of the corridor they'd just entered and stared at him. "Oh no. That means they'll have everything, including my family."

"Yes."

"Lord, that was fast." Uncle Ted was looking less happy and a lot more anxious all of a sudden.

"Before he left, Tate and I did a very thorough job destroying records, but there's every possibility they'll demand answers from him. I'm sorry, Ted. You were on the bus with Anna and me. We'll be reeled in, one way or another."

Andre, who'd stayed this whole time beside Anna, put a hand to his ear. "Elisa and Elen are out of London now. The driver believes he picked them up early enough that MI-5 was not on to them yet."

"They'll be here for dinner," Sophie said brightly.

Ted let out a breath, and his expression became a little less tight.

"What about Livia?" Anna said. "How come they aren't tracking her talking to you?"

"Right now she's contacting me from a surplussed computer, running the messages through several dozen countries to hide her location and mine. That might not last long." Mark's eyes were worried as he read the latest text. "They've completely shut out our section on this, so all she's getting is bits and pieces, and she has retreated to her office."

"Can't she delete everything about us?" Anna felt she should have thought to ask that question ages ago.

"These systems are automatic," Mark said. "She could delete the record, but there are backups of backups. Keystrokes are recorded, along with computer identifications that can tell exactly which computer someone uses to do anything. Better to accept what cannot be changed and plan accordingly."

George, who like Andre seemed to spend half his life listening to people speaking in his ear, held out his hand to Mark. "I'll dispose of that, if you like."

Mark typed, *I'm destroying this phone. Get out now if you can,* after which he typed in a string of numbers that hopefully meant something to Livia. Then he handed the phone to George. "Thank you."

He nodded, while Sophie said, "Mr. Treadman is very focused on security. The UK has more CCTV cameras and listening devices per person than any country in the world. People are used to it, but they don't realize all the ways they can be tracked."

"People think they don't care because they're not doing anything illegal," Mark said.

"Which at this point we're doing?" Anna asked.

Mark made a *maybe* motion with his head. "That depends on your point of view."

"It's like we're back to the bad old days," Anna said. "The farther down this path we go, the more likely things are to go wrong."

Mark nudged her elbow. "You'd think we'd be used to it by now." He was trying to joke.

Anna managed a slight smile. After all they'd gone through together, he was like a brother to her. Time traveling had a way of clarifying everything and everyone around a person and making clear what was important. Maybe that was what Uncle Ted had been trying to get at, back at Callum's flat.

"You're safe here." Andre was still with them. "You have my word."

The elevator had taken them to a long corridor that was decorated much like the foyer at the castle's entrance, except for the interior wall, which consisted of a bank of windows and faced west to let in the afternoon sun. What had looked like a solid square keep from the outside where the car was parked proved instead to be open in the center, with a garden on the ground floor. Every floor also had access to a balcony that overlooked the garden.

Sophie took them to a conference room, which took up most of the width of this level. It overlooked the garden and had its own balcony and bank of windows. When they entered, a man was seated at the end of a long, slightly oval, table. At the sight of them, he stood, grinning, and held out his hand. He was older than Anna had expected, in his late thirties, of average height, slender, with sandy-brown hair and brown eyes.

"I'm Chad Treadman. So glad you could join me."

Anna reached for his hand out of habit and politeness, but as she shook, she found herself saying, "I wouldn't have said we had much choice."

Chad's expression faltered, and he put his free hand on top of Anna's so he was holding her right hand in both of his. "I'm sorry about that. I really just wanted to meet you. Ted has been keeping me up to date on the investigation into your arrival and disappearance." He looked around at all of them. "You've had reassurances from my staff, but you truly are safe here. I wouldn't let you stay if you weren't."

Anna gazed at him. He looked genuinely contrite, giving her sad eyes that made him resemble a puppy who'd just been kicked. "Thank you." She wet her lips. "It's been a crazy day."

He perked up at her apparent forgiveness. "Hasn't it, though!" He finally released Anna and turned to Mark, shaking his hand vigorously. "I've heard so much about you."

Mark blinked. "You have?"

"Of course! Of course! The man who made the sacrifice to stay behind!"

"That isn't ... quite what happened."

Chad waved a hand. "You are too modest."

Anna felt a hand on her shoulder, and she turned to see Uncle Ted smiling gently down at her. "None of this is working out at all like I meant it to. If it wasn't your choice to come here, please forgive me for presuming I knew best."

Anna let out a long sigh. "It's okay, Uncle Ted. It seems as if we really might be safe here, so you weren't wrong." Just then, one of the stark white walls went dark, and a moment later turned into a movie screen, the full height and width of the wall that it was on. A silent movie of what was unmistakably Snowdonia National Park began to play.

Anna also hadn't missed the significance of the code Sophie had given Mark. Cilmeri82 could only be a reference to the place (Cilmeri) and year (1282) that Papa should have died and hadn't because of her and David. Chad had made it the internet passcode for his personal castle. If it was indicative of his enthusiasm about history, Anna could understand, but it also felt creepy and stalkerish.

Andre approached. "Mark gave up his phone. Have you used yours?"

"No."

Andre held out his hand. "You can never be too careful, especially now."

Uncle Ted relinquished his too, and at this sight of Ted's phone, Chad gave him a stern look. "You should know better!"

"It's a burner like hers!" Uncle Ted protested. "How else was I supposed to talk to you? I wouldn't bring my regular phone here. I left it in my car on the outskirts of London."

Chad harrumphed. "The key to staying off the grid is to ditch all your electronics. They can be tracked, as our friend here well knows." He clapped a hand on Mark's shoulder. "Laptop."

Mark looked just a bit uncomfortable with the familiarity, but he managed a rueful smile. "It isn't connected to anything." He took it out of its bag and reluctantly relinquished it. "I wouldn't have brought it otherwise."

"Still—" Chad passed it off to Andre, sending Anna careening back towards distrust. "We'll put it in a secure place until you need it again." Then he rubbed his hands together. "We should get started! I'm so excited you're here!"

A far doorway opened, and three people came in wheeling food carts. They approached the table and began laying out the food they'd brought.

Chad gestured to the spread. "In all the excitement, I wasn't sure you got lunch, and I didn't know what you liked, Anna, or what you missed most. I had them bring a variety."

He'd even ordered Welsh cakes, possibly in an attempt to make her feel at home, though the only reason she knew they were Welsh cakes was because of the fancy card that labeled them. To her, they were currant cakes, which admittedly the cook at Dinas Bran made in quantity every morning, and everybody ate with butter and honey at any time of day as a shot of energy. Those and the Eccles cakes, with their sprinkled sugar, looked excellent, and although Anna felt it might be a bit of a betrayal of David to cave so easily and over food, she took one of each and sat down at the table.

Chad rightfully took her acceptance of the food as a capitulation of sorts and grinned. "So ... the pitch!"

He waved a hand at Sophie, who dimmed the lights and pressed another button so the windows darkened. Chad then whipped out a tablet and started working on it furiously, and the reason for the stark white walls became clear: the ceiling had turned into swirling sky, like they were in a planetarium, something Anna had gone to on a school field trip back in middle school. Big words suddenly plastered themselves on the wall in front of her. "TIME," it read, "THE LAST GREAT FRONTIER."

"I thought that was space," Anna said.

Ted shushed her, and truthfully, Chad was so excited about the audio-visual tour through history he embarked them on—battles, cures for diseases, great people (she particularly noted he gave equal billing to women)—she didn't have the heart to be snarky again. Ten minutes later, the lights came up.

"So—" Uncle Ted, who was sitting behind her, poked her in the shoulder. "What do you think?"

"What do I think about what?" She spun around in the chair to look at him. "Is that a pitch for investors?"

Chad looked a little uncomfortable, and Anna gave a cynical laugh. "Who have you showed it to?"

"Nobody! I just thought—" he faltered.

Anna gestured to the now-empty screen. "What exactly does *that* have to do with *me*?"

Chad swallowed hard. "It was my understanding Ted had talked to you about how the past can help the present—how perhaps you can personally help the present."

"He did a little." Anna spread her hands wide. "I don't get it. Nobody in this room can time travel except for me. And it isn't even time travel, you realize. It's a different world we go to."

"That's the great thing. If it were real time travel, everything we know about the way the world works would have to be thrown out, but it isn't. It's an alternate universe!" Like Ted earlier, Chad was practically jumping up and down. "Think of what we can learn from what you do!"

A headache was forming above Anna's left eye. "What exactly are you proposing?"

Chad made a calming motion with his hand. "I know the circumstances under which your traveling happens. Your life has to be in danger. I'm not suggesting in any way that you should travel any more frequently than you already do, or do anything differently from what you're doing now. All I'm suggesting is that instead of calling MI-5 or the CIA or your family—because you know their phones are tapped, right?—from now on when you arrive in this world, you call me."

Anna stared at him. "That's it?"

"That's all I'm asking." He handed her his card, which was plastic rather than made of paper, so it wouldn't disintegrate in water. Thoughtful of him. The card had one word on it: *Treadman,* and two numbers, one for the UK and one for the U.S. He gestured towards the card. "Call me any time, day or night. Here, take a dozen."

She studied him. "That's really all you want?"

"Well, of course I want you to talk to me. And if you're willing, to let me provide you with everything you need." He glanced at Mark. "No more bargaining with MI-5, not that they appear to be interested in that anymore."

Anna tapped the edge of the first card he'd given her on the table. "Why should I?"

"Because I can help!" Chad went up on his toes and came back down. He really did look like a fifteen-year-old excited about playing Dungeons & Dragons and reminded Anna of a much younger, less worldly, David. "Whatever you need: medicine, weapons, technology. I have it all, and I can get it to you anywhere on the planet, no questions asked." He leaned in. "Have you considered what toll your traveling might be taking on your body at the cellular level? Are you exposed to radiation? Is there anything science can do to mitigate the effect?"

Anna stared at him, knowing that if David were here, he could speak Chad's language, and he would know better than she if what he was saying made sense.

"Another thing—" Chad hastened to a different wall, which suddenly became a white board, "—have you considered you might not be the only ones this has happened to throughout history?" He turned to look at her. "Maybe, in fact, there are other people even now who are traveling as you are."

"We've thought about that. MI-5 did too, but if so, they're hiding better than we are." Then she mumbled under her breath, "Way better."

Meanwhile, Chad took out a marker and drew a long horizontal line on the board. This he labeled "Earth Zero" and put points on it like it was a number line, with arrows pointing infinitely in both directions. He labeled zero and put an extra tick at 1208 AD, a date which had no significance to Anna, and she wracked her brains for anything that had happened that year. David's great-grandfather, Llywelyn Fawr, had been Prince of Wales, but beyond that, the date meant nothing to her.

Then Chad drew a branch, which he labeled "Earth One," off the first line beginning at 480 AD. It went off at an angle, and it too had an additional mark, this one at 1996. Then he drew a third line, labeled "Earth Two", as a branch off the Earth One line starting at 1268 AD. When he finished, he turned around and grinned.

Anna looked from Chad to the chart and back again and said in an even tone, "I have no idea what I'm seeing."

"I do." Before Chad could deflate completely, Mark rose to his feet and went to the board. "Our earth and your medieval earth are 728 years apart in time, yes?"

Anna nodded, though warily. She didn't feel like admitting to anything before she knew what the end result would be.

Mark picked up a pen. "There have been lots of approaches to the concept of time travel, all of them fiction until you. First, there's time travel where time is fluid and can be changed: you travel to a past which you can affect, and what you do there makes the present, once you return, different."

"David always said that approach was wrong," Anna said. "You shouldn't be able to travel to the past in order to change the present because it was your personal past that made you go to the past, in which case, changing the past might eliminate your ability to time travel. If that makes any sense."

"To us, it does." Chad gave a little bow. "We agree. The only theory of time travel that makes logical sense is one where you travel to the past but can't change it because time is a continuous loop. You always traveled to the past, so what you did in the past always happened. Time is a one massive pre-existing event."

"David didn't like that one either because it eliminates free will. In fact, I think those were his exact words," Anna said, recalling that first conversation in the woods outside Cilmeri. She and David had been completely freaked out, made even more so when she realized they'd saved Papa's life. Although Mom had assured them that Avalon hadn't changed because of what they'd done, David's additional journey with Ieuan in 1285 had proved it outright. It had been a relief to know they didn't have the burden of all those lives on their shoulders.

Not to say they weren't responsible for lives now, because they were, but at least there was no obligation to somehow preserve what they thought would be better off changed.

"Then there's this theory." Mark gestured to the board. "It says an alternate universe splits off from an earlier universe as the result of a catastrophic event, creating an entirely new timeline."

Anna sat up straighter. "That's what we have."

"Some people even postulate that every decision a person makes creates an alternate universe where the person didn't make that decision," Uncle Ted added.

"But we're not going there today." Mark took up the explanation again. "In this case, Chad is postulating that Earth One—that's us here—" he drew over Chad's second line with a different colored marker, "—was created when someone in 1208 time-traveled to 480 AD, thus breaking off from the original timeline known as Earth Zero. Earth One's timeline continued uninterrupted until your mother time-traveled in 1996 to 1268, creating a second timeline we're calling Earth Two."

"That's my Middle Ages," Anna said.

"Yes." Chad nodded happily. "Your family has continued to travel back and forth between Earth One and Earth Two."

Anna frowned. "What's with Earth Zero then?"

Chad turned to look at his board. "I figured if it happened to your family it probably happened before. I didn't want to imply that your time traveling was unique or the earth we're in now, which you call Avalon, was the first earth and thus somehow original or more authentic."

"Why 1208 and 480?"

"Like 1996 and 1268, they're 728 years apart," Mark said.

"Well ... that's not the only reason I chose those dates." Chad's expression grew sheepish. "It occurred to me that if the powers that be—" using the same turn of phrase as Elisa had used back at Callum's flat, "—care so much about Wales, then maybe—" He paused again, clearly embarrassed.

"Maybe what?" Anna prompted.

Chad wrinkled his nose, still embarrassed but finally choosing to answer, "Maybe King Arthur was a time traveler too."

Anna gaped at him. "King Arthur?"

"Yeah, you know, the sword and the stone and all that."

"I know who King Arthur is," Anna said patiently. "I'm not questioning his existence, though many do. I'm wondering about your logic."

"King Arthur is a powerful story that has lasted nearly two thousand years. Do you ever wonder why that is? How many stories outside of religion have lasted that long?"

"Not many," Ted said.

Anna assumed he'd heard this all before, and in that sense the question had been rhetorical.

"He's also really hard to pin down. The historical sources are imprecise most of the time, but occasionally very specific. He defeated the Saxons for a generation—that we know—but he is surrounded in every story by magic." Chad gestured to Mark. "Magic is simply unexplained technology, and what better way to explain what went on in the Dark Ages with Arthur than technology the people didn't understand?"

Anna tipped her head. "If that's what you're going with, I would be more inclined to think the time traveler was Merlin, not Arthur, in which case your timeline would need to be adjusted."

Chad gaped at her. And then he laughed and swung around to look at the white board. Hastily, he rubbed out 1208, changing it to 1188, and the earlier date to 460. Then he stepped back and studied it with a critical eye. "I don't think that really changes anything."

Anna leaned forward, getting into it now. "If you change the first date to 1170, that was the year King Owain Gwynedd died and his son, Madoc, set sail for the New World. Maybe he time traveled instead. And maybe the 728 years isn't set in stone. The only important thing is what needs to happen."

"Saving Wales from extinction." Mark had retaken his seat, and was studying the board, his finger to his lip.

Chad scratched the top of his head. "Mark, I hope you know if MI-5 fires you, you have a job with me." He glanced at Anna. "You too."

Anna laughed. "I think you've made that clear." Feeling a lot better, she bit into an Eccles cake. Sugar was an extremely rare commodity in medieval Europe, and her tongue luxuriated in the sweetness. It was too sweet for her now, really, but somehow she was going to eat this whole cake anyway. "Though whether or not this is even close to right isn't something we'll ever know."

"Isn't the need to explain the time traveling the reason David has accepted the mantle of Arthur?" Chad said.

"Partly. It started as a way to explain why he disappears." She shifted in her seat. "We started out calling this world the Land of Madoc. How's that for irony?"

Chad nodded. "And that's also why you refer to this world as Avalon?"

Anna sighed. She still didn't like the name, but it appeared she was stuck with it. "Yes."

"See." Chad looked inordinately pleased. "You were reaching for this idea and you didn't know it."

Her eyes still on the white board, Anna put one elbow on the table and her head in her hand. Her wrist hadn't hurt for the last twenty minutes, so at the very least she could thank Chad for the distraction.

Uncle Ted rubbed her shoulder. "You okay?"

Chad was gazing at her with a hopeful expression.

Anna studied him, a large part of her wanting to give in, just so she didn't disappoint him, but then she shook her head. "I don't mean to offend you, but I need to say what I'm thinking: you're the stereotypical evil genius. You're incredibly rich, incredibly smart, and incredibly successful. When was the last time somebody told you *no*? What would you do if I did?"

Chad stuttered, "What-what do you mean?"

"Would you lock me up?"

His expression cleared. "Why would I do that? What purpose would it serve? You're no good to me locked up! I want you free and doing your thing."

Anna drew in a breath, trying to reconcile all that he'd said with her fears and her certainties.

Ted whispered in her ear, "As long as you get home, what's the downside to being protected by Chad?"

She couldn't think of a way Ted was wrong, and there was no doubt Chad's castle was a haven right now. "Just so we're clear, what exactly are you proposing? If I'm going to speak to David and Mom, I need it laid out plainly."

Chad gave a sharp nod of his head, his enthusiasm giving way to the businessman Anna knew lurked inside. "As I said, when you arrive in Avalon, I want you to call me, nobody else. I will provide you with medical care, equipment, supplies—whatever you need."

"And in return?" This was where the rubber hit the road.

"In return, you give me the same courtesy you gave MI-5. You allow my researchers to examine you, test your blood, pick your brains. I want to know everything about everything that's happened to you, there, here, and in the transition."

It was essentially what Anna had expected. "What do you get out of it? I don't see a profit in this for you."

"Not everything is about money."

But when Anna narrowed her eyes at him, he shrugged. "The world is a complicated place. It may be that in working with you, we discover something that leads to other discoveries. If there's money to be made, you will receive royalties for your part in it. Say the word, and we'll draw up a contract."

Ted stepped in again. "The moment you agree, there's a trust fund ready to go, solely in your names. Even if you agree today, and then break off the agreement next week, the money will still be yours."

This was not a decision to be made lightly, and Anna really didn't want to make it without consulting her family, both medieval and modern. It wasn't that they were beholden or overly dependent. It was rather that they were interdependent. They trusted and relied on one another other.

It was like somebody had poured a bucket of cold water of her head. Their unity gave them strength, and even though Anna's family wasn't physically beside her, they were with her in spirit. She would make the decision in her own time, on her own terms—and whether or not it ultimately turned out to be the right one, it was still her decision to make.

21

19 March 1294

Math

In the late afternoon sunshine, Math and Ieuan, along with twenty men, collected their horses from where the beasts were cropping the grass in a field near the barn and set out. On the one hand, Math felt a huge sense of relief: they knew (they thought) where Anna was, and they knew for certain where the company had gone.

On the other hand, as Math had outlined to his men, any approach to FitzWalter was fraught with peril. Because Beeston Castle was afforded such views, secrecy was limited, which was why, in order for Math and Ieuan to leave without being seen, they'd had to ride south until they reached the main east-west road through this region of Cheshire. Following it west took them to Lyons Castle, Warenne's seat.

It was also a significant relief that, with their problem starkly before them, they had Warenne as an ally. Beeston was not going to be an easy castle to take. It was built on a high rock for a reason, and regardless of what FitzWalter planned and who he was planning it with, they had to deal with him. Math didn't see any way to do that without an army.

Keeping their approach to Beeston secret was hardly Math's biggest problem either. With Dafydd in Ireland, Nicholas de Carew was receiving petitions at Westminster Castle, but London was many days' ride away. As Welsh lords, Math and Ieuan had less trust from the English barons than Carew, though with Lili's support and as Dafydd's brothers-in-law, they were *de facto* regents of both England and Wales.

They could start a war if they wanted to. The real question was whether they could avoid one.

The ten-mile ride to Lyons took nearly two hours, in large part because the horses had been going all day already. By the time they came up the last rise before the castle, the sun had set behind the Welsh hills to the west. They also found the road teeming with men and horses, all milling around as if waiting for something. Or someone.

As it turned out, they were waiting for Math himself.

"My lord!" An Englishman Math didn't recognize ran towards them, his cloak billowing behind him.

The men in the road bore a dozen torches, allowing Math to do a quick accounting of their number, echoed a moment later by Ieuan. "I count twenty. I'd rather talk than fight or run."

Math and Ieuan urged their horses a few yards down the sloping road to meet the Englishman.

"I apologize for the discourteous greeting, my lords," he said. "I am Peter Beech, steward to Lord Warenne."

"What has become of your predecessor?" Math asked.

Peter bent his head. "Of course you would know my father. He is ill."

Math canted his head. "I'm sorry to hear that."

"Thank you, my lord. May I speak of my errand? I am here to assure you that Lord Warenne is at your disposal, along with his men and resources."

Math surveyed the castle a quarter-mile distant. He'd kept his eye on Warenne over the years, but even when Warenne's brother-in-law, William de Valence, had rebelled at the start of Dafydd's reign, or his distant cousin, Fulk FitzWarin, had leagued with Red Comyn fifteen months ago, or Gilbert de Clare had risen in rebellion nine months ago, John de Warenne had stayed resolutely faithful.

"We were just riding to him," Ieuan said. "We have much to talk about."

Peter bowed. "Allow me to escort you, my lords."

Math turned in the saddle and made quick disposition of his men. He sent three homewards to Dinas Bran, to tell Bevyn what they were facing at Beeston, what they'd done about it, and where they planned to spend the night. He directed a dozen to make camp right there alongside the road, to maintain a watch and intercept any of his own scouts who might come this far. And he kept the remaining five, plus Ieuan, with him. If Warenne chose this moment to rebel, to violate the laws not only of hospitality but of common sense, their twenty men wouldn't be enough to stop him anyway.

Lyons Castle sat on a slight mound on the western bank of the River Dee. King Edward had built it initially as a defensive outpost against marauding Welsh. Then in 1282, though before Dafydd and Anna had come to Wales, he gave the castle to Warenne. In 1285, when Wales became a separate kingdom, Lyons Castle had been on the wrong side of the border between the two countries. Although the bulk of Warenne's lands remained in England, he'd improved this stronghold at great expense, so he'd bent a knee to Llywelyn rather than give it up. Pentagonal, with five huge towers, a moat, and a gatehouse with three portcullises, it was easy to see why Warenne had thought long and hard about his loyalties and realized they were flexible.

They had to ford the Dee south of the castle's village and then approach the castle from the west, since the Dee had been diverted to create a moat around the curtain wall. They trotted across the drawbridge and into the inner ward. Unlike most Norman bastions, Lyons had no second wall and outer bailey, so they were immediately thrown into the heart of the castle.

Warenne himself came out to greet them, which indicated how seriously he was taking their arrival. It was full dark by now, and the bailey was lit by two dozen torches, an extravagance that was perhaps for Math's benefit rather than customary procedure.

"You honor my house with your presence, my lords." Warenne bent his head.

Born within a year or two of Carew, Mortimer, and Clare, Warenne had been approaching forty when Wales had become independent from England. Nearly ten years on, age had set in, most notably in his gray hair, paunch, and receding hairline. This wasn't a man who rode out with his men any longer.

And as his eyes flicked from Math to Ieuan and back again, Math read in them a certain wariness, the reason for which Math wasn't entirely sure, other than having Dafydd's two brothers-in-law within his keep.

"Have you dined this day?" Warenne said.

Math almost laughed. His last substantial meal had been the evening before. He'd been too sick to his stomach to eat anything at Dinas Bran and had managed a few bites of bread and cheese while riding. He realized now he was starving. "No, we have not."

"All is prepared. This way." Warenne himself led them up a flight of stairs and into his great hall, which was built against the curtain wall of the castle, the windows of which overlooked the River Dee to the east.

In the morning, the rising sun would shine through the windows and brighten the hall, but tonight it was lit with more torches and candles. Math and Ieuan followed Warenne to the high table. Now that it was dark and no daylight would be wasted by resting, many of his people were eating their evening meal.

They rose in a wave of respect as the noblemen passed, a courtesy Math was pleased to see. In the past, many Norman lords on the border of Wales had ruled by fear, but Warenne didn't appear to be one of them.

Math knew from Meg that in Avalon Warenne had been on the leading edge of King Edward's war with Wales. Math believed her, which was why he'd continued to hold Warenne at arm's length. Tonight, however, the bill of allegiance would come due.

With the meal set before him, Math didn't waste any time in pleasantries and laid out what had transpired over the course of the day. "What did you know of this?"

Warenne had been listening with ashen face, and now he shook his head. "If I have been remiss, it is in not watching my neighbors closely enough. You must believe me!"

"The company of soldiers who tried to abduct Anna is not here, that is plain, and did not ride by today," Math said. "We know now they've taken refuge at Beeston, and I have sent men to find their way inside and determine the truth. But again I ask, what do you know of this plot?"

"FitzWalter is not my friend." Warenne's chin firmed. "Whom did you send?"

"William Venables," Math said. "He is of Kinderton, and FitzWalter should admit him."

Warenne stood, clearly restless at the disturbing news. "If you will excuse me for a moment, I must confer briefly with the captain of my garrison. The threat is too serious not to have my men prepared and waiting in case an enemy turns in this direction."

"Of course." Math leaned back in his seat, his primary duty for the night done.

Once Warenne was gone, Ieuan and Math put their heads together. "We must send word to Dafydd," Ieuan said. "He will be angry if he learns about Anna's disappearance and rebellion in England from someone else."

"I was hoping to wait." Math looked around the hall. In the last few minutes, many of Warenne's people had retired for the night. "May FitzWalter rot in hell for his role in this plot."

"I truly cannot imagine what he was thinking," Ieuan said. "He couldn't have thought this would end well for him."

"All men have delusions of their own grandeur," Math said. "Some just reach higher than others."

Eventually Warenne returned, followed by a servant with a fresh carafe of wine, with which he filled each man's cup. Warenne accepted his and sat heavily at the table, looking even grayer than before. Ieuan leaned forward to speak past Math to Warenne. "What can you tell us of Balliol?"

"My daughter and I were never close." Warenne put down his cup in order to spread his hands wide. "Her loyalties were to her husband, as they should have been. But at Christmastide, when I went to Edinburgh to see my grandson, I was not well pleased with the ambience. Something was afoot, but I could not discern what, though I was aware it involved Red Comyn."

Math groaned internally. "Why did you not speak of this to me or King Dafydd?"

"Red Comyn is always plotting something, is he not? I did speak to Fulk, who was so roundly put down by the king last year, and he denied all knowledge or contact with Red. He was grateful to have been let off with his life and lands. He wanted nothing further to do with the Scots."

"And what about you?" Math said.

Warenne pressed a finger to his temple as if his head ached him. "I understand why you might be at times distrustful of me, but if FitzWalter planned to abduct Princess Anna, he said nothing about it to me." He looked directly at Math. "I can tell you something has changed in John Balliol in this last year or two. He is feeling his power—and believes England restricts it. He was not always this restless."

"King Dafydd has not appreciated his delegations to King Philip of France or to the Pope, but as far as we knew, his machinations have never gone further than diplomacy." Math took another sip of wine. It was rich and fruity, imported no doubt from Warenne's relations in France.

"As far as I knew as well."

"So then what is Balliol thinking?" Ieuan said. "If it is indeed he who's behind it."

Warenne shook his head. "I cannot tell you."

Math took in a deep breath. "The question now, John, is what are you prepared to do about it?"

Resting his elbows on the table, the Norman lord clasped his hands before his lips and studied his hall over them. What Math wanted from him was not going to be easy, and his next words showed that he understood that.

"What are you asking? Do you want me to speak to FitzWalter?"

"I do."

"And say what?"

"Find out if he has Anna, first and foremost," Math said. "I am all but certain he does not, but until I see her face again, I cannot know. Then, at your discretion, speak to him of whatever course of action he intends to follow next. Imply you are in Balliol's confidence. He should believe that."

Warenne bobbed his head. "What if I were to offer FitzWalter my support?"

Math found himself astonished. "I would never ask that of you."

"That's why I'm offering." Warenne leaned back in his seat. "I have no son to succeed me, no wife to comfort me, and all my children are dead. What do I have to lose?"

"You have grandchildren," Math said.

For the first time, a smile crossed Warenne's face. "Henry turns twenty-one in a few days. Before he left for Ireland, King David gave me permission to knight him." He gave a deprecatory laugh. "His birthday is the only reason he didn't go to Ireland with the king. Henry would have preferred to be knighted by the king's hand rather than the hand of an old fool like me." Then he frowned. "In fact, I expected him yesterday."

Math was suddenly concerned. The Warennes and Percys together comprised two of the most powerful families in the north of England, holding many castles between Chester and York. "Have you sent riders to inquire for him?"

"He is preparing for his knighting. He pledged to spend three nights on his knees in the weeks before his birthday. I assumed he'd found a church to do so in."

"When is his birthday?" Ieuan asked.

"The twenty-fifth of March."

Ieuan looked at Math. "Should we be worried something has happened to him? Or that he has joined FitzWalter himself—" he stopped at the way Warenne's face turned utterly pale.

Math put out a hand to Ieuan, but his eyes were on Warenne. "Has he joined FitzWalter, John?"

But before Warenne could answer, Math found himself blinking rapidly at the way his vision had turned blurry. Ieuan crumpled forward onto the table, and Math managed to stay upright long enough to ask, "What have you done?"

"What I must," Warenne replied.

22

19 March 2022

Anna

Anna and Mark were alone in the expansive gardens outside the castle proper, though still inside the massive curtain wall which surrounded not only the hill on which the castle had been built but the fields around it. Probably there were guards posted along its length, but Anna didn't feel threatened or held against her will. Uncle Ted was in the house, discussing business with Chad. Perhaps she should have been there, but she was too tired to worry about what they were saying.

Instead, she relaxed against the backrest of the bench upon which she and Mark were sitting. "You realize he's out of his mind, right?"

"Maybe."

"Maybe?"

Mark looked at her. "You do travel back and forth to an alternate universe, do you not?"

Anna laughed and adjusted the sling, which was chafing the side of her neck, more comfortably so her shirt lay between her skin and the strap. "I suppose you have a point."

"I stayed in Avalon—" Mark shook his head, "—I'm doing it too. I stayed here because I thought—assumed, really—having an ally in MI-5 would make a difference when one of you returned."

"It has!" Anna said. "It did! For me and for Arthur and Gwenllian."

"But like David always says whenever he comes here, one man can do only so much." Mark sighed. "And that means if I am to have any kind of future, I must leave the castle."

Anna's hand went to her mouth. "You're going to go to London?"

He nodded. "I must face them head on. I have a life here, a good one. Even were I to hide out on Earth Two for a couple of years, the moment I stepped foot in Avalon, I'd be on the run again. I don't want to live like that. I don't want my parents to live like that." He pressed his lips together for a moment as he thought. "All those papers Livia read that allowed her to learn what was going on? I have copies too."

"Is that how you kept your job? You threatened to expose them?"

"Oh no. They don't know I have them." He looked at her steadily. "I'm thinking I will give the key to the safety deposit box to Chad."

Anna bit her lip. "Aren't those documents classified?"

"They were, but if Five are going to throw me into a deep pit for rescuing you, I will expose them."

Anna looked down at the ground. "So Chad really is my only hope at this point. Uncle Ted knows about Callum's apartment, so I couldn't go back there anyway." She scuffed at the gravel that formed the garden's walkway. "I don't know what to make of my uncle."

"Whatever he's done, you know he's trying to do the right thing and has what he believes to be your best interests at heart."

"That's the issue, isn't it? What are our best interests?"

"That's up to you." Mark looked around the grounds of the castle. "Look, this place is a fortress. At the very least, if anyone comes for you—MI-5 or the CIA or some new organization we don't yet know about—Chad can protect you. And you know Ted isn't going to let anything happen to you." He lifted his chin to point to the field below the castle, which she could just see from where she sat. A strange looking airplane with fat tires rested on the grass, though she saw no airstrip. "Chad has all the toys. He could probably take you to the moon if he had to."

Then Mark stood. "Stay here, Anna. Have dinner with your family. You need to sleep and heal that wrist." He gestured to a point behind Anna. "Your uncle is coming now."

Anna turned to look. "Okay. Good luck." His chin was set, so she didn't try to talk him out of what he was planning.

"Who knows? Maybe I'll be back later tonight. At the very least, I'll ring. If you don't hear from me by tomorrow morning, you'll know it's because I can't contact you, and Chad will know what to do."

"So will I," Anna said. "I'll climb up to the tower and jump off."

Mark's face paled a little, and Anna put out a hand to him. "It's okay. Thank you for everything you've done."

"We'll see if I did you any favors." He started down the path, stopped to speak briefly to Ted, and then continued on his way.

Ted kept coming. "Traffic has been atrocious, but Elisa and Elen are almost here. All of us will stay with you for as long as you're in Avalon—and then go home with you when you're ready."

Even with that last remark, which Anna chose to ignore, she found herself more calm than before. "I'd like to spend some time with you when we aren't running around madly evading government agencies."

"Mark hopes to put that to rest." He sat on the bench next to her where Mark had been sitting. "Are you mad at me?"

She sighed. "I was never mad, and I know you were doing what you thought was right. I love you for it." She'd had to acknowledge that even she was having trouble figuring out a better way for Chad to have presented his ideas to her. He'd known he had limited time, and even with his company's vast resources, Uncle Ted had been his only option, short of springing her himself from the hospital. He undoubtedly could have done that too, but her arrival may have been more of a surprise to him than it had been to Mark.

"Are you sorry I brought you here?"

"Could I be sorry about this?" She gestured to the beautiful grounds that surrounded them. It was the middle of March, but it had been a warm day, though with the sun disappearing behind the hills, she needed the coat around her shoulders.

"At the same time, Uncle Ted, I have to wonder if this is really going to work out. Chad seems too good to be true."

"He isn't. You have no idea what having you here means to him. For him, your presence here, the knowledge that not only is your traveling real but he can play a small part in it, is worth any cost. Like that ad says, it's priceless."

"That's what he gets out of helping us? Knowledge that alternate universes exist?"

Ted laughed. "When you're Chad Treadman, all you think about all day is the next great thing. He has a hundred irons in the fire. We're talking about a guy who has a serious plan to land a manned ship on Jupiter's moon, Europa, and the money to make it happen. All he needs is the technology."

"So, my family is just one more cog in his machine?"

"No, Anna." Ted shook his head emphatically. "You ask what he's hoping to get from Earth Two? Knowledge. He wants to change the world and our perception of it. He wants to be a part of something great. On top of which, what Chad hates more than anything is being bored."

"So he's offering to help us for the entertainment value."

Ted laughed again. "You could say that. But then, why not? Don't sell him or yourself short. Besides which, you may have noticed governments are fickle."

"Chad Treadman isn't fickle?"

"Oh sure. But like I said in the conference room, what's the worst thing that could happen if he lets you down?"

Anna raised a hand and dropped it. "He doesn't answer the phone, and we go back to doing what we did before."

"Exactly. With Chad, you really have nothing to lose." Uncle Ted smiled gently. "And maybe a whole lot to gain."

23

19 March 1294

Constance

The day Constance had joined David's men as the only woman among them, her father, rather than turning his back on her as the priest had urged, had given her a brand new bow, one he'd apparently spent the last eight years making without her knowledge. *I was saving it for the right time. I can't think of a better time to give it to you than now.*

Constance had been an only child, having lost her mother at her birth, and her father had never remarried. Perhaps if he'd had a son, he would have lavished his hopes on him, but he had only a daughter, and for that reason Constance had grown up learning to sew and cook and care for her father—and in his spare moments, he'd encouraged her to shoot. At the time, he'd treated it as the most normal thing in the world, and when some of the men had told them the archery butts were no place for a woman, he'd insisted she continue, and she'd gotten the better of them by outshooting them.

Nobody in her village had practiced harder than she, and when she'd won the archery contest at the King's tournament last summer, it was the culmination of years of work. She'd cried tears of joy and relief, and her greatest happiness had been when she'd given her father the silver-tipped arrow she'd won. At the end, she'd even had the honor of standing between Queen Lili and Sir Morgan, King David's chief archer, and shooting a final round, just the three of them. Though Constance had defeated all of the men in the contest, she'd been more nervous in that moment than the whole rest of the day.

And though Queen Lili denied it, she'd shanked her last shot to allow Constance to defeat her. She and Constance had been neck and neck up until then.

Constance had told the king that if he had a mind to outfit an entire company of archers just like her, she knew women who could fill the posts. He hadn't yet taken her up on her offer, but she had seen the interest in his eyes. Though since the birth of Alexander, Queen Lili hadn't spent as much time shooting, her husband was fully supportive of her art. Constance had the feeling a seed had been planted that might soon bear fruit.

For her part, she enjoyed the company of the men she worked with, and once they'd become accustomed to the idea of a woman in their midst, none objected to her presence. But she wouldn't be sorry to be able to share this life with other women— and for others to have the same opportunities she'd been given.

Being able to shoot when one was nervous or afraid was the entire purpose behind practicing so hard, but as Constance gazed at Beeston Castle ahead of them, she acknowledged that the fear she'd felt the day of the contest was nothing compared to what she was feeling now. That fear had been based on hope for a better future if she won. This was sheer dread, and she had to clench her hand into a fist to contain it. The battlements were bristling with soldiers, and she and the men with her were a paltry few by comparison.

"I know I don't need to tell you we must be careful," her husband said from just beside her.

"When am I not careful?"

Cador snorted under his breath, and Constance grinned, easing some of the tightness in her chest.

Along with Rhys and Mathew, they were pretending to be Venny's retainers, while ostensibly he was here as a representative of his father, the Baron of Kinderton. They'd left their bows behind, thinking they would only call attention to themselves, and instead wore long knives at their waists—except for Mathew. He was acting as Venny's captain, so he wore a sword.

As Constance had suggested to Lord Ieuan, she was with them not for her prowess as an archer but because she was a woman. It went without saying that an armed company riding with a woman amongst them was less threatening than if they'd been five men. Constance always carried a dress in her saddle bag, though she'd never had cause to wear one before in the course of her duties.

Venny turned in the saddle and surveyed his companions. "Remember, this is just a scouting mission. We want to determine if the company we followed is still here, and more importantly, if Princess Anna was ever among them. At worst, if she is here, and they are in the midst of plans for war, likely the guard won't admit us."

"And we must be prepared, if he does admit us, not to be able to leave until morning," Mathew said.

Constance's mouth was dry, and she glad she was surrounded by such stalwart friends. They trotted up the road to the castle, arriving at the gatehouse a quarter of an hour later. Beeston Castle was not only built on a high rock, it was protected by eight massive towers built into the curtain wall. Furthermore, if assailants made it past the gatehouse into the vast outer ward, they were prevented from reaching the inner ward and the keep by a great ditch cut into the rock that was traversable only by the wooden bridge that spanned it.

Lord Mathonwy had instructed them to wait until dark to begin their approach to the castle, so it was nearing eight o'clock in the evening by now. The guards weren't expecting visitors, though they hadn't yet closed the gate, and the portcullis that allowed entrance into the castle was still raised.

At their approach, a guard in a shiny helmet with a wide nosepiece stepped into the road just outside the gatehouse, effectively barring the way. Why a rider would be mad enough to run him down in an attempt to escape *into* the castle wasn't clear, but his stance was probably intended to put the fear of God into any visitor. They were only five, however, and the guard rightfully didn't view them as much of a threat.

In response to the guard's stance, Venny removed his helmet and introduced himself. "I am William Venables, heir to Kinderton. I come seeking shelter for the night."

The guard visibly hesitated. Constance would have thought someone would have prepared him with an answer for such an occasion, but he wasn't ready with one. He did step back, however, and bow slightly at the waist. "I must speak to my captain. Please wait a moment."

Constance had been in this position before at other castles, and it was rare to be kept waiting on the doorstep and not admitted at least into the outer ward. Someone inside obviously thought so too, since a moment later the guard came hustling back. With another bow, he said, "Please enter. Someone will see to your horses."

They crossed under the gatehouse, thankful none of the portcullises dropped to trap them, and headed into the outer ward. It stretched the entire length of the mountain top, all the way to the bridge across the ditch seven hundred feet away. Lord Mathonwy had explained that a previous Earl of Chester had built this castle, and Constance could see why he'd chosen the spot. The real stronghold, the castle itself, was a fraction of the size protected by the curtain wall, and the whole arrangement bore a strong resemblance to Dover.

The outer ward was so large, in fact, that the space could have housed an entire town. A dozen shops and huts, a guest hall, and a barracks clustered together along the eastern wall between the bridge and the outer gatehouse. Otherwise, the outer ward contained dozens of tents and campfires around which hundreds of men sat. At the sight of her small group coming through the gatehouse, several men at the nearest fire circle, which was fifty feet away, stood to look at them.

Venny ignored them, as did Constance. Cador, however, lifted a hand to one of them and trotted his horse closer. In the night air, his words carried, "How goes it?"

Nobody answered him.

"Nice night," Cador added.

"Could be," one of the men replied.

Cador took his curtness as a signal to veer back towards his companions, who had directed their horses to walk towards the inner gatehouse. In an undertone, he said, "Not very friendly, are they?"

"They don't seem to be," Venny said. "If I wasn't suspicious already, I would be now."

The stables were a stone's throw from the ditch, so it was reasonable to allow riders to cross the large space on horseback rather than having them walk it. Knights and men-at-arms didn't walk if they could help it, as Cador had informed her when she'd first joined the company. By becoming a member of King David's retinue, she didn't walk much herself anymore either, which was a far cry from her past life as a farmer's daughter. Horses meant for riding were expensive, war horses even more so, and most villagers never went more than five miles from home. When they did, they rode in a cart, not on horseback.

Once they reached the bridge, Venny waved everyone off their horses and tossed his reins to a stable lad. Then he stood for a moment surveying the tents and fire circles scattered throughout the outer ward. Mathew stepped up beside him. "How many men do you count?"

"Hundreds more than are needed to defend this castle." He looked at Cador. "Could you tell from those brief words if the man you spoke to was Scottish?"

"Not from his words, but his clothing was unfamiliar. Rather than a cloak, he wore a blanket wrapped around his shoulders, like Highlanders do."

"I don't like this," Venny said.

"Are you rethinking our plan?" Mathew said. "It isn't too late to leave."

"Yes, it is." Venny strode across the drawbridge towards the inner gatehouse, and after a moment, the rest of them trailed after him. As at the outer gatehouse, the defenses of the castle remained down, and they encountered no resistance.

24

19 March 2022

Anna

Everyone was preparing for bed, but while Anna was exhausted, she wasn't quite ready to call it a night. After dinner, Chad had given them a more complete tour of his castle, which included an observatory of sorts on the top of one of the towers. Remembering the way he'd taken them, she found the right elevator and rode it to the top. She stepped out of the elevator, pleased it came out where she thought it would, but hesitated when she realized the tower wasn't as empty as she'd hoped.

Chad stood with his arms folded across his chest, looking at the stars above them. The night was cold enough that he hadn't pressed the button to open the tower completely to the sky but was looking upwards through the transparent bubble. "If you were thinking of jumping off this tower, I'll have you know I've locked the doors to the wall-walks."

"That wasn't my intent," Anna said, a little stiffly. "Are you here because I am? Did you see me leave my room?"

Chad turned to look at her, and his expression told her that was exactly what had happened. "Why did you come up here if not for that?"

"It seemed silly to waste any of my short time here asleep."

"You're no good to me exhausted," Chad said.

"I wouldn't have said I was any good to you at all."

"You're doing it again." Chad made a motion and somehow upped the light inside the bubble. The difference turned the bubble opaque so nobody outside could tell that the light was on inside. The top of the tower was decorated like an outdoor living room, though Anna was pretty sure the only rain that ever fell here was from the watering can of a gardener. It was one more futuristic piece of technology in an entire day of similar absurdities.

"What is it you think I'm doing?" They were sparring with words, which hadn't been Anna's intent either.

"Selling yourself short. Do you really think if your brother or mother were here either of them would be doing so much better?"

Anna scoffed under her breath and made her way to one of the squishy chairs to sit. She wasn't interested in a confrontation with Chad, and she felt as if one might be more easily avoided if she was sitting down. "No, that isn't what's happening either."

"Then what is happening? I really do want to know."

Anna gestured to a chair opposite, wanting Chad to sit so she didn't have to crane her neck to look up at him. "You must have read the reports of what happens when we come here, so you know David gets treated like a delinquent. He's been locked up, interrogated, abducted, drugged, and alternately ignored and abused by anyone in authority who comes into contact with him. As has been the case today for me, his survival has depended on the kindness or position of others. In fact, it might even be that, because of who he is and how he thinks, if he were here instead of me, he might be doing quite a bit worse."

It was a truth she'd come to realize over the last few hours.

She shook her head. "It's never clearer to me than when we come here how power in Earth Two is personal, where here it's faceless and nameless. That cop at Westminster was just some random guy doing his job, but he killed my horse and arrested me, even though he's near the bottom of a very elaborate food chain. But it seems it's a food chain there's no avoiding."

Chad spoke gently, "Normally we consider our nameless bureaucracy an asset. We don't have kings in America because personal power can be abused."

"I know! And I approve. But as we say to David whenever he complains about his burdens and talks about democracy, *we're against the monarchy except when it's you.*" She put out a hand to him. "I appreciate what you're trying to do here, believe me, but the lessons to learn from Earth Two are ones either everyone already knows—like family is important or life is short—or aren't lessons people in Avalon want to hear. And even if people did, who is going to believe we are who we say we are, even with your backing? We'd come off like a crazy cult."

Chad eased himself farther into his chair, and Anna felt like he was finally looking at her as a person, rather than as a time traveler only. "Thank you for speaking to me so frankly, but there has to be a way to make the transition from one world to the other easier. Earth Two exists. It isn't magic! You're in an alternate universe. We *can* science the hell out of it."

"Of all the things you've said, David would agree with that the most. But I have to wonder what would happen if we were believed. It's why we were reluctant to work with MI-5 initially or with your company before you bought it: if traveling between worlds became easy, like beaming from one place to another in Star Trek, what would happen to Earth Two? What *always* happens when humans come across a place that is pristine?"

Chad made a grumbling sound deep in his chest that made him sound a bit like Bevyn. "We destroy it." But then he immediately brightened. "We do have national parks. The moon hasn't been mined."

"It's a miracle the national parks haven't been strip mined yet—at least I assume they haven't—and the only reason the moon hasn't been mined is because the costs are prohibitive. Face it, if public opinion would allow private interests to buy the moon, someone would have sold it already. Except in rare cases, political power in Avalon is about enriching yourself and your friends."

Chad barked a humorless laugh. "So young and yet so cynical."

"You have to admit my experience with the government hasn't been pleasant. For a brief moment, we thought MI-5 was going to come through for us—and then policies changed." She paused, studying him.

Chad eyed her. "What?" His expression had turned hopeful again.

On one hand, there was so much here that had Anna out of her depth. The technology in Avalon was routinely mind-blowing to her, and she didn't know anything about trust funds or royalties or contracts. On the other hand, she did know people. Anna was sure now that David would think agreeing to any of this was akin to selling out. He might argue—and she didn't know that he'd be wrong to do so—that linking up with Chad might in the end be worse than MI-5.

For all that David had hardened a bit about the edges, he still sometimes had trouble putting what was practical above what was necessary. She'd known him to be devious only once, when he'd prepared for William de Valence's treachery. And even then, David had given Valence a chance to surrender. For her brother, it always came down to principle, and were David in her shoes, he'd have walked away hours ago, regardless of what terrifying agency was on his trail.

But Anna wasn't David. Although she didn't know where right and wrong began and ended, she knew in this moment that it didn't matter. *This* was the reason she, rather than her mother or David, had been put in this particular place at this particular time. Sometimes it was the job of the king's sister to do what the king could not.

So she met Chad's gaze and took what he was offering. "Perhaps you're right, Chad. It *is* long past time we approached this differently. It seems you really are the only one who can help us now."

25

19 March 1294

Constance

Robert FitzWalter sat in his seat at the high table, surrounded by diners even at this late hour, and sneered down his nose at Venny and his small party. FitzWalter was not well pleased to see the heir to the barony of Kinderton in his hall—and Venny was just young enough and not quite noble enough for him to show it. If FitzWalter had known that the companion to Venny's right was a commoner from London, or that Constance was an equal member of King David's guard, he would have been even more disparaging. But Constance kept her mouth shut, as did the rest of Venny's supposed retainers.

Venny simply bent his head in greeting. "We are seeking shelter for the night, my lord."

To Constance's horror and dismay, FitzWalter was not alone in his superiority. Humphrey de Bohun had a seat next to FitzWalter, and Henry Percy was two seats down from him, both gazing over their cups at the newcomers.

"Sweet Mary, where will it end?" Cador whispered low in Constance's ear.

After Clare's betrayal last year, David had examined the loyalties of every Marcher lord, and neither Henry Percy nor his grandfather had ever given any cause for doubt. On top of which, Henry was a sometime companion of Venny, though far more elevated in rank, both young men having been raised in the north and openly supportive of King David.

Meanwhile, FitzWalter began to question Venny. "You're hardly five miles from home. Why come here?"

"We are heading home, not coming from it, and one of our horses went lame at the same time my servant here—" he gestured to Mathew, "—spiked a fever. I was hoping he could consult with your healer about what ails him."

FitzWalter narrowed his eyes at Venny, but the boy gazed at him with an innocent expression he'd probably spent years mastering. FitzWalter couldn't have found anything suspicious in his face, and he had no cause to throw him out, so he finally nodded, accepting their presence and inviting Venny to join the high table. While his friends had no wish to be separated from him, that was an offer Venny could not refuse. Before he left them, he drew them a bit away from any listeners and lowered his voice so he wouldn't be overheard. "Find the healer, as I said."

"We can't leave you alone in here." Mathew's voice was urgent.

"You have to. I will search the inner ward on my own." He glanced towards the high table.

"If this is because I'm a woman—" Constance started to say.

Venny cut her off. "It isn't. Lord Mathonwy needs to know that Bohun and Percy sit beside FitzWalter. The conspiracy is far more widespread than we'd hoped."

"It might even include Warenne, Henry's grandfather," Cador said.

"I fear it," Venny said. "Set up camp in the outer ward, and then as the night draws on, probe the defenses. Maybe there's a way out for at least one of us."

"What if you aren't allowed to join us?" Mathew said.

"Then leave without me at first light."

Mathew pressed his lips together. "I don't know if I can do that."

"If I don't find you, you'll know I'm a prisoner. Please—" he looked at each one of them in turn, "—do as I ask."

"FitzWalter shouldn't have let us inside his castle in the first place if he was so concerned about strangers knowing what he was doing," Constance said to Cador as she headed off with him and the others a few moments later to find the healer. She had to admit the four of them were hardly enough to protect Venny against any concerted effort on FitzWalter's part to harm him, so leaving him with no guards shouldn't make a difference.

The four companions left the hall and walked across the inner ward to the gatehouse. A query to the guard there directed them to the healer's hut, which was on the far northern side of the outer ward, as far from the bridge as it was possible to be and still be inside the walls. The location made sense, since if an army managed to breach the outer curtain wall, they would hardly be concerned with herbs and ointments. The healer could always retreat inside the keep with his satchel of supplies.

"I'm surprised they let us go off by ourselves," Rhys said, still in an undertone though nobody was close by. "If they had something to hide, you wouldn't think they'd let us out of their sight."

"Maybe FitzWalter really doesn't have anything to hide," Cador said.

"You saw the look in his face," Constance said. "He was not pleased to see Venny. And he has too many men for a garrison."

"It may be, rather, he thinks he has nothing to fear from Venny. He isn't going anywhere, and from the looks—" Rhys gestured towards the outer gatehouse. The portcullis had been dropped. "Neither are we."

Since they weren't leaving the castle, they didn't collect the horses, and they walked through the outer ward on foot. During the day, the healer's garden plot would take the greatest advantage of the sun, which much of the year crossed a southerly portion of the sky. Thus, the northern curtain wall could provide some residual heat for tender plants overnight, and there were no buildings or walls to block the sun from shining on the garden.

With Constance beside him, Cador pressed his ear to the door of the hut before giving it a sharp rap. Arms folded across their chests, Mathew and Rhys waited a few paces away. Mathew was a bit disgruntled because Venny had told FitzWalter that he, ox of a man that he was, had a fever. A man as big and strong as Mathew, who relied on his physical prowess, viewed illness as weakness.

When there was no answer, Mathew said, "I'm not sick. Why are we even here?"

Constance poked him in the ribs. "We need to not raise suspicion, and it was a good way to get us out of the hall."

Mathew grumbled under his breath, admitting she might have a point. With that, the door opened, and the healer, a wizened man with gray hair and a bent back, appeared. "What is it?"

Even from three paces away, Constance could smell the beer on him.

"This man is ill." Cador gestured to Mathew. "We were hoping we could acquire a tincture for fever for him."

The healer looked Mathew up and down, clearly disbelieving, but then Constance said, "Sir Robert sent us."

"Very well. Wait there." He lit a lantern, and despite the request for him to stay where he was, Mathew moved towards the doorway.

Cador stepped back to allow Mathew to enter the hut and then bent to speak to Constance, "Is it just me, or are we being watched?"

"I would be surprised if we weren't." A hooded man had definitely followed them from the great hall, though Constance didn't see that particular man anymore. It was dark, however, with the only light available to them coming from cooking fires and a handful of torches. Truthfully, which of the three hundred men in the inner ward was tasked with keeping an eye on them hardly mattered. They had nowhere to go, and the men facing them wouldn't be here if they weren't loyal to FitzWalter—or another of the lords in the hall, like Bohun or Percy. Constance and her friends were truly in the lion's den.

Rhys took the short period of waiting to stroll in a large circle around the outer ward, greeting the men who were willing to look him in the eye and making an accounting of the various lords they served. This late in the evening, many were asleep or drunk, which made those who remained awake all the more noticeable for watching them.

Then Mathew reappeared, ducking under the frame of the door so he wouldn't bang his head. "I have what I came for." And then he added in an undertone, "Let's get moving."

As one, the four of them headed to the blacksmith's works, one of the few deserted spots in the outer bailey. The fire was banked for the night, but it still glowed orange, and Constance moved towards it to warm her hands.

"I can tell you this castle has held too many men for a while," Rhys said. "The latrine ditch has an offensive odor and can't accommodate this many people for much longer. The men who are still awake seem to be on watch, which I wouldn't have thought necessary inside the curtain wall, and if you see here—" he indicated a rack of weapons on the far side of the workshop they were in, "—this is as much an armorer's hut as a blacksmith's. They are preparing for war, and by my guess it should happen soon."

"Did you hear anyone speaking Scots?" Constance said.

Rhys laughed low and without humor. "Ten Scotsmen cluster around their own fire pit. A few more were dotted here and there." He frowned. "Did any of you see Scotsmen in the hall? I didn't."

"I didn't either," Constance said. "If it's true John Balliol has something planned for England, such a small number of men isn't a large commitment."

"It's plenty enough for a raid, though," Cador said. "And we know Scotsmen were among the riders who entered Wales."

"So what do we do now?" Mathew asked.

"We do what Venny said: find a place to camp in the open so everyone can see us and be certain we have nothing to hide." Constance paused. "And when we get a chance, we slip away."

26

19 March 1294

Venny

Venny's friends left the hall, but instead of making room for him at the high table, FitzWalter directed him around the back and out a side door. Before leaving, Venny shot a glance over his shoulder to Henry Percy, who from all appearances was very drunk.

He lifted a cup blearily to Venny. "Godspeed!"

That did not give Venny confidence.

With a word in the ear of Bohun, who stayed where he was, FitzWalter made his way towards the doorway too. Venny's stomach was in knots—and that was before Henry had raised his cup to him. Something very bad was about to happen, but he honestly had no idea what it was. He didn't think FitzWalter would kill him outright. Venny was a minor lord in FitzWalter's eyes and hardly worthy of his attention.

As it turned out, the place to which he was led was not a dungeon but a chapel, up one floor from the great hall, with a beautiful stained-glass window behind the altar. Although everyone knew Thomas Becket had been murdered in his own church on orders of King Henry, generally lords preferred to keep their evil deeds out of the direct sight of God, and Venny was a little bit heartened to think he wasn't going to die just yet.

So he threw back his shoulders and said as innocently as he could, trying to project a confidence he wasn't feeling, "What am I doing here?" Likely the men who faced him knew he was putting up a false front, but bravery in the face of utter despair was the only way he was going to survive this.

"You are here to pledge your loyalty to me."

This was a voice Venny had never heard before, and he turned to face the one who'd spoken. Before him stood a dark haired man of medium height, similar in age to these other barons. He had high cheekbones and narrow shoulders, and when he walked forward, it was with a limp.

"You have the advantage of me, as I don't know you."

The man stopped in front of him. "Roger Mortimer."

Venny had heard of him, of course. He'd been a favorite of King Edward, even before his eldest brother died and the middle son, Edmund, ascended to his title. It had been Roger's message that had lured King Llywelyn into an ambush at Cilmeri. His presence explained Humphrey de Bohun's too, far more than FitzWalter's marriage to Bohun's niece. Before Edward's death, Roger Mortimer had been a force to be reckoned with.

It also explained the behavior of FitzWalter, who'd married twice above his station, and thus risen to the master of Beeston

Castle by the efforts of men other than himself. He always looked to a more powerful man above him.

Still, that Roger was the leader of a rebellion against King David was surprising. Since David had been crowned King of England, Roger had proved far less concerned about power in England than the status of his estates in France, which he'd gained courtesy of King David. As with Balliol, the king had attempted in a not-so-subtle way to distract the Norman lord from all he'd lost in the March—and the fact that David did not trust him. The last time Roger had been in England, rumor had it he'd petitioned King David for a high-ranking wife, since his first wife, a very minor noble named Lucy, had died in childbirth. Even with the dangers that women faced in the birthing room, that same rumor said Roger had hurried her along.

"Roger, didn't you know this young man is in the service of the king?" FitzWalter had his shoulder propped against the wall, and his words came out a drawl. "He isn't going to swear allegiance to you."

Mortimer looked down his nose at Venny. "He is if he knows what's good for him."

Then a new voice spoke from the shadows, and Venny's father stepped into his view. "He is my son. He will do what he must. He will do as I command." His father's hand came down on Venny's shoulder and forced him to his knees.

If Venny's stomach had been in knots before, now it was a five-pound weight in his belly. White-haired, thin but still vigorous, the Baron of Kinderton had never been a loving guide as much as a force to be reckoned with in Venny's life. While Venny's decision to become one of King David's men had been made with his father's approval, that approval had been grudging. Because his father never approved of anything he did, Venny hadn't taken his attitude as anything unusual. And of course, serving the king had been an honor. It would have made no sense to keep the family aloof when doing so came with the real possibility of causing it harm.

Venny ducked his head and said exactly that. "I served King David because what other choice did I have?"

Mortimer guffawed. "See, Robert. Most men feel the same. They serve David not because they wish to, but because they have to. The Venables family knows upon which side of the bread the butter must be spread—as we all have up until now." He turned again to look at Venny, who was doing his level best to look humble and self-effacing—and to ignore the pain in his knees from kneeling on the hard floor and the anger that shot through him hearing Mortimer speak of the king so dismissively. "I did the same, did I not?"

"I didn't," FitzWalter said.

Mortimer sneered. "Don't go all high and mighty on me, Robert. You went to London on bended knee too, and you did it again when David handed you Beeston Castle on a silver platter."

FitzWalter didn't like being reminded of his obeisance, and he put his nose into the air. "I didn't prostrate myself like this one."

"He is of lower rank. He had no choice." Again Mortimer turned to Venny. "Isn't that right?"

Venny nodded vigorously. "That is absolutely right. He is the king, but ... perhaps not for long?" He wasn't trying to sound sly. He wanted desperately to hear their plan from Mortimer's own lips.

Mortimer obliged. "We have an alliance with Balliol of Scotland."

"Roger!" FitzWalter threw up his hands. "He hasn't pledged yet."

Mortimer was still looking down his nose at Venny. "But you are going to, aren't you?"

"Of course, my lord. I was awaiting an opportunity that made sense. Gilbert de Clare—" He deliberately left the sentence hanging, and Mortimer again obliged by finishing it for him.

"—was a fool. He reached too high. He thought to kill both David and the King of France in one blow." He laughed mockingly.

"So ... you don't intend to become king?"

"My royal blood is thin, though not as thin as our current king's." Again the mocking laugh. "I will marry Princess Elizabeth, however, and then we'll see." The glitter in his eyes was definitely dangerous, and Venny had a feeling Balliol should watch his back.

King David had taken the throne of England five years earlier after the murder of King Edward's eldest living daughter, Princess Eleanor, and the subsequent refusal of her younger sister, Joan, to marry William de Bohun, instead finding herself called to the Church. Five years ago, those two had been the only daughters of marriageable age, but Edward had more daughters: Margaret, who'd married a Duke from the Continent once she came of age; Mary, who'd joined a convent; and Elizabeth, who was the same age as King Llywelyn's daughter, Gwenllian, both of whom would be twelve years old this year. Venny thought marrying a child to a fifty-year-old man was obscene, but that wasn't to say it hadn't been done before.

"We have her," Venny's father said. "Or rather, King John has her."

"Balliol will give her to me as soon as David is dead, and the English crown is on his head," Mortimer said.

"I am confused," Venny said, leaving aside the fact that no word had reached his ears—or King David's—that Elizabeth's guardian had lost her to Scotland. "Why do you ally with Balliol at all when you could do this for yourself?"

"Our aims are the same." Mortimer paused. "And he can do some things I cannot do myself." He spoke as if he hated admitting he wasn't all powerful.

Venny still didn't understand Mortimer's plan, but it was clear from his expression that he wouldn't welcome more questions in that direction. So Venny tried another tack: "The king is in Ireland. How will you reach him there?"

The look that came over FitzWalter's and Mortimer's faces was positively gleeful. "As I've said, Balliol can do some things for me I cannot do for myself. His forces should have already consigned David to hell where he belongs."

Venny's heart sank into his boots. He should have known, given FitzWalter's attempt to capture Princess Anna, that the conspiracy went farther than Beeston Castle, but to know they had co-conspirators in Ireland meant they truly did have wide-ranging support. The knowledge hardened his resolve, however, and he rose to his feet, straightening his shoulders and implying that his earlier cowering had been feigned. "Then it is time I told you the truth of why I am here."

That was the last thing FitzWalter and Mortimer expected. Despite their arrogance, they gaped at him, and Venny's father said, "What is this, son?"

"I come to you now as a warning and a courtesy. My father thought to keep secret from me his alliance with you, but I learned of it and have stayed close to King David ever since, in an attempt to protect my father, knowing I would ride to him the moment the king or his allies got close." He looked darkly at Mortimer and FitzWalter, who were still gazing at him open-mouthed. "Lord Mathonwy knows you sent those riders into Wales to abduct Princess Anna. He is coming."

That had everyone's attention in a way nothing else could have. "How could he possibly know?" Mortimer said.

"This morning, in the saddle bag of a man who was killed during Princess Anna's abduction, Lord Mathonwy found a tunic sporting the FitzWalter crest. But even without that, the riders left a trail a blind man could follow. Lord Mathonwy has some of the best trackers in Britain."

The stunned silence this last statement caused had Venny's knees trembling. He had brought out the news of Lord Mathonwy's coming to elicit a response—and because he didn't believe it could possibly come as a surprise. But it was also to save his own skin, and when Lord Mathonwy questioned him about how the evening had gone, he would be straightforward about it.

When the barons still didn't respond, Venny cleared his throat. "Is Princess Anna here?"

"No." Gone was Mortimer's expression of superiority and complacency, replaced by fury. He turned to FitzWalter and spoke through gritted teeth. "They were supposed to leave no witnesses and nothing behind." The two men glared at each other.

While Mortimer berated FitzWalter, Venny turned to his father and spoke in an undertone for his ears only. "Are you sure about this?"

Venny had avoided eye contact with his father before now, but if Venny was to get himself and his men (and woman) out of the castle in one piece, preferably sooner rather than later, he needed allies, and Hugh Venables was possibly the best option.

This conspiracy had gone miles too far already, and Venny's story was painfully thin. He feared it wouldn't hold up for long.

"Of course I'm sure. It is unconscionable you would ask such a question."

"You are betraying the king and yet you question my judgement? How did you become involved with Roger Mortimer in the first place?"

"FitzWalter approached me." Hugh put his nose into the air. "He knows I am the most powerful baron in the Kelsall area. If Balliol is to succeed, he needs the north of England to stand with him. We have ever been neglected by London."

It was an old complaint, and not one Venny in principle disagreed with. "How can you support Balliol's claim to the throne of England?"

"It is long past time the two crowns were united. Besides, if Balliol does not counter him, King David will claim Scotland. He has to be stopped."

"Why? Why not unite the crowns under King David instead of Balliol?" The question was out before Venny could stop himself.

But it was exactly the right question to ask, because it allowed his father to look at him with the same disdainful expression he'd directed Venny's way a thousand times while Venny was growing up. "Don't you realize by now that a strong king is the last thing we want?"

"You think Balliol is weak?"

"Of course he's weak. Haven't you been paying attention?"

Venny thought he had been, but he could admit to himself that his head felt a bit like mush trying to make heads or tails of what was happening here. "If I understand correctly, Mortimer is supporting Balliol's quest for the throne because he thinks he will be able to control Balliol. And—" he paused a moment to think, "if it comes to the point that the barons demand Balliol's head, Mortimer will be the last one standing, since he will be married to Elizabeth. Because Mortimer himself has neither the power nor the reach to murder David in Ireland, Balliol controls Mortimer by holding Elizabeth hostage—until the crown of England is placed on Balliol's head."

Almost for the first time in Venny's life, his father looked at him proudly. "You understand now." He smiled. "Mortimer insisted you not be told the whole story, but you put the pieces together yourself, and very quickly too."

"And because you support Mortimer now, you will ride the hem of his cloak to more power and land for yourself."

"I do this for you and your heirs. I had feared you'd fallen under the king's spell, or worse, that of his witch mother, but I'm pleased to see you have come to your senses in time."

"I am still not clear as to why Mortimer thinks King David wants Scotland," Venny said, trying to sound musing. "He could have taken it a few years ago and didn't."

"Hasn't King David gone to Ireland to force his rule upon the barons there? Everybody knows he would like nothing better than to wear the crown of the High King."

Venny bit his lip, wondering how much he could say. "Last I heard he wanted to give Ireland back to the Irish."

"Pah. He said that to put everyone off their guard. When his father dies, he will have Wales. Through his mother, he will claim Scotland. He rounds it out with Ireland because he descends directly from its great kings as well."

While Venny had been talking to his father, Mortimer and FitzWalter had been conferring closely in heated tones, but finally Mortimer gave a sharp clap of his hands. "It is time to swear."

He waved his hand at a servant, who'd been standing in the doorway. The man left for a moment and came back with a priest, who went to the altar where an open Bible lay. Venny's father came forward to stand at Venny's left shoulder.

Venny allowed himself to be urged forward and then again onto his knees. A moment later, he found himself pledging life and limb to Roger Mortimer.

That detail taken care of, Mortimer headed for the door, but before he reached it, it swung open to reveal an agitated Henry Percy. "I have had word from my grandfather." His words came out slurred. "He sent a rider."

Not a man to suffer fools, Mortimer glowered at Henry, who was weaving on his feet. "Spit it out!"

"Lord Mathonwy sent William Venables here as a spy." Henry pointed a finger. "He still serves the king."

Mortimer swung around to look at Venny, who backed up, hands raised defensively. "Did I not just swear? I already gave you this exact news!"

Mortimer's nostrils flared as he looked between Henry and Venny.

Venny's father stepped between them. "He did just tell us this. Lord Mathonwy believes my boy is faithful, so that's what he would have told Warenne."

Mortimer looked at FitzWalter for a rare piece of advice, and FitzWalter shrugged. "It's up to you."

"Collect his men from the outer ward and confine them to the barracks." Mortimer then turned to Venny and his father. "You two will be confined to the keep for the time being."

"But, my lord—" Venny's father started to protest, but Mortimer held up a hand.

"It's late, and I'm of no mind to make any more decisions tonight. Be grateful you're not in the dungeon." He gave everyone, including the drunken Henry Percy, a long look. "God willing, we will hear from Balliol's men in Ireland in the morning."

27

19 March 2022

Mark

"What do you want me to do?" Andre said.

"Stop here, out of the light." Mark indicated a spot not lit by the lamppost in the layby, located roughly halfway between Chalfont St. Giles and London. He had a map of every CCTV camera in Britain on his laptop, and so far they had avoided all but two of them. The moment they entered the motorway, however, cameras would proliferate, taking pictures on the fly of every vehicle passing underneath them, along with images of their drivers and passengers. These were sent to a central database at GCHQ. Mark had known this before he'd set out, but had done so anyway until Livia had sent yet another urgent warning *not* to come to London, and Andre had turned off the road.

Mark slouched in the passenger seat of the car, which had been the most obscure vehicle in Chad Treadman's massive parking garage, in large part because it wasn't Chad's at all, but his cook's. They'd borrowed it (with permission), in hopes that Mark could get all the way to London without being noticed. Thankfully, MI-5 was still keeping the hunt in-house, so as of yet his and Anna's images had not been plastered across every news outlet and web page.

Mark had also taken the precaution of transforming his appearance, having shaved his beard and mustache before getting into the car. The beard hadn't been MI-5 sanctioned anyway. He'd started growing it nine months ago after Christopher had left for exactly this reason. Nobody had confronted him about it, despite how daft he looked with a beard. In retrospect, it was an indication of how little regard his bosses had for him.

Livia had left Thames House, having been released from questioning and told not to return until the crisis was over. She'd been followed home, but the tail had been desultory. It seemed now that Mark's decision to accept her help had been inspired. The two of them had never rung each other, they'd emailed only about work matters, and had engaged in no social contact before today. Even the hyper-paranoid MI-5 could see that she'd been doing only as he'd asked her and could not be faulted.

Mark liked to think that if he'd been running the operation, he would have detained Livia until Anna was in custody. As it was, once her tail departed, Livia had changed clothes, ducked out of her flat through a back door, and returned to a bench at the bus stop across the street from the exit of Five's parking garage. With yet another new phone, her first act had been to contact Mark and warn against his grand plan to return to MI-5.

Her voice had been only the latest in a loud chorus, including Chad's, who believed that by turning himself in, Mark ran the risk of exposing where Anna was. In turn, Mark had argued that the men running the operation remained behind the curve. Mark was the only one left from Callum's days, which meant they'd have more to gain by listening to him and working with him than throwing him in prison. In truth, Mark himself had been over the video showing Anna's arrival in the middle of Westminster Hall a dozen times. It was shocking to *him*, so he could imagine what anyone who didn't know the truth would think. By working with Five rather than against it, he could mitigate their tendency to think the worst.

Regardless, Mark was regretting his earlier hubris. Not quite twenty-four hours earlier, he'd been remarking to himself how important all those CCTV cameras were to the safety of his nation and that a surveillance state wasn't really all that bad. Now, he was furiously sifting through all the images taken from around the embassies and the museum, accessed via Chad Treadman's resources, knowing it was only a matter of time before someone wondered about the Treadman Global cars that had driven by that morning.

As far as Livia knew, Ted, he, and Anna hadn't been caught on camera getting inside the cars or later on one of the motorways. But Livia was out of the loop now, which was why she was sitting across from Thames House trying to get a feel for what they were going to do next rather than reporting to him from inside Five.

Chad's estate could even be monitored, if only because the British state monitored everyone. It wasn't a question Mark had thought to ask before today, and Livia hadn't been able to query that herself without exposing herself or Chad to her superiors.

Andre rested his elbow on his armrest and looked at Mark's screen. Currently playing was a video Livia was taking of the entrance to the parking garage, showing the arrival of a darkened SUV with diplomatic plates. "CIA."

"That would be my guess," Mark said.

"This went up the chain of command faster than it should have," Andre said.

Mark laughed. "Five would have to be thick to ignore a dead horse in Westminster Hall and the disappearance of its rider with the aid of a Security Service officer. Too many others saw Anna. A bobby killed the horse. And anyone who heard her would have known she's American."

"The official secrets act covers many ills."

"Sure, but between the ambulance, the hospital, and the knackers, that's a lot of people to enforce silence upon. It was on the news." He looked at Andre. "I'm sorry I bungled this so badly. It's going to lead to your boss. He could be charged with harboring a fugitive."

"Chad Treadman is a big boy—and he's more powerful than you know. Nothing will come of it. You'll see."

After another few minutes, Livia had to move her location to an all-night coffee shop that gave her a less good angle on the garage, but at least she could now work openly on her laptop. People kept coming to Thames House, and so far nobody notable had left. It was a really bad sign for the director of the CIA to arrive at MI-5 after hours and not leave. Something big was going down. Mark had already spoken to Chad Treadman several times. The tech genius had put out feelers too, but if Five were moving in a particular direction, they weren't telling anyone else about it.

Then, near midnight, a car pulled up behind them. Andre straightened in his seat, where he'd been dozing. "Copper."

"You've got to be kidding me." Mark turned in his seat, and at the sight of the flashing lights, he closed all of his electronics and slid them into his backpack. He'd left his go bag at the castle in case Anna needed anything in it, which at this point might be just as well, since he had put a gun at the bottom of it.

The bobby knocked on the window, and Andre pressed the car's power button in order to slide the window down. "May I help you, officer?"

"What are you doing here?" He pulled out his torch and shined it into the car.

"Talking," Andre said.

The light was bright in Mark's eyes. The officer also wore a camera as part of his gear, so Mark's face was now broadcast to every law enforcement agency in the country, should they choose to access the feed. "What about you?"

"I'm the one he's been talking to," Mark said, trying project the right balance between innocent and flip that wouldn't be suspicious.

The muscles around the cop's eyes tightened. He was thinking Mark and Andre were a couple. Andre realized it too, and he put a hand briefly on Mark's knee to better sell the idea. The officer's eyes tracked to the motion, and then Andre moved his hand away. They were fully dressed and had the appearance of being and doing exactly what they'd said.

Still, the officer couldn't let it go, "Let's see some ID."

There was no help for it. Andre took out his driving license. After a pause and a canter around the idea and the possible consequences, Mark handed over his journalist's badge, the same one he'd used in the hospital. It was a risk, especially if the officer looked up the number, which was backstopped by MI-5, but it was better to deal with this problem now, even if it created a bigger problem later. The cold knowledge settled on his shoulders that returning to London had become a nonstarter. He was on the run, maybe for the rest of his life. "We were just talking, officer. Surely there's no crime in that?"

The officer continued to look stern. "Why have you been sitting in this layby?"

"It seemed a quiet place to meet," Andre said.

"Does this have anything to do with what happened at Westminster last night?"

Inwardly, Mark cursed that the officer had asked that question, since the conversation was being recorded by the officer's personal surveillance gear. Mark had to hope the mention of Westminster would get lost in the shuffle of a thousand people saying the same word over the course of the day. What with the dead horse, maybe more like a million. It would be too many to follow up with every encounter.

Meanwhile Andre made his expression very serious. "It does."

Andre's answer was finally enough to convince the officer that no crime was being committed. He nodded, returned their IDs, and headed back to his vehicle.

Andre looked at Mark. "We should go back to the castle. Your presence at Thames House will do nothing more than pour oil on the fire. You know too much, and they'll break you."

Mark took in a breath. "I keep making mistakes. I thought I was cut out for spy work, but I'm not."

Andre studied him. "What could you have done differently?" And then at Mark's disgruntled look, he added, "No, I mean it. Anna arrives at Westminster Palace on a horse and is immediately placed in police custody. What do you do differently?"

"I should have disabled more cameras at the hospital. We should have left the city immediately."

Andre shook his head. "In a movie, sure, but you take down the entire suite of hospital cameras, and the security staff are going to notice and respond immediately. I know the protocols for that hospital, because London police use them. The cameras there are linked directly to the Victoria embankment headquarters. Bringing down those cameras would have brought attention sooner than if you and Livia had waltzed in there and flashed your MI-5 badges. It was six hours at least before any paperwork was filed."

Then he canted his head. "As to leaving the city, you could only have done so if you had a vehicle and some place to go."

As Andre started the car, Mark stared out the window. "I should have arranged months ago to garage a car. I wasn't as prepared as I thought."

"You needed a team and more time to plan, and it was just your bad luck she arrived when and where she did. If she'd ended up in some farmer's field, she could have ridden the horse to the nearest house and simply rung you."

Mark turned to look at him. "So why didn't she?"

Andre frowned as he executed a three-point turn and headed back the way they'd come. "Why didn't she what?"

"Why didn't she appear some place where she wouldn't have ended up in police custody right away?"

Andre snorted. "Because she didn't."

"No." Mark shook his head. "You don't understand. She ends up where she's supposed to."

"Well ..." Andre was focused on his driving, backtracking across the countryside exactly as they'd come to avoid cameras. "I said she could have rung you, but could she have? How would she have reached you—or her aunt and uncle? They'd moved to England, so new numbers all around, yeah? And you changed your name, not to mention the fact that you work for MI-5. What could she have done ... rung up Thames House and asked for you?"

"I used to work out of Cardiff, so that location might be the last thing she knew." Mark settled back in his seat, the tension easing out of his shoulders. He felt all of a sudden as if he'd been here before.

Andre noticed too and shot him a look through narrowed eyes. "What just happened?"

"What do you mean?"

"You relaxed."

"I stopped worrying. I've been looking at this the wrong way round. My job isn't to understand what's happened. It's to go with it, even if that means I end up back in the Middle Ages." Mark managed a genuine laugh. "It may be I'm supposed to."

Andre's expression indicated he thought Mark had gone mental.

"Just you wait." Mark settled farther into his seat. "It's like David always says. You do what you can and what is right—and let the chips fall as they may."

28

20 March 1294

Math

Math could barely breathe for the hay dust, and it irritated him to no end that not only had Warenne completely fooled him, which was indignity enough, but he couldn't be bothered to cover his head with a woven bag. Wool would have been better than this hemp sacking that was making him sneeze.

He was guessing his wine had contained poppy juice because the events of the rest of the evening had completely passed him by. He groaned and shifted his legs, to find his feet butting up against something with some give to it.

Then Ieuan said, "Stop it, man! It's bad enough that my head hurts without you poking your boot into my ribs."

Pleased to find his friend alive and irritated, Math sat up. His ankles and wrists were bound, but knowing he was with Ieuan improved his chances of escape enormously. He wriggled closer. "Get this thing off my head, will you?"

"My hands are tied behind my back. You?"

"Same."

The pair managed to maneuver around each other so that Ieuan's fingers could grasp the sacking over Math's head, and then Math rolled over to free Ieuan. Gasping at the effort, they lay on the floor of their cell, which turned out to be a genuine prison, with stone floor, iron bars, and dampness seeping down the walls. At least they hadn't been thrown into the pit of the dungeon Math knew lay in the basement of each of Lyons Castle's five towers. Perhaps those black pits had been reserved for his men. If they weren't dead.

Still, Math saw no reason to suffer more than necessary and worked to free Ieuan's hands. "In retrospect, Warenne chose his words very carefully last night, did you notice? I'm not sure he even openly lied. I wasn't mindful of the danger."

"We were completely fooled. Hospitality doesn't appear to be what it once was."

Math snorted laughter, pleased Ieuan still had the ability to mock, and then he laughed again as the rope around his wrists loosened. Ieuan's hands were tied even tighter behind his back, which told Math that the hemp sacking and rope bonds were purely vindictive, given the bars that separated the prison cell from the adjacent guardroom. Math hadn't realized he and Ieuan were so hated. Or maybe that was Dafydd.

They ended up side by side against the wall. They kept their hands behind their backs with the ropes held loosely in their fingers. It wouldn't pay to be complacent now, not when they'd come this far towards freedom in so short a time. They didn't address their ankles because loosened ropes there would be impossible to hide. If they were to have a chance at escape, it would be only after the cell door was opened and they were moved somewhere else in the castle. In that case, someone would have to cut the ropes around their ankles for them.

Ieuan used his bent knee to brush away a piece of straw that had caught in his hair and was hanging in front of his face. "I don't see the play here. I understand Balliol wants to rule Scotland without fear of English interference. But Warenne? What's he reaching for?"

Before Math could answer—if he had an answer—the door to the outside swung open, and Warenne himself appeared. He laughed out loud when he saw them. "It isn't often I win a wager with my garrison captain. I assured him you would not still be wearing those sacks."

Math found himself even more irritated, but Ieuan repeated the question he'd asked Math, this time for Warenne's reply.

"The throne, of course." Warenne's boots scraped on the stone floor as he approached the cell. He was warmly dressed to ward off the damp Math was trying not to think about, since then he'd start shivering.

"You lured us here with false promises," Math said.

"I did not lie outright."

"It seems an odd thing to care about," Math said, "given that you've betrayed the king."

"There is no king to betray. King David is dead."

"You lie." Math licked his lips. He was already very thirsty, and he tasted ash at Warenne's assertion. He should have known the plan involved an attack on Dafydd, and in the face of Warenne's certainty, Math needed to be on his feet. He scooted up the wall to a standing position so he could look Warenne in the eye. He wasn't sure why Warenne was bothering to speak to them at all, but he'd always struck Math as an intelligent man, so he had to be keeping them alive for a reason.

Warenne raised one shoulder in a half-shrug. "Time will tell. If David isn't dead already, then he soon will be. Balliol sent his nephew to Ireland, and the countryside has risen in rebellion."

"Balliol sent Red Comyn? The Irish follow him?"

Warenne scoffed. "The Irish barons follow whoever offers them wealth and power, which King David did not."

Math couldn't deny Dafydd hadn't done much to woo the Norman barons in Ireland. To him, the warfare in Ireland had been a sticky problem that had dogged him throughout his short reign. If what Warenne said was true, then Dafydd's attempt to deal with the problem was too little too late.

Ieuan had stayed on the floor, and he looked up at Warenne. "I gather you're reaching for the throne yourself? You have no royal blood."

"Since when does that matter?" Warenne clenched his right hand into a fist. "King David has none by his own admission. The one who rules is the one who is strong enough to take the throne and hold it against all comers."

"If the plan is to divide the world between you," Ieuan said, still from the floor, "Comyn gets Ireland, Balliol Scotland, and you England, that doesn't leave much room for men like FitzWalter."

"FitzWalter does as he is bid. As you should."

Math and Ieuan exchanged a glance. Now they were getting to the meat of the matter and why they were here—and also why they weren't confined to the damp dungeon below their feet. Or dead.

"You want us to walk away." Ieuan spoke with a kind of awe in his voice, as if he couldn't believe Warenne's audacity.

"King Llywelyn is dead alongside his son. Wales is yours now, but only if you don't fight me."

Math laughed, though with an aching bitterness. The scope of Warenne's plan made William de Valence's and Gilbert de Clare's schemes look paltry and under-reaching by comparison. His gut twisted at the thought that even now Dinas Bran could be under siege as Bevyn had feared. Lili and Arthur, the heir to the English crown, plus the twins, the heirs to the throne of Wales, were there, not to mention his own children, who had claim through Anna. He swallowed hard. That was the reason Bevyn had stayed behind, of course, and Math had to believe the old warrior knew what he was doing and would protect them.

"I'll have you know that going after Anna was foolhardy and not my idea," Warenne added, oddly continuing the conversation and offering unrequested information. "You two are the far bigger prize. FitzWalter and Mortimer tried to take Anna because they thought to use her as leverage against you, but imagine my pleasure when you walked right into my arms. In a few days, all of Britain will fall in line behind us."

"Wait. Did you say Mortimer?" Ieuan said. "Are we speaking of Edmund?"

"Roger."

Math let out a breath. "Roger Mortimer allies with you? That must not have come cheap. Who else?"

Warenne's expression soured slightly. "Humphrey de Bohun."

"You have competition for the throne then," Math said. "How are you getting around that?"

Warenne gave him a hint of a smile, though it lacked humor—or perhaps conviction. "I don't have to. They have all pledged to support my grandson's claim."

"Why would they do that?" Ieuan said. "Henry has no more royal blood than you do."

"Because Henry is betrothed to Elizabeth, King Edward's youngest daughter."

Math gazed at Warenne. His words were completely believable, and for the first time in many years, despair entered Math's heart. They would need a true miracle to get out of this one.

29

20 March 2022

Anna

"**W**ake up, Anna. It's time to go."

Anna came out of a deep sleep, a product of the pain pill she'd taken so she could fall asleep in the first place, to find Aunt Elisa shaking her awake. She looked into her aunt's troubled face. "What is it?"

Elisa put a hand to her heart. "You were so deeply asleep, I was afraid something had happened to you in the night." She was dressed for the road in jeans, boots, and a weatherproof jacket.

Anna rubbed the last of the sleep from her eyes and swung her feet out of bed. "I'm fine."

"MI-5 is coming."

Rather than panic, which by rights she should, Anna's eyes went briefly to the ceiling before she headed to the bathroom. "I don't know what they're so afraid of."

She stripped off her pajama shirt, a new one brought to her last night by one of Chad's assistants, since she'd left the previous night's outfit at Callum's apartment. Her modern clothes were piled on the counter, and she started pulling them on. "At this point, it would be way better to let the world know what we can do, even if it means everyone thinks I'm crazy."

"That would put you in danger, Anna," Elisa said, with evident patience in her voice. "Not all countries are friendly, you know."

Anna laughed, her voice muffled by her sweater as she pulled it down over her head. "As compared to the governments ostensibly on our side?"

Elisa gave her a rueful smile, acknowledging the irony.

"Where's Mark?" Anna said. "When I fell asleep he hadn't yet reached London."

"He turned around and came back."

That was a relief—to Anna if not to Mark. "Why?"

"Livia got in touch with him again and made him see that no amount of explanation was going to make this right." Elisa took in a breath. "Chad's been on the phone to his contacts in the government, but there's nothing the commerce department can do, and the CIA is involved, so—"

"So they don't want to help, or they can't." Anna checked the clock on the bedside table. It said five in the morning. Dawn was in an hour or so, provided the UK hadn't gone to daylight savings time yet. Earth Two, as Chad called her world and Anna had grown used to hearing over dinner last night, had no use for such a thing, thank goodness. Its absence was a blessing to all mothers everywhere, even if they didn't know it. "How are we getting out of here?"

"Chad has a plane. He has the pilot preparing to leave now."

"I saw a plane parked on the grass below this hill yesterday. I didn't see an airstrip though." Anna pulled on her boots. The leather was soft as butter and hand-stitched, as it would have had to be since they'd been made by a craftsman in Llangollen. When Mark had given her a pair of shoes yesterday, she'd opted to keep her own, since the lamb's wool insoles were so nicely molded to her feet.

"Apparently it doesn't need one."

"So it's more like a helicopter?"

Elisa shrugged. "I don't know how these things work, and I've given up asking. Chad just needs us down there when the plane is ready."

Anna and Elisa met everyone else in the corridor, shivering a bit at the early hour, despite the central heating. They all had bags on their shoulders, not dissimilar to the go bag Anna carried, the same one she'd brought from Callum's apartment. Sophie was there too. As before, she herded them onto the elevator, but this time, they went down.

"I am so glad to see you," Anna said in an undertone to Mark as the doors closed. "Did you return because you knew we had to run? I thought I was safe here."

"I told you about the CCTV cameras, right?" Mark said. "It took them most of the night, but they found us."

"Why do they care so much?" Anna swallowed down the wail that rose up in her throat, since she didn't want to upset Elen more than she already was. "Will they never leave us alone?"

"Apparently not." Mark shot her a look that was almost sad. "It's all about control, Anna—control of information and people."

"And ideas," Uncle Ted said from the far side of the elevator, apparently having overheard despite Anna's and Mark's efforts to speak quietly.

"I get that, sort of," Anna said. "I just don't see why they're so intent on me. I didn't do anything."

"You appeared at Westminster Hall on a horse," Mark said. "That was more than enough."

"You would think they'd be happy I'd disappeared, so they could sweep my existence under a rug. They've denied all knowledge of the Time Travel Initiative, right? Why dredge it all up again?"

"Because the initiative isn't dead so much as resurrected in its original form," Mark said. "Pre-Callum."

"And around it goes again." Ted gave Anna a sad smile. "I'm glad I'm smarter now. I just wish we had a Callum in charge at MI-5."

Mark grunted. "These days it's politicians all the way down."

"What about Livia?" Anna said.

Mark looked up at the numbers blinking by on the elevator, which seemed to be taking a long time to get them to where they were going. "She isn't going in to work today, but all anyone knows is that she drove me to the hospital and dropped me off in the vicinity of Hyde Park. She was only following orders, and that's the story she's sticking to. I think she'll be okay."

"I hope so. I hate to leave her out in the cold."

"She won't be left out in the cold. She has a job with us, as soon as all this blows over."

Anna turned at George's voice. She hadn't noticed him in the corridor, and she realized he'd been in the elevator when they'd gotten on.

"That's only if Chad survives this," Anna said.

George scoffed. "Of all the things you need to worry about, Chad Treadman isn't one of them. The security services will come to their senses sooner or later. Treadman Global designed half their tech."

"You should have left a back door into it," Elen said, and when everyone looked at her, she added, "What? I'm not allowed to say what I think?"

"You are allowed," George said kindly, "and we would have if it wasn't illegal and might cause more problems than it solved."

But Anna could see his eyes turning thoughtful. She was almost afraid to think what the consequences of today might be in the future.

"We have to live in this world, Elen," Ted said. "It's a constant series of compromises to survive."

"I suppose it can be like that everywhere," Anna said, realizing she hadn't told her family yet what she'd agreed to last night with Chad. "Everyone makes compromises. The key is to keep them to ones you can live with."

The elevator dinged and dumped them out into a sub-sub-sub-basement. Chad Treadman was there to greet them, along with Andre, back again in his immaculate suit and tie. Chad, by contrast, wore khakis and a U Penn sweatshirt, implying he'd once lived in the same neck of the woods as Uncle Ted and Aunt Elisa.

"Welcome to the bat cave!"

The man clearly had been watching too many superhero movies. Anna hadn't seen one of those in ages—only in passing that Christmas Eve at Aber, when David and Christopher had been multi-tasking, downloading stuff off the internet while watching videos. Anna frowned, regretting that she hadn't yet gotten to a computer—or, more reasonably, had Mark do so. She could have added reams of paper to her backpack by now.

Mark had his backpack slung over his shoulder, the larger of the two they'd brought to Chad's castle, and Anna eyed it. Too bad it wasn't possible to have internet on a plane, or she could have gotten to work once they were on board. Then she remembered the tablet with a library full of information on it. This world had moved on since she'd lived in it and didn't use paper.

They set off at a quick pace across the giant garage/warehouse/bat cave they'd entered. The reason for the sub-sub-sub-basement access was clear, as Chad really had carved himself a hangar out of the base of the hill upon which his castle perched. It occurred to Anna that perhaps he'd actually created the hill from scratch, which on the whole sounded more likely than getting a permit to hollow out an existing one.

Anna jogged a few steps in order to come abreast of Chad. "Where are we going?"

"I figured we'd start with my castle in Ireland. I have a bigger plane there we can take anywhere in the world if need be." He glanced at her. "I'm sending you with George, Andre, and Sophie for now. I need to stay here and run interference."

"Are you sure that's wise?" Mark said from behind them.

Chad glanced over his shoulder. "I am as committed to Anna's welfare as you. I consider it my job. I'll sort things out here and then join you tomorrow."

As he hustled them through his bat cave, Anna looked left and right. He had at least twenty fancy cars in his underground lair: black cars like those they'd driven out of London yesterday, a half-dozen SUVs that wouldn't have been out of place at MI-5, several buses like the ones that took passengers to and from airport hotels, and a helicopter. David would have loved everything about it, but for once, she didn't wish he was beside her. He was better off where he was, leaving this to her.

In the predawn light, the plane looked normal enough, if small. The wings were a slightly odd shape, with more flaps than she was used to and fat tires. It definitely wasn't a helicopter, so Anna didn't know how it was supposed to take off without an airstrip. Chad had no such reservations, and he trotted up the stairway to the door, and the others followed.

Once inside, the plane proved to have eight seats in pairs facing each other with tables between them, plus a couch, all in white leather. There were even throw pillows and flowers on the tables, though a quick check revealed the vases were affixed to the tables and the flowers were kept moist through a green fibrous block rather than a cup of water.

This was a smaller plane than the one they'd flown in several years ago from Oakland, California, courtesy of MI-5, and Chad implied as much when he said a second later, "This is just my puddle jumper. I traded fuel capacity for getting in the air quickly. I'll bring the bigger one when I come."

"It still can fly five thousand miles without refueling," Ted said in an aside as he sat down next to Anna.

She had taken a chair in the middle of the plane, opposite the couch, on which Elen and Elisa chose to sit. Mark hovered for a moment and then chose a chair opposite Anna. Sophie and George entered the plane last.

After a quick check to make sure everyone was seated and safe, Chad stopped in front of Anna and held out his hand. "It's been a pleasure. Good luck."

She shook without hesitation. "Thank you."

Then Chad bent to Andre, who was sitting in the pilot's seat, the two men spoke briefly, and Chad left. George sealed the door behind him.

Anna craned her neck to see that Sophie had settled into the co-pilot's seat next to Andre. George, meanwhile, disappeared into the back of the plane, only to reappear a minute later with an apron on. "Can I get anyone something to drink before I finish preparing breakfast?"

Anna laughed outright. "MI-5 is coming, but you're preparing breakfast?"

George checked his watch. "Well, they're not here yet." It appeared his amusement was genuine. "Mr. Treadman is not one to go anywhere on an empty stomach."

And then the engines fired up, and Anna gripped the armrest of her seat.

George put up a hand. "I'll get those drinks for you after we take off. Is everyone buckled?" He himself took a jump seat at the back of the plane. Then Sophie's voice came over the intercom. "This can be rough." She laughed. "You'll see in a second why we haven't gone into full production yet."

Anna peered out the window. They were moving across a field that looked nothing out of the ordinary. It was mowed, she supposed, but it could easily have been eaten down by sheep. It was lumpy, and they bounced around as they picked up speed. Then with a burst that sucked her back into her seat, ten times the pressure of a normal take off, they shot across a last fifty feet of grass and were in the air.

The plane barely cleared a stone wall and afterwards a stand of trees—and then they were soaring over the castle, circling around the Treadman property. The sun wasn't yet up, and Anna realized it was the morning of the spring equinox. She looked through the window at the ground, searching for Stonehenge, which she knew was somewhere off to the west of London, hoping to see the people dancing around it.

After circling over the castle once, the plane flew northwest. Once they steadied, George set out their meal, and Anna soon found herself with another full English breakfast in front of her, much like the one Mark had cooked the previous morning in Callum's apartment. The food was very good and without a doubt the best airplane meal she'd ever eaten. Mark spent the whole time he was eating studying the screen of yet another phone, which he'd set beside his plate.

"What are you doing?" Anna finally asked, having finished her meal.

"Downloading a file Chad sent me." He didn't look up.

"From the plane? How?"

He looked over at her, his brow furrowing in puzzlement, and spoke slowly, "Through ... the internet?"

"Oh." Anna frowned. She could tell by the way he'd ended his comment with a question mark that her question had been clueless. She remembered that her mom had talked to Aunt Elisa on the phone from MI-5's plane, but—

Sophie's voice came again over the intercom, interrupting her astonishment. "Friends, if you'd look outside ..."

Anna obeyed, gazing down at the landscape that was taking shape in the gray light of morning.

"We've just crossed into Wales, which, I'm sorry to say, in this world means nothing to those fighter jets trailing us."

With a gasp, Anna pressed her face to the window, but she couldn't see them. "Would they shoot us down?" She looked anxiously at Mark.

"No." Mark shook his head vehemently. Then he paused. "But they might force us down. There's a military airstrip on Anglesey. I think that's the closest one."

The plane flew on, and Anna could hear Andre speaking into his headset, presumably talking to the men controlling the fighter jets, though he didn't share any information with his passengers.

Earlier, while they'd been eating, Sophie had kept up a running commentary on the details of the plane. From that, Anna knew the plane could fly over five hundred miles an hour. If they'd crossed the border between England and Wales two minutes ago, they could be on Anglesey in another seven, since it was only seventy miles from Llangollen to Bangor. Even she could do that math in her head.

"More news," Andre said. "They've just informed us of the arrest warrant for Anna and Mark. I'm sorry to say we can't ignore it."

Anna stood up and moved towards the front to a pair of seats behind the cockpit. A moment later, she found Mark in the seat opposite, and Ted standing in the aisle between them. George, Elisa, and Elen stayed in the back of the plane.

"Do what they say," Anna said to Andre. "None of you have done anything wrong. This isn't your fight."

She felt Ted's hand on her shoulder. "That's where you're wrong, Anna. We're in this together. That's what family is."

Anna spoke even more urgently. "Chad runs one of the largest companies in the world. People depend on him. He can't be in trouble with the law." She looked at Mark. "And you. I got you into this—"

"I got myself into this a long time ago when I boarded that bus in Cardiff, knowingly intending to help Callum and you against the wishes of MI-5. I've been working for you ever since."

Anna had no answer to that. She looked at each of the people with her in turn, and then faced front, to what lay before them. She accepted that she shouldn't second guess their past life-changing decisions.

Instead, she presented them with another one. "Do you see what I see?"

They all looked ahead to where she pointed.

"What?" Ted said.

"That's a mountain, and we're in a plane."

There was a moment's pause as everybody reconciled her words with what she could be suggesting. All of a sudden, it seemed obvious what the answer was: there was trouble in medieval Scotland, and here she was in a plane that could take her there, just like a plane had taken her mother and Cassie.

"I'm not saying you have to," Anna said. "I'm just laying it out there as a possibility. My family wants to come with me, but the rest of you didn't sign up for this."

"We did, actually." Sophie flipped some switches above her head.

"You signed up to drive this plane into Mt. Snowdon and come to the Middle Ages with me?" Anna had hardly spoken two words to Sophie since they'd met. She didn't know her at all—and yet, she was agreeing without hesitation to this. "You *can't* have."

"Mr. Treadman didn't tell you that he filled the cargo hold." Her eyes were bright. "You're going to love what we're bringing."

"You have to be sure." Anna decided she'd deal with that bit of news at a later date. "There might be no coming back."

By way of an answer, Sophie tipped her head to Andre, who calmly turned the plane and flew straight for Snowdon's peak. It wasn't a big mountain by American standards, but it rose into the clouds, and was plenty big enough for their purposes.

"Buckle up!" Andre took off his headset, from which loud squawking sounds came. Presumably the fighter pilots weren't happy with the change of direction.

Anna fought for the seat belt in her new seat.

Meanwhile, Ted shouted to Elisa in the back that she should secure herself and Elen. "It's time!"

Anna, who was both sick and excited about what was going to happen, couldn't mistake his glee. "What about George?" Until this moment, she'd forgotten him. "He's in the galley!"

"He agreed to this too!" Sophie was alight, hyped up and panicked at the same time.

Anna bent her head, her hands clutching the armrests of her chair. She had led, and everyone else had followed. She didn't think her idea to evade the fighter jets was wrong, but like her decision to accept the help Chad offered, it had been a bit more ruthless than she felt comfortable with.

And still, Anna wouldn't take any of these decisions back—even as Andre dove the plane towards the nearest peak at five hundred miles an hour.

30

20 March 1294

David

David stood at the base of the Hill of Tara and looked to the eastern sky. On this first day of spring, the morning of his crowning as High King of Ireland, the sun was going to be visible as it rose above the horizon. How many rainy spring equinox mornings had there been since the Stone of Destiny had been put up by those ancient Irish three thousand years ago? How many thousands of people, at those hundreds of cairns scattered on mountain tops all across Ireland, had left disappointed at not seeing the sun rise and shine on the exact spot they wanted it to?

So it was a huge relief this wasn't going to be one of those cloudy mornings. David would have been crowned anyway. He'd agreed to be Ireland's new High King because the alternative was continued warfare, and if he was going to take the crown—in many ways against his better judgement—then the occasion might as well be as memorable as possible. David was the first High King of

Ireland in over a hundred years, since 1169 when the Normans had arrived and overthrown the prevailing social order.

A crowd had come, bigger than David had hoped for. The fields around Tara had already been filled with men who'd fought in the battle yesterday, but since the fighting had ended, their families had come as well, any who lived within twenty miles of the hill. Never to be left out of a good story, Rupert, the twenty-firster news reporter, had arrived near midnight, and he'd spent all night interviewing everyone about the battle. Christopher was again a favorite, though David thought his cousin's jubilation was more tempered than it might have been even a month ago. Men had died. He'd almost died. If a man was decent, it made him think. If Christopher was anything, he was a good man.

"It's time, my lord." Gilla O'Reilly bowed before David. Beside him were the other great lords of Ireland—Hugh O'Connor, Niall MacMurrough, James Stewart, John de Verdun—each holding one of the marks of David's new office. These included a staff, a shield, a brooch, and a crown (of course). There had been a great deal of jostling as to who should have the honor of putting the crown on David's head, and since everyone believed in the divine right of kings, it had ultimately fallen to the Church. David had put in a good word for Abbot John of Bective Abbey, who now found himself at the center of attention—a place with which he was not entirely comfortable. He was waiting for them on the top of the Hill of Tara, beside the Stone of Destiny, or *Lia Fáil* in Gaelic.

Hugh and Niall together draped the fur-lined robe around David's shoulders. The ritual had been orchestrated to be as inclusive as possible, not in terms of religion, since everyone here was Christian and Catholic, but with each kingdom having a piece of the action. David had hoped more women would be involved—or any woman, for that matter—but none of the women he'd encountered, Gilla's daughter, Aine, among them, had consented to participate in the traditionally all-male ceremony. It was irksome that David hadn't had time to make them understand his goals, because he'd wanted to start as he intended to go on.

David's father was still playing the role of neutral facilitator, though obviously he was far from neutral in this matter. He led the procession out of the tent and through the lines of watching people, who fell silent as an Irish trumpet played, announcing David's approach. As he left the tent, David glanced out of the corner of his eye at the horizon, thinking they were cutting it a little close to sunrise, but the Irish didn't hurry and processed up to the top of the hill in good order.

Unlike in modern times (according to David's mother), the Stone of Destiny did not stand upright at the top of the hill. It had always been intended as a base upon which the high king would first kneel and then stand when he was crowned. Legend had it the Stone of Destiny would roar when the king put his feet on it, which wouldn't be possible if it were a three-foot-tall oblong pillar.

Because Tara hadn't been used as a seat of the high kings in several hundred years, all that remained of the various buildings that once housed a royal court were the turf walls and ditches that protected it. Today, people stood on them, trying to get a better view of the coronation. They'd left an open pathway heading east, however, so the sun, when it rose, would strike the top of the hill and the crown on David's head.

As he walked, David was very conscious of the smell of newly cut grass and the fresh breeze that marked the rising of the sun. Since David's back was to the east, he couldn't see the eastern horizon anymore. Instead, he focused on the not-quite-half-full moon hanging in the sky above him. It was the one white thing in a land of endless blue and green.

David approached Abbot John, and the music ceased. Next, a bard was supposed to have sung a ballad, but a quick wave from David's father, who came to a halt on John's left, told him they had, in fact, timed the coronation a little too closely, and the crown needed to be put on David's head immediately, lest they miss their moment. David strode towards the stone and knelt on it. It didn't shout with joy, which he hadn't expected but some in the crowd might have.

Then Abbot John raised the crown above his head, quoting from Samuel: *Then all the tribes of Israel came to David at Hebron and said to him, "Look, we are your own family. Even when Saul was king, you were the one who led Israel in battle. The Lord said to you, 'You will be a shepherd for my people Israel. You will be their leader'."* And then first in Latin, then in

Gaelic, and then English, he said, "May God bless David, the High King of Ireland!"

He settled the crown on David's head at the exact moment the sun rose above the horizon to the east. It was too early in the year to be warm, but the light was bright, and since David was facing him, he saw Abbot John blink as the rays of the sun hit him full in the face. Their figures also cast long shadows in the grass, and the crown atop David's head looked larger than life. With a nod, Abbot John stepped back, and David rose to his feet to stand directly on the Stone of Destiny. He turned in a circle, away from the abbot and towards the sun, and in the same motion pulled his sword from its sheath to raise it above his head. "*Chun onóir na hÉireann*! For Ireland!"

The crowd shouted its approval, which David thought expressed sufficient joy to please anyone who was disappointed the stone hadn't screamed. That is, until a plane burst from the sky in front of the sun, its engines roaring, and soared over Tara a hundred feet above their heads.

Half the crowd dove for the ground, terrified, while the rest gaped up at it, David included, though it was William de Bohun, of course, who said what was on everyone's minds. "You've got to be kidding me!"

"I'll get your horse, shall I?" Callum was beside David in a half-second. He hadn't played a significant role in the crowning because there'd been so many other men who'd needed to participate. One of the headaches of being king and having as much power as David was that men vied for his attention. Callum had no ego in that regard, so David had willfully put him at the back of the line.

But when a crisis came, Callum was the man David trusted most here in Ireland, other than his father, who would want a horse of his own too. Abbot John was bent over, his hands over his eyes, and appeared to be praying. David put a hand on his shoulder and raised him up. "Do not fear. I know what this is, and I will see to it."

"Yes. Yes, of course." John stared at David with an amazed expression that he also saw on the faces of most of the people who surrounded him.

If things had gone as planned, there would have been a receiving line and a feast, and David would have accepted the obeisance of the lords here. As it was, the ceremony would have to wait. He'd stepped off the stone while the plane had circled the hill, but he went back to it and raised both arms, sword still in hand, signaling to the crowd for silence. They wanted reassurance, and they quieted to listen to him. He didn't even have to shout. "Please don't be afraid. All is well. Someone has come from Avalon."

Before last year, he would have assumed that someone was his sister, since both he and his mother were here, but now he had a twisting in his gut that it was Arthur again, and that something catastrophic had happened to his family in Wales. That anyone was here at all was horrifying enough. Time travel happened to his family members when their lives were in danger. It was sickening to think that, while he'd been fighting here, his family had been suffering at home.

He left the stone and loped down the grassy slope towards the royal tent. The crown fit well enough that he didn't have to worry about it falling off his head, but the robe was heavy and hot, and he needed to do something with the relics before he mounted his horse.

Fortunately, Gilla had followed him, and when they reached level ground, David was able to hand him the scepter, the brooch, and the shield. Aine helped take off the cloak. When David turned to thank them, Gilla spoke before he could, "The stone roared, my lord. I've never heard such a sound."

His expression was one of awe, as if he'd just seen a miracle. By his standards, he had. David could tell him that a hundred-thousand planes flew every day in Avalon, but it was unlikely to help.

"It wasn't the stone but the plane, which isn't magic. I want to tell you about it, but I don't have time to explain right now."

"Is it from Avalon?" Aine asked.

"Yes. Christopher has told you?"

She nodded. Then Christopher edged his way through the crowd, the rest of his friends in tow. "Do you think—" He cut off the sentence, his eyes to the east where the plane had gone to land, unable to articulate his hope.

"We'll find out soon enough," David said.

William stepped closer. "May I come?" He had been David's squire, so he'd rubbed shoulders with the twenty-firsters almost more than any person from this world, barring Lili, Ieuan, and Math.

"Of course." David looked around at his companions. "All of you can come. We have nothing to hide."

By then, Callum had arrived with David's horse, a white one, which had been a gift from Hugh O'Connor. David swung himself into the saddle and then reached down to Christopher to help him mount behind him. "Let's go find our family."

31

20 March 1294

Anna

"Did we do it? Did we do it?" Elen was wide-eyed and gasping. "Who are all those people down there?"

Anna flung herself towards the window and pressed her nose against the glass. She couldn't make out individual people necessarily, but a crowd of thousands had gathered on a green hill. Many were prostrate or cowering, their hands over their ears, but others craned their necks to look up at them. There were no power lines or radio towers anywhere, so she was able to answer Elen, "Yes, I think so."

"Do I put down?" Andre's voice trembled slightly, which was the first hesitation she'd heard from him.

"We could fly on, but I don't know to what purpose," Anna said. "It isn't as if a thousand people didn't just see us come in."

"*Where* do I put down?"

"There are a lot of fields," Mark said dryly. "I thought this plane could land anywhere. Pick one."

Anna glanced back at him. This was exactly what he hadn't wanted. "I'm sorry."

He gave her a rueful smile. "How could it have ended any other way?"

By Anna's reckoning, there were lots of other ways it could have ended—if this was, indeed, an ending, but she saw no reason to disrupt Mark's evident equanimity with her doubts.

"Is that an airstrip?" Andre had circled the plane around the hill by now.

Anna bent over with a hand on the co-pilot's chair. "It can't be." They were in the Middle Ages. There were no airstrips.

"Where are we?" Sophie's nose was pressed to the glass of the window beside her. "I caught a glimpse of the ocean a second ago. Is this medieval Wales?"

"I don't think this is Wales. I don't know where we are." Anna glanced back to where Elisa and Ted were sitting together, hands clasped tightly, though Anna had the sense Elisa's wide-eyed look was due to horror and Ted's to excitement. Anna refused to feel guilt, though that might come later depending on what happened next.

Fortunately, Andre had remained focused on the task before him. "I don't care what it is. It's close enough to an airstrip not to matter. Buckle up again." He nosed the plane down towards what had to be a road, though Anna had rarely seen such a good one in the Middle Ages. The Romans had built many, some still in good repair, but none that looked like this as far as she knew.

Andre was right, however, that the only important thing was that it was wide enough for two carts to pass and was built up above the surrounding terrain.

She returned to her seat and hastily buckled her seat belt. The engines roared, louder than before, but when the plane approached the ground, it settled onto the road as light as a feather.

Sophie turned in her seat, recovered enough to talk up the airplane again. "The landing is much better than takeoff, as you can see."

Anna found laughter welling up in her chest, and she put the back of her hand to her mouth, shoulders shaking.

Ted was bent forward to look out the window, but he turned to look at her. "Are you okay?"

Anna struggled to sober. "I'm fine. More importantly, how are you?"

"I told you I wanted to come with you," he said. "No doubt theory and reality are two very different things."

"I did warn you." She spread her hands wide. "Are you all okay? George?" Regardless of what they'd stated—and done, truth be told—she couldn't help but think that George, Sophie, and Andre had been coerced into accepting this assignment.

"We're fine," Sophie said in a tone that brooked no argument. The somewhat sticky sweetness of their first encounter was long gone. "Even if I wasn't, would there be anything you could do about it?"

Anna hesitated and then said straightforwardly. "No. Not right away." There was no point in sugar-coating the obvious truth.

"I assume I will stick out like a sore thumb," Andre said.

"You will," Anna said. "There's no way around that. You can ask Darren how it's been for him."

"Who's Darren?"

Mark answered for Anna. "He worked for Callum. He came on the bus a few years ago and stayed."

There was a sourness to Mark's tone that Anna didn't like, but she didn't respond to it. Mark was going to have to come to terms with being back here against his will, but it wasn't going to happen through anything Anna herself said.

Lastly Anna went to Elen and crouched in front of her. "What about you?"

"School sucks," she said matter-of-factly. "I'm glad not to have to go back there ever again."

"We have schools here," Anna said.

"Yeah, but I bet they aren't anything like mine."

Anna gave a low laugh. "You're probably right."

Elen looked hopefully at Anna. "Maybe Christopher is here."

"Only one way to find out." Mark rose from his seat and looked at Anna. "You're a princess of Wales. I think it's down to you now to see this through."

Anna took in the faces looking back at her. All of them had turned eager, and she saw no point in diminishing their enthusiasm with cold reality right away. They would find out soon enough what this world was like and if their decision to ride with her had been a mistake.

"Give me a second." Anna grabbed her pack from the storage compartment and pulled out her medieval clothing, which Mark had stuffed into the top back at Callum's apartment. "I think it would be better if I looked a little more the part when we open that door."

It was a delay that could be a bad thing if the people out there were hostile, but Anna didn't see that they had any great alternatives. In the back of the plane, with Elisa's help, since Anna still had the broken wrist, she pulled off her modern shirt and pants and exchanged them for wool leggings, underdress, and overdress. It took close to ten minutes, but still she hesitated before pulling back the curtain and reentering the main cabin. She'd put on the uniform. Now she had to act the part.

Then she found Aunt Elisa's hand on her shoulder. "Thank you. Thank you for giving us this chance."

Closing her eyes, Anna took in a deep breath and let it out. Once again, she'd arrived back where she belonged and where she did make a difference every day. It wasn't everything, but it was enough to be going on with. She flung back the curtain. "Let's get that door open."

The order had come out before she thought about it. In Avalon, every one of the people here but Elen outranked her in every way. Anna hadn't even graduated from high school. Uncle Ted was the CFO of a huge corporation, Andre was a pilot, and Sophie and George had depths they hadn't yet plumbed. But here, her brother sat atop the medieval food chain.

And she was a princess again—in her own right.

The plane had settled in the middle of the road, and the wings had folded themselves back so they were out of the way, much like a bird when it came to rest.

Sophie opened the door, and Anna stuck out her head ... somehow, of all the crazy things that had happened today, seeing her brother looking at her from the back of a white horse was the least of them. They'd arrived in Ireland, not Scotland, but it would do. "Hey."

"Hey to you!"

She and David stared at each other for a second, and then his eyes went to her arm. "Is that a cast?"

"It's a long story." Then Anna looked at Christopher, who was mounted behind David. "Your family is here. Come on in."

David maneuvered his horse closer to the side of the plane, and Anna got out of the way so a tearful Uncle Ted could hold out his hand to his son. Christopher reached up and half-leapt, half-clambered into the plane, ultimately flopping on his stomach in the doorway. Then he scrambled to his feet, and a second later was enveloped in his father's arms. Elisa, naturally, started crying.

Christopher wrapped his arms around his mother's waist and lifted her six inches off the ground. "I'm sorry, Mom. I'm so sorry."

"You have nothing to be sorry for." Aunt Elisa's words were slightly muffled by Christopher's cloak. "I was at fault."

Then Ted wrapped his arms around both of them. "It's nobody's fault and everybody's. How about we leave it at that. I'm just so glad we're all together again."

"Me too!" Elen hugged her brother from behind.

Christopher laughed. Having put down his mother, he reached out an arm to Elen in order to bring her into their circle.

Tears tracked down Anna's cheeks to see them so joyful, and she found herself accepting her role in reuniting them. It wasn't her job to keep them apart or make their decisions for them. Then, as she'd come to expect from her cousin's family, all of them started talking at once, still too excited to have a thought for anyone else. Anna edged past them to sit in the doorway with her legs dangling outside the plane.

David had walked his horse to the front of the plane and back to calm it, and now he gazed up at her with a big grin on his face. Since she'd wiped away her tears, her smile was probably just as big.

"Do you want to come down here?" he asked.

"Not yet. I don't dare leave everyone. You'll be thrilled to learn I brought more people to acclimate."

"Me among them." Mark poked his nose through the doorway above Anna's head.

"Oh. Wow." David hesitated, clearly not knowing what to say. "You came."

"It's what you wanted, isn't it?"

"Yes." He met Mark's gaze. "I'm guessing I have you to thank for keeping Anna safe in Avalon, broken arm aside."

Mark actually blushed a little. "That happened on the way in." Then he shrugged. "To tell you the truth, she did just fine all by herself."

"It was chaos," Anna said flatly.

"I figured. Are you going to tell me how you got here? Or more importantly, *why?*"

"You want that now? Because the details don't matter just this second." Anna's eyes went to the top of his head, finally realizing she didn't recognize the crown he wore. "Where'd you get that?"

David touched his temple. "I've just been crowned High King of Ireland."

Anna laughed. "Of course you have."

"It was to avoid outright civil war. We fought in a terrible battle yesterday."

Anna sobered immediately. "I'm sorry. Are Mom and Papa okay?"

"Yes. They're coming."

Anna bit her lip. "Were Scots involved?"

"Yes." He stared at her, not at all happy with her dead-on guess.

She nodded. "We do have a lot to talk about."

They left the plane where Andre had parked it, for lack of a better place to put it. Although its arrival came a little too close to making David look like a god, the end result was as spectacular a crowning as was possible to imagine, including if the Stone of Destiny had, in fact, roared.

Once Mom and Papa showed up, and everyone had been hugged sufficiently, or in Christopher's case, enough for now, they headed back to the Hill of Tara. Even though David had his hands full with the Irish, on the ride back to his pavilion he demanded to hear about Scotland.

Riding pillion behind him, Anna obliged, concluding, "I'm just sorry I couldn't bring you an immediate solution to all this."

David laughed, at first under his breath, and then more fully such that Anna could feel his stomach clenching, since her arms were cinched around his waist.

"What's so funny?" She had expected a cloud of disapproval, not laughter.

"And people say I take too much on myself." He put his hand over hers. "Just the fact that you're here is a miracle. You went to the right place at the right time. You made hard decisions. You talked Mark into coming home. And you, apparently, haven't seen the cargo hold."

"Sophie mentioned that Chad had filled it."

"I had a quick look around in between being hugged. Sophie wasn't kidding." David paused. "I don't know if I could have done what you did. For starters, I have a feeling I would have handled the cop all wrong and either gotten shot or ended up in jail."

"So you don't hate that I agreed to work with Chad?"

David lifted his chin, his eyes, as hers were, on the Hill of Tara ahead. "I do hate it, but that doesn't mean it wasn't the right decision—and certainly it was your decision to make. What I hate most is that you were put in a situation where a decision had to be made."

"You say that I did enough, but even so, I'm hoping for more."

"What are you thinking?" Despite the fact that he had thirty barons waiting for him in his pavilion, she could hear real interest in his voice.

"Chad wasn't wrong to think that it's time we did things differently. What we need more than anything when we go to Avalon is a position to bargain from."

David nodded. "An alliance with Chad might give us one." Then he paused. "The very fact that I'm alive is due to the efforts of an army of people who have been loyal to me even though they didn't have to be. I intend to thank every one of them in due course, and to honor them, but I want you to know that above all, I'm grateful to you for everything you've been to me and done for me. I don't think I've ever said it, but even before you showed up with an airplane, I couldn't have managed half of what I've been able to do if you hadn't been beside me."

Anna swallowed down the rush of tears that threatened to spill down her cheeks again. "Thank you." She patted him on the shoulder. "We'll talk later. Right now, you're High King of Ireland." She found herself laughing just to say the words. "It's utterly typical of you to come to Ireland to divest yourself of your authority—and end up with even more than you started with."

"I'm instituting a more equitable Parliament."

"Yeah." Anna half-scoffed and half-laughed. "Hope springs eternal."

Just because Anna found humor in David's new status didn't mean that Ireland's needs were any less pressing, however. On one hand, the people of Ireland knew already the King of Scots was up to no good, since he'd sent Red Comyn to fight against them. On the other hand, nobody had thought David would need to leave Ireland quite so soon. He had huge qualms about departing immediately for Wales, but he didn't believe he had a choice in the matter either, not now that he knew of rebellion not only in Scotland but England too.

So he spent a long day with his new constituents, while the twenty-firsters attempted to come to grips with their new reality. Only Papa and Callum stayed beside him as his closest advisers. Mom would have, but she had to catch up with her sister and hug Anna approximately ninety-seven times.

Once the sun set, the barons departed to their tents, exhausted. All and sundry would need to get an early start in the morning, most to scatter throughout Ireland to spread the news of the victory and David's crowning, take stock of the families and lands they were left, and begin to discover what a united Ireland really meant. David had sworn to return within three months, by the summer solstice, a promise he intended to keep.

"We'll take the plane, of course," Anna said, her words cutting across the general chatter of the late evening meal in David's private pavilion.

That got everyone's attention. Only twenty-firsters were among them. Sophie, George, and Andre were family now whether they were ready for it or not. For all that Chad Treadman was both a nut and a genius, which could either be a good combination or turn out to make him as dangerous an ally as MI-5 had been, he'd certainly chosen his staff well. If they were willing, they could transform Earth Two, a name even David was starting to call it.

For Anna, the better word for this world was *home*.

"How much fuel is left in the plane?" David said.

"It has a five thousand mile range. We came a few hundred, and that's including if we expended fuel getting from Wales to Ireland." Andre paused, his expression troubled.

"You probably didn't," Callum said, an old hand when it came to time travel.

"Anyway," Sophie said, "the gauge still reads essentially full."

"So we could use it," David said. "It's hugely tempting, for more than just this one trip."

"Take-off and landing use the most fuel and are the hardest on the plane," Andre said. "Longer flights are better than shorter ones."

As Andre had spoken, Mom's eyes had gone to him. "So you're a pilot in addition to a security expert. What else?"

"My degree was in agriculture." Andre gestured to Sophie. "Hers is mechanical engineering, like Mr. Treadman—and of course she can fly the plane too."

"Oh thank goodness. We surely need you," Mom said. "I've regretted sending all those twenty-firsters back almost from the moment we did it."

"I have a Ph.D. in electrical engineering." George had both elbows on the table and was behaving as if he'd had a bit more wine than he was used to, or maybe the wine here was more potent than what they were currently drinking in Avalon. Regardless, the words came out in a drawl he hadn't exhibited before. "That's how I started, tinkering in my dad's garage."

"Again, we surely can use you," Anna said.

"I know I'm not useful, but I'm staying anyway." Elen folded her arms across her chest.

"I don't know about that," David said. "I haven't yet given you permission."

Anna laughed. David had spoken pompously, like the worst caricature of an overbearing school principal, a play on the conversation they'd had at Rachel's father's house fifteen months earlier.

He grinned at her, but nobody else laughed, and most looked back at him with expressions of genuine concern.

His face fell, and Anna reached for his arm, as disconcerted as he was. She'd had a front row seat to the way his power had grown over the years, but it was a sad day when even his family didn't know when he was joking.

So now she looked around the table, standing up for him like she'd been doing from the beginning, whether she'd realized it or not. "You're all looking at David as if he was about to behead Elen. You know that was a joke, right?"

There was uneasy laughter around the table, and Uncle Ted said, "Oh yeah, right."

Anna smiled gently. "He's still David."

"It's just—" Elisa shook her head. "Things have been a little intense lately."

Anna found herself easing back in her chair. Elisa wasn't wrong, and not only about what was going on tonight at the table. "I am sorry you—all of you—were caught up in this again. I never intended for anyone to come here unless by choice."

Mark wet his lips, but when he spoke, his expression was lighter than earlier in the plane. "It isn't all bad. If I were back home, I'd be in a cell in the bowels of Five."

Anna wasn't sure that made her feel any better. "Mark—"

He put out a hand before she could say more. "Hey—there are worse things—a lot worse things, than being here among friends. How many people have a chance to make a difference to an entire world the way I have? Just ... do your thing. All of you. I'm along for the ride to wherever the ride takes me." He gestured to the newcomers, all three of whom were nodding. "Maybe we can get started on some serious R & D."

"The research lab in Llangollen is always open to you." Anna said.

Then she looked at David, who'd eased back in his seat too, to see how he was taking the conversation. The sadness had left his eyes, and then suddenly they brightened further. "That reminds me of a real bone I have to pick with *you*." He stabbed his finger in Christopher's direction. "Traitor."

Christopher put a hand to his chest. "Me? What did I do?"

"Other than save Ireland, apparently," Anna said *sotto voce* to her brother.

David glanced at his sister, his lips quirking, and then turned back to his cousin. "While your mom was hugging you—" he grinned at Elisa, who for the first time in her life grinned back at him, "—I glanced through the plane's entertainment options. How could you not have told me they'd made more Star Wars movies?"

32

20 March 1294

Humphrey de Bohun

Yesterday evening had turned to hell far more quickly than Humphrey would have thought possible. He hadn't known FitzWalter and Mortimer had sent a band to capture Anna or he would have found a way to warn her and Math, but once FitzWalter's company had returned without her, he'd cornered the two barons. "What were you thinking?"

Roger snorted. "The attempt to take Princess Anna, even if unsuccessful, will distract Lord Mathonwy from our true purpose. Nothing has changed."

"If we had succeeded, we would have gained powerful leverage against the Welsh. Lord Mathonwy wouldn't dare interfere with the succession if we held his wife," FitzWalter said. "It was worth the attempt."

Humphrey snorted. "Offa's Dyke is no barrier anymore, you do realize? Beeston Castle is a paltry quest in comparison to what he would have been willing to sacrifice to avenge the loss of his wife. Math would have hunted your men to the ends of the earth if he had to. But all he has to do is come here!"

Pride was the downfall of so many lords. William de Valence had been stuffed full of it—that and his own importance— and he'd ended up dead. The same could be said (and had been) of Gilbert de Clare, whom Humphrey had hated most of his life anyway, since he'd betrayed Humphrey's father by running back to Edward rather than standing like a man at Evesham.

Humphrey had learned to swallow his pride when it came to King David, and he'd been rewarded for his practicality a hundred-fold. In fact, he would have said his pride was far more warranted now than it had ever been.

His loyalty to David would have driven him out of Beeston Castle within an hour of his arrival yesterday morning, but every moment he stayed had garnered him more information to take to the king—or to Math in his stead. With David's blessing, Humphrey had spent the past six months wooing Roger Mortimer, and it would have been foolish to squander all that work too soon. But now he could no longer put off his departure. England needed him like it never had before. David needed him.

Humphrey's pride reared its head and preened.

He resolutely squashed it down. First, he had to accomplish what would gain him those accolades. He hadn't bothered to see William Venables, who was in an impossible position. If he was loyal to his father and Mortimer, he shouldn't be imprisoned, but if he was loyal to David, Humphrey would be unable to convince William of his own loyalty. Better to leave him where he was. Regardless of Balliol's plans, Mortimer intended to take the throne. He wasn't going to win over the rest of England if he started killing minor barons.

As Humphrey headed across the inner ward, more men were about than might be warranted at this early hour of the morning. He merely noted it and with purposeful stride crossed the bridge to the outer ward. He'd been told once by his father, may he rest in peace, that if a man wanted people to believe he knew what he was doing and was where he was supposed to be, first and foremost he needed to act like it.

Humphrey had spent his life acting like it. Every lord did. But as he'd realized with the demise of Valence and Clare, the danger was in believing, even for a heartbeat, in one's own legend. Humphrey himself, on behalf of his son, had reached for the throne before David had been crowned king. David had even supported William's marriage to Joan. And yet, there had been something inevitable about the way Humphrey's plans had fallen apart, and when David had been crowned king instead of William, even Humphrey had been blinded by his light.

How Mortimer, FitzWalter, and Warenne couldn't see it, Humphrey didn't know. Maybe they were so blinded by their own greatness they couldn't see anyone else's. But they were fools to think their Irish plan had worked. Humphrey wasn't going to believe David was dead until he saw the body. And even then ...

Humphrey was a long way from being ready to concede to Roger Mortimer an ounce of power he didn't deserve.

Instead of heading to where his people had camped, over a hundred of them, Humphrey detoured to the stable. Henry Percy had promised to meet him at dawn, which was now. If anything, Humphrey was late.

He'd taken only one step through stable doorway, however, when he found himself swung around by the lapels and pressed up against the interior wall.

"Damn it, Henry. It's me." Humphrey was not a tall man, but he was burly, and yet he had no counter to the forearm pressed against his throat.

Henry released him and took a step back. "You're late. I thought you'd betrayed me or been captured."

Humphrey straightened his tunic with a jerk, pleased Henry's drunkenness of the night before had been an act. "Why would Roger throw me in prison? He thinks he has his traitor in Venny." He narrowed his eyes at the Warenne heir. "What were you thinking, giving him away like that?"

"My grandfather sent a rider with word that Lord Mathonwy had tracked FitzWalter's men here. It was either share the news or flee."

"Why did your grandfather imprison Math and Ieuan?"

It was bad enough that Mortimer had gone after Anna, thinking to use her as leverage against Math and hoping, with David dead, that none of the Welsh lords would seek to involve themselves in England. Roger was right that Anna's captivity would have ensured Math's compliance. Mortimer's plan, in fact, was carefully calibrated to make acceptance of his rule the path of least resistance. In the aftermath of David's death, he wanted to isolate the Welsh, not incite them to violence—which the capture of Math and Ieuan might well do.

"I don't know!" Henry's voice was almost a wail.

Humphrey quickly shushed him, and then, belatedly, while he waited for Henry to calm himself, walked down the aisle between the horse stalls, looking for stable boys or spies.

"I already did that," Henry said from behind him. "There's nothing to worry about."

Humphrey looked anyway, and found Henry was right. Humphrey hadn't expected trouble. The drink had flowed freely last night, as if victory was already theirs. If Humphrey hadn't known already that FitzWalter didn't deserve his niece, he did now. He was surprised, in a way, that Roger had allied with FitzWalter so fully—but Roger was ever one to use the tools at hand. FitzWalter was a connection to Balliol, and if nothing else, Balliol was committed to overthrowing King David.

Balliol was also spineless and deluded, but that had only made Roger all the more happy to ally with him.

Humphrey returned to stand in front of Henry, who began to pace back and forth. "We're taking a terrible chance."

Humphrey narrowed his eyes. "You're having second thoughts?"

Henry looked up. "Not about betraying Mortimer, but my grandfather—"

"—has lost his reason on this issue. He may appear as sharp as ever to outsiders, but you know how false that impression is. He sees traitors around every corner and refuses to admit what is plain before his face if it doesn't suit him." Humphrey studied the boy, realizing only now how young Henry was. "Your grandfather told Mortimer that he could have his support if you married Elizabeth. Mortimer agreed." Humphrey tipped his head. "He lied, of course."

Henry was aghast. "My grandfather spoke about putting me on the throne, but I thought he was dreaming out loud."

"I tried to tell him not to trust Roger, but he wouldn't listen. He thinks he has the upper hand, when he does not."

"That's half the reason why I went along with Roger in the first place, to protect my grandfather."

"Your grandfather was easy pickings for a man like Roger Mortimer. King David will understand that when I tell him of it."

"You don't know that." Henry appeared very close to tears.

Humphrey found himself irritated at the need to reattach Henry's spine. "I know the king; I know your grandfather; and I know you." He bobbed his chin at Henry. "You can do this."

"What are we going to do about Roger?"

"We are going to bring him down, after I rescue Math and Ieuan."

"I hadn't thought whatever Mortimer was planning would come to a head this soon."

Humphrey tsked through his teeth. His son, William, was younger than Henry, but far more competent, as a Bohun should be. Again, the pride flared, but this time he didn't suppress it. William had become a man any father would be proud to call his heir, unlike Henry, who was proving to be disconcertingly fearful. Thus, Humphrey decided he could share his own uncertainties if it would help Henry manage his. "Neither did I. In truth, Mortimer cornered me, and it was either pledge support or go the way of Venny." Then his chin hardened. "Roger forgets that after Evesham, my own father was taken to this very castle and died of his wounds here, a prisoner. *Roger's* father was among those who sealed his fate."

Henry clearly hadn't known that history either, because his face paled. "If that's true, why isn't Mortimer worried about betrayal from you?"

"King David is dead, hadn't you heard?" Humphrey didn't bother to keep the scorn from his voice. "What else do I need to know?"

Henry laid out the entirety of the situation beyond the walls as he'd heard it from his grandfather's messenger. Oddly, instead of raising his anxiety, the direness of the situation calmed Humphrey and gave him focus. He went to the doorway of the stable to look out at the growing light. "Given the stakes, I can't wait another hour. I'm leaving with my men now. *You* must stay here and keep an eye on Mortimer and FitzWalter. They are awaiting word from Ireland before moving. I need to know the instant any word comes."

"Where are you going to be?"

"At your grandfather's castle, of course."

Henry's face was white. "Will Mortimer let you leave?"

Bohun looked down his long nose at the boy. "I am Constable of England and Earl of Hereford. Roger cannot take the throne without my approval. I dare him to stop me."

33

20 March 1294

Constance

Constance rested her head against the wall at the back of the stall in which she'd been hiding half the night. When Mortimer had ordered Venny arrested, she'd been probing the defenses, as Venny had asked, and she'd hidden herself in time to see her husband and the others taken away. Either Mortimer had forgotten that Venny had brought a woman with him, or he'd dismissed her as unimportant and not worth looking for. Either way, she'd remained free.

She'd seen Henry Percy come into the stables, and he'd paced around for quite some time before Humphrey de Bohun had arrived. Henry had been less observant than Bohun, who'd seen her and ignored her. That had been the first inkling that maybe he was not the traitor he'd appeared to be in the hall.

And with the conclusion of the men's conversation, she was breathing easier than she had in hours, and she poked her head above the wall of the stall in time to see Henry Percy leave.

Lord Bohun walked back down the aisle to where she was hiding and opened the stall door. "You heard all that, I presume."

She bobbed a curtsey. "Yes, my lord." When Bohun had first seen her, she'd feared reprisals, but he'd merely given her a long look and walked away. In retrospect, he couldn't have known for certain where her loyalties lay, but he'd taken a risk—they both had—and now she met his gaze with more determination than fear.

"I didn't want to scare poor Henry by revealing your presence. You're Constance?"

"Yes, my lord."

He grunted. "I saw you shoot at Windsor. You serve Queen Lili."

"Yes, my lord." She couldn't seem to say anything else, and all his questions were really answers anyway.

"I'm taking you out of here with me."

She wasn't one to defy the Constable of England, but she shook her head. "I need to stay. They have my husband."

"Your husband would want you free, and I need you to speak to whoever is waiting outside Beeston for you to return. You are my safe passage to him."

Constance's mouth fell open in surprise. "You know about that?"

"I know Lord Mathonwy. He wouldn't have sent only the five of you here, not without anyone to back you up." He paused. "It was a risky move."

"We volunteered."

Bohun scoffed. "Don't we all." He tipped his head to indicate outside the door, where the sun had risen high enough to light the interior. "Where are your horses?"

"This one here is Venny's. I hid with him after the soldiers came for Cador and the others."

"I'll have you know they're still alive. They're in a room in the barracks, unfortunately far from Venny, who is in the keep with his father."

Constance pressed her face into the horse's neck, her relief so great she was embarrassed to have it show on her face. "Is that your doing?"

"Mortimer has no interest in killing English soldiers. Henry will look after them."

Constance looked up, a dubious expression on her face. "Are you sure you can trust him?"

"He's young, but he'll do the right thing in the end," Bohun said bracingly. "Get your things and come with me."

"How can you be sure King David's alive?" The question came out before Constance could stop it.

Bohun had taken a step towards the stable door, but now he stopped and turned back. "I have to believe it. My son is with him."

As Bohun had asked, Constance connected him with Sir Cadwallon, who remained with his ten men in the barn near

Beeston. That was an awkward reunion if there ever was one, since Bohun had been responsible for almost killing Cadwallon ten years earlier. But Cadwallon was more gracious than Bohun deserved, and as much as Cadwallon wanted to either storm Beeston or come with Bohun to Lyons, he agreed that he should continue to keep watch where he was. In particular, Bohun needed to know if Henry Percy sent a messenger to his uncle instead of to Bohun as he'd promised.

Whether because Constance had brought it up or out of his innate skepticism, Bohun was hedging his bets and seemed to think that Henry Percy's loyalty remained an open question.

Now, Bohun leaned forward on his arms, which he'd crossed and rested on the pommel of his saddle, his eyes on the battlements of Lyons Castle. It was late morning by now, and the sun had chosen that moment to come out from behind the cloud cover and shine down on them.

Instinctively, Constance's hand went to her bow rest near her saddle bags, but Bohun put out a hand to her. "No. Remember why we're here? Warenne doesn't know I still serve King David. We need him to trust me."

"You think to go in there?"

Bohun let out a puff of air. "I think I have to."

"Out of the frying pan and into the fire, that would be, my lord," Constance said, speaking with more familiarity than was perhaps wise with a Norman lord—albeit under her breath.

Bohun released a laugh. "You have the right of it."

Then Bohun's captain, a tall man with jet-black hair and black eyes, indicating foreign blood, pointed south of the castle, along the road that followed the Dee. "I see movement, my lord!"

Bohun frowned and peered ahead. "Who is it?"

Before leaving Beeston, Constance had taken Venny's binoculars from his saddle bag, and now she put them to her eyes. "My lord, those are Mortimer colors."

Bohun's head whipped around to look at her, his hand reaching for the binoculars to see for himself. "Roger?"

"No, my lord." Her heart beat a little faster. "Edmund."

"Excellent." Even as he took the binoculars from Constance, Bohun waved a hand to one of his men. "Ride to intercept him."

"What will you do, my lord?" Constance asked.

Bohun had the glasses to his eyes, and he turned them from Mortimer's company towards the castle itself. "Now that we have more men, I will ride to the front gate, as I told Henry I would."

"Isn't that exactly what Lord Mathonwy and Lord Ieuan did?" the captain said. "Warenne tricked them. Trapped them."

"What if the castle were instead to become a trap for Warenne?" Again, Constance spoke with some trepidation, even though Bohun hadn't objected to her outspokenness so far.

All of the men nearby looked at her with interest, and Bohun asked, "How so?"

"Tell him you won't enter the castle until he proves to you he hasn't switched sides and now serves the king. Tell him you have reason to suspect that his grandson is a traitor to Balliol, and you want to know if he is too."

Bohun's captain gaped at her, but Bohun himself laughed a deep belly laugh. "I like the way you think."

Another man, this one Saxon like her, said, "I don't understand, my lord. What is she suggesting?"

Constance turned to him. "By accusing Warenne of betraying the cause, Lord Bohun deflects any suspicion that he might have done the same." She looked at Bohun. "You could even say you've convinced Lord Edmund to join you, since Roger is his brother and King David is surely dead by now. Roger Mortimer isn't here to gainsay you, and Warenne has no means to discover the truth without sending a message that goes through you first, since you have brought an army to his doorstep."

"How does any of this help Lords Mathonwy and Ieuan?" the captain said. Constance didn't know if his questions reflected genuine confusion or if he simply didn't like hearing good ideas from a woman.

It was Bohun who answered. "Warenne will be forced to produce them one way or the other. Either they are unharmed, indicating he has sided with the king, or they have been imprisoned. If the latter, then he proves his loyalty to me and disloyalty to the king. If the former, then they go free."

"Either way, we will know if they're alive and in what condition," Constance said, glad Lord Bohun, at least, understood her plan.

Lord Bohun's company reached the River Dee and met Edmund and his men at the crossroads just past the ford south of the castle. Lyons was on the Welsh side of the river, which was what had necessitated Warenne's decision to bow to King Llywelyn in the first place.

As Bohun related all that had transpired, Edmund's expression changed from one of suspicion to relief. "I am appalled by the plot, but more glad than I can say to hear this from you, my friend. I was worried. Why didn't you tell me what you were doing?"

"I begged the king to keep my secret. Nobody could know my true intentions. Nobody. Besides, neither of us knew if it would ever come to anything."

"But your wife? Your son?"

"Why do you think I sent William to Ireland? I could not bear for him to think I was a traitor."

Edmund put a hand on Bohun's shoulder. "I knew my brother was up to something. After all these years, why does he choose this moment to revolt? King David has never been stronger or more beloved."

"King David chose to go to Ireland. Regardless of how necessary that decision was, it left the field open for men with treacherous minds," Bohun said. "Besides, the Scots are involved."

Edmund spat on the ground. "Balliol." Then he lifted his chin to single out Constance. "And what's this I hear about William Venables? His father betrays the king, and yet he does not?"

Constance drew in a breath. She'd spent the last few hours specifically avoiding thoughts of Venny's father. He was involved in a plot not only to overthrow the king, but to assassinate him. And believed his co-conspirators had already done so. It was heartbreaking. "I know Venny well. He is not his father."

"And we can be grateful for it." Edmund looked down his nose at Constance, but not in an arrogant way—more as a man who understood, and she supposed that Edmund, the second son destined for the church before his elder brother died, would know all about what it was like to try to fill too-big shoes. In Edmund's case in particular, King Edward had favored Roger, the third and youngest brother, and confirmed him in his holdings before he'd grudgingly done the same for Edmund.

Bohun gazed around at the men who surrounded him. "None of you are making a mistake in holding to the king."

"What if King David really is dead?" This came from one of Edmund's men, echoing Constance and who-knew-how-many-others in the last hours since they'd learned of Roger Mortimer's plans. The moment he spoke he looked as if he wanted to take back the words.

"If he is gone, we defend the true king, Arthur, David's son, with our lives," Bohun said. "But until someone other than Roger

Mortimer tells me David is dead, I will count him among the living."

Edmund gave a sharp nod of his head. "As will I." Then he grinned, though it made his expression look more villainous than happy. "Now let's see what Warenne has to say for himself, shall we?"

At the head of their greatly expanded host, Bohun and Edmund rode towards the castle gates. Lyons Castle was built so the main entrance was on the north side and included a drawbridge across a moat fed by water diverted from the Dee, forcing the road to circle even farther to the west before curving to meet the castle road. This close to the Dee, which flowed north towards Chester at this location, the land was relatively flat, and the men were able to spread out, not in a threatening way, but so they weren't jostling each other.

Once they approached the drawbridge, Bohun urged his horse ahead of Edmund's. He didn't set foot on the bridge, however. He couldn't. Its end was raised two feet above the ground. Warenne had seen their company coming and wasn't in a mood to be hospitable—but he wasn't such a fool as to close the gates entirely, especially since Humphrey de Bohun was known to be on his side.

As he'd done in the road on the other side of the Dee, Bohun rested his forearms on the pommel of his saddle and leaned into them. He spoke without shouting to the three men who stood on the other side of the bridge. "You know who I am." It wasn't a question.

"Yes, my lord Bohun." As a sign of respect, their apparent leader took off his helmet to reveal his face. With brown hair and beard shot with gray, he looked to be the oldest of the three men.

"But I see I am less than welcome."

"That isn't the case, my lord." The man shook his head. "These are dangerous times."

"So it seems. Is Earl Warenne within? I would speak to him."

"He is and asks you to choose five men to accompany you inside but leave the rest without."

Bohun studied the guard. "I would first like to speak to John. Will you ask him to come out himself?"

The man hesitated, clearly discomfited at keeping such a great lord waiting, but Bohun's request was outside what he'd been instructed to answer without further consultation. He bowed. "I will ask."

It took some time, perhaps a quarter of an hour, which felt to Constance like a long time to wait when Warenne should have been aware of them and prepared to greet them. It made her think Bohun might be right that Warenne's mind had faded. The wait did give Edmund time to move among the men, whispering the rest of the plan if things didn't go their way. Warenne had no archers on the wall, but Bohun had many at his back, not just Constance.

Eventually Warenne came, and when he appeared, he was dressed formally in full armor and a thick maroon cloak, which looked too heavy for the relatively warm spring day. "Humphrey."

"John."

Then Warenne looked beyond Bohun to Edmund, and his eyes widened.

Bohun grinned. "I have brought another into the fold, John, but we are concerned about our reception here. We hear you have Lords Ieuan and Mathonwy hidden within. Could it be you have betrayed our cause and now side with the king?"

Warenne's control was good, as one might expect from such a powerful baron, but Bohun's opening parley was not what he expected. It set him back on his heels, and he took a moment to answer.

"The king is dead, Humphrey, I assure you. He is no longer a man one can side with."

"Then you have turned Lords Ieuan and Mathonwy to our cause?"

Warenne's expression soured. For some reason, he'd dismissed the guards who'd greeted them initially, though soldiers crowded the wall-walk above him and could hear every word. There was something masterful and brave about him standing all alone beneath the gatehouse. "They have been recalcitrant."

"I would speak to them. Perhaps I might convince them of their folly. They have been my friends."

Warenne was offended. "You don't trust me?"

"Trust is a rare commodity, in royal politics more than most." Bohun gestured impatiently. "Produce them and show your loyalty."

"How dare you question me!"

"It is not I but Roger Mortimer who doubts. Your grandson has not comported himself well."

That gave Warenne pause. "What do you mean?"

"Roger suspects he still serves the king, at your command. Even now Henry sits in prison in one of Beeston's towers."

Warenne's nostrils flared. He hadn't expected that either, and he knew now that he was cornered. After a moment, he gave a sharp nod of his head. "Wait here."

34

20 March 1294

Ieuan

Whenen Warenne had spoken to Ieuan and Math sometime in the night, he'd pontificated at them, sounding less and less reasonable with every sentence, before being called away. Once they were left alone, perhaps a result of the continuing effects of the poppy juice, Ieuan had slept until morning, at which point he found Math kicking him in the leg again.

"Someone will come soon," Math said.

"My head hurts."

"Warenne really believes he can be king."

Ieuan didn't want to think about it, but it seemed he had no choice. "How many men are going to die for that to be possible, especially if Roger Mortimer and Humphrey de Bohun are part of this?" A hint of Ieuan's old animosity for Bohun stirred in his chest. He had thought he'd have to bury it forever. He'd been wrong.

"What do you think the messenger asked Warenne? He looked very concerned when he left."

"I'd be pleased if I wasn't so worried about our position." Ieuan had been in his fair share of tight spaces before, some of them with Dafydd and some of his own making. In the past, he'd always escaped, but Lyons Castle didn't have a Thomas Hartley in residence to burn down the stables for them like at Carlisle Castle all those years ago.

Ieuan took a tighter hold on the ropes that were supposed to be binding his wrists, though his hands were, in effect, free. "A chance will come to escape. We have to be patient." They'd been speaking Welsh, so the guard in the next room couldn't understand them.

Math turned to show Ieuan his wiggling fingers. "Leaving us in hoods and bindings was petty. It isn't as if we can get through those iron bars." Then his expression turned thoughtful. "Perhaps they fear us."

"They fear our association with Dafydd. Their masters tell them he is dead, but we are not behaving as if he is, are we?"

"No, we are not. And we will not." As Math finished speaking, the door to the outer guard room opened. Ieuan was incredibly thirsty, but it didn't appear they were going to be fed and watered just yet.

The man who entered was one of the garrison's leaders, and he strode to the cell. His expression was so intent, at first Ieuan feared for their lives, but then the soldier unlocked the door.

Three guards remained at his back, so when he pulled out his knife and cut the cords that bound their feet, neither Math nor Ieuan attempted to take the weapon from him.

"Get up!"

Two nameless soldiers, faceless too since they wore helmets, grabbed Ieuan's upper arms and forced him to his feet. It was a relief to be able to walk, and with each step as he moved from the cell, he flexed his ankles, trying to get the blood moving in his feet. Unbound was a huge improvement, but it wasn't yet running.

The guards took them outside, and again Ieuan feared they were headed for the block or the hangman's noose, but the reality was much better. Passing under the three raised portcullises, they arrived at the entrance to the gatehouse, with freedom so close Ieuan could smell it.

He and Math hadn't exchanged a word since they'd left the cell, and they didn't now, even in Welsh, though the sight of Humphrey de Bohun, Edmund Mortimer, and Constance staring across the slightly raised drawbridge at them had his heart lifting.

That is, until Bohun sneered in that way of his and said, "I commend you, Warenne. It seems you do speak the truth."

Back at Dinas Bran, they'd speculated on Bohun's allegiance but to have these three whom they'd thought loyal smiling at Warenne had the pit of despair Ieuan had refused to acknowledge gaping wider, and he tasted bile at the back of his throat. If he couldn't trust Bohun or Edmund anymore, despite all

Dafydd had done for them—and they'd done for him—over the years, then the contagion that had infected Gilbert de Clare was endemic. Dafydd would have to fill his court with only Welshmen, and even the loyalties of Nicholas de Carew would be suspect.

Mortimer added, "Drop the drawbridge, if you will, Warenne. I haven't breakfasted, and I'm hungry."

Each of the castle's defenses worked on a system of weights and pulleys. To lower the drawbridge required winching it down. All that was necessary to raise the drawbridge was to allow the giant counterweight to run free. It was the opposite for the portcullises, which had been raised when they'd come through. Truthfully, Warenne should have dropped the outermost portcullis to pen Ieuan and Math inside the castle. That he hadn't done so was probably because he himself remained one foot off the drawbridge, and he, or his men, hadn't wanted to risk having him caught outside the safety of the castle, stuck between the last portcullis and the bridge.

With a wave of his hand, Warenne gave the order, and the drawbridge was lowered down onto the wooden supports on the other side. "You and Edmund may come in with your guard. Leave the rest outside. We're a bit cramped, as you will see."

And then all hell broke loose.

But (as Bronwen would say) in a good way.

The forward ranks of Bohun's cavalry parted, revealing twenty archers, and a heartbeat later, twenty arrows were shot from bows that until now had been lowered and hidden. Bohun and Mortimer had been among those to wheel their horses to get themselves out of the way of the archers, but others of the cavalry stayed behind in support, dismounting to protect the archers, who were otherwise undefended. In an old Saxon move, one that predated the use of cavalry, they formed a shield wall in front of the archers.

All this Ieuan took in with an encompassing glance, and he inwardly cheered as an arrow from Constance's own bow pierced the neck of the soldier next to him, who'd been stunned into inaction by the sudden movement of Bohun's men. Someone else shot the guard next to Math, who immediately took off at a run across the drawbridge. Another soldier had covered Warenne, saving his life, since the soldier fell to the ground with an arrow sticking out of his back, Warenne beneath him.

Fully aware of the crossbowmen hiding in the gatehouse towers and shooting through the arrow slits, Ieuan opted to split their attention so he and Math weren't in the same line of fire. Dropping the rope he'd kept around his hands, he dived into the moat. Thankfully, it wasn't as filthy as some, since when the sluice gates were open, as they were today, cleaning the daily waste the castle residents dumped into it, the River Dee flowed continually around the castle. The water was unpleasant, but not putrid, and as he came up, he wasn't puking.

But a crashing sound from the front of the castle had him swinging around and treading water. The drawbridge had been raised. From down in the water, Ieuan couldn't see if Math had reached the far side or had been thrown backwards towards the castle's entrance at the suddenness of its return to a closed position.

Math wasn't in the water, so Ieuan forced himself to focus on his own swimming. The moat was only fifty feet wide, but it had been many years since Ieuan had done anything more strenuous than paddle about in a pond with Catrin in his arms. Still, he stroked vigorously towards the far bank.

Though Lyons was a grand castle, it didn't have an outer curtain wall, making the moat its last defense. Moats were designed to prevent an enemy from getting close to the walls, either with grappling hooks or a siege engine. They weren't intended to prevent a lone man who'd escaped the dungeon from swimming to freedom.

And then Edmund himself was there in the reeds that had grown on the edge of the moat, reaching down with a hand to pull Ieuan from the water. Ieuan had aimed his jump to take him away from the gatehouse towards the main course of the Dee in hopes of using the current to sweep him away from the castle—and take the bolts of the crossbowmen away from Math.

His gambit had worked a little too well, in fact, since as he came out of the water, a bolt hit the reeds right where he'd been a heartbeat earlier. Ieuan surged up the bank, gasping from the effort, but more determined than ever to escape. Fortunately, the disadvantage of a crossbow—they had to be wound and reset for firing—gave him the breathing room he needed. In the time it took

Constance to fire ten arrows, the crossbowman managed two at most.

Ieuan's boots were full of water, so he was lucky they hadn't dragged him down. They would have if he'd had to swim much farther. As it was, he ran despite them, sloshing away from the castle towards the bulk of Bohun's army some three hundred yards away, having moved out of bowshot of the walls. He glanced behind him to see the archers, Constance among them, retreating with their shield wall, one step at a time. After they reached a point a hundred yards from the moat, no more bolts came. Edmund realized it too and barked an order.

Like Ieuan, the archers turned and ran.

A small group kept to a hobble, however. As they came closer, Ieuan saw Math at its center, his arms around the shoulders of two of Bohun's men, hopping on one foot and cursing with every step.

Ieuan crouched low to the ground to make himself a less obvious target, in case a crossbowman tried another shot, and waited for the group to reach him. Then he replaced one of the soldiers beside his friend. "What happened to you?"

Math cursed again. "You were smart to dive into the water."

"You almost made it cleanly, my lord," one of Bohun's soldiers said.

Math snorted. "I was just at the end of the drawbridge when they dropped the weight. It sprang upwards and tipped me end over end. It would have been beautiful if I hadn't landed on my ankle wrong."

They reached the edge of the woods where Bohun stood with Edmund. He greeted Ieuan with a bear hug, which without a doubt was the most exuberant greeting he'd ever received from the Norman lord—or any Norman lord. "Praise be to God you're safe."

"Your timing is impeccable, Humphrey," Math said.

"I regret to say we must withdraw, however." Bohun proceeded to relate all that had transpired to reach this point. "We are at war."

"Warenne delighted in how our loss was his triumph," Ieuan said.

The men helped Math to an overturned log, and he removed his boot to massage his ankle. "I wondered why you didn't take Warenne up on his offer to enter the castle, but you made the right decision, Humphrey. Warenne cannot be talked from his treason, and you risked being captured as Ieuan and I were. We don't have time for a siege, and this war won't be won at Lyons Castle."

"Nor Beeston," Ieuan said, "as much as it pains me to leave friends in captivity."

"If we besiege Beeston, my brother would hang Venny from the battlements before he surrenders—out of spite," Edmund said.

"David wouldn't thank us for that." Bohun grimaced at the sight of Math's swollen ankle, already purpling. "We won't take it without far more men and resources than we have at our disposal today, and we could lose the war if we besiege it and don't take it."

Edmund looked at Ieuan. "Can we get word to David that he is needed?"

"If Warenne was telling us the truth about the maneuvers in Ireland, I imagine he knows by now," Ieuan said dryly. He gestured to Math's ankle. "Can you ride?"

"I'll have to, won't I?" He reached for his boot to pull it on again. "We have a war to plan."

35

21 March 1294

Gwenllian

Gwenllian sat at breakfast with Arthur on her lap. Since their adventure in Avalon, they'd become inseparable. Their bond was making her reconsider her decision to go to university—not because she didn't want to learn, but because it meant she'd spend months and years away from him.

They'd all spent a fairly terrible night, again without Anna, of course, though Ieuan, Math, and the Norman lords had hobbled in by yesterday evening with the grim news of the day. It was disheartening to find English barons once again chafing at Dafydd's leadership. Gwenllian herself was half-English, the great-granddaughter of King John of England, though usually nobody talked about it. She also would never have trusted Warenne, since he'd allied with, and then betrayed, her grandfather, Simon de Montfort, leading to his death.

When Lili had shared Dafydd's message that he was alive—as of three days ago--

Math had cheered briefly, before turning to the other lords with that grim expression men wore when they feared the worst. Having been to Avalon and seen what was possible, it was aggravating to Gwenllian how poor communication remained. They could talk to London, which in itself was a miracle, but not Ireland. Not yet.

"I miss Mama." Elisa had been sitting by Lili, but she and Padrig, who did everything together, moved their dishes to sit next to Gwenllian.

"I know. I do too."

The children had overheard the adult conversation, though nobody was saying outright that if Dafydd hadn't survived whatever onslaught the conspirators had prepared for him, then it was highly possible, as Roger Mortimer insisted, that everyone else—Gwenllian's mother and father, Christopher, Callum, Darren and Rachel—was dead—and those were just the people Gwenllian loved in particular. The loss for England and Wales if Mortimer's allies in Ireland succeeded would be impossible to recover from.

And that meant as they breakfasted around Dinas Bran's high table, the few of them here were the center of the known world, as Aaron had put it yesterday during Gwenllian's lessons.

Last night, Gwenllian had eavesdropped on Bohun raging at Edmund in his quarters, though not *at* him so much as towards his sympathetic ear. This morning, from the haggard look on Bohun's face and the circles under his eyes, she wasn't sure he'd slept at all. Still, he raised his cup. "To David!" It was only then she remembered that Humphrey's son, William, was in Dafydd's company too. If Dafydd was dead, William undoubtedly was also.

"To Dafydd." Everyone drank, but it was a distinctly sober group that put down their cups and stared around the table at each other. The mood was a far cry from the last time Gwenllian had sat like this with so much family, at Christmastime after the birth of her nephew, Alexander, when it had been joy all around.

Arthur, sensing the mood of the room, turned in Gwenllian's lap and put his arms around her neck. She pushed back from the table so he wouldn't knock her breakfast to the floor. Padrig leaned in, and with more wisdom than Gwenllian ever would have given him credit for, said to Arthur, "Your dad's okay."

Gwenllian looked down at her little brother, and she whispered, "So is ours."

"I really do believe that." Lili, with Alexander in her arms, sat down on the other side of Gwenllian, who found tears pricking at the corners of her eyes, despite her best efforts to fight them.

"Have you *seen* him?" Hope sprang in Gwenllian at the thought Lili may have been visited with *the sight.*

"No, *cariad.*"

"Then how can you know?"

"Because I haven't seen him. Don't forget, like Anna, they could have gone to Avalon. They're safe. You have to believe that."

Gwenllian nodded, though she had to tip back her head a little to stop the tears from overflowing. To cover her emotion, she brought Arthur's little hand up to her lips and kissed it.

Then Gwenllian heard a sound coming from outside the keep. As it grew louder, she stood up so abruptly her chair tipped backwards to the floor, and Arthur in her arms squawked.

A moment later, Ieuan surged to his feet too, and he put out a hand to silence everyone else. By then, the noise from outside was loud enough to hear over the talking. Bohun looked from one to the other. "What is that?"

As she looked around the table, Gwenllian realized that other than Bronwen, who had been busy nursing Cadwaladr, and Arthur, who was too young to know, she and Ieuan were the only ones at the table who'd been to Avalon. That was why they'd been the first to realize the noise they were hearing was unnatural in a very specific way.

"It's a plane." Releasing Cadwaladr from her breast, Bronwen hugged him to her, listening hard. "It's close too."

"A plane?" Bohun said.

"A carriage that flies," Bronwen said.

And then the door to the hall flew open, and two soldiers hurtled into the room, gasping and incoherent. A bus was one thing, but an airplane was the stuff dreams were made of. Everyone was on their feet by now, and Gwenllian, Arthur on her back, took off running for the door, followed closely by Cadell, who'd pretended all was well up until now, but as he came abreast, she saw a tear on his cheek.

It was only then Gwenllian realized the tears she'd thought contained were falling down her own cheeks as well.

"It's Anna. It has to be!" With Alexander clutched to her chest, Lili stared up at the people on the battlements, which were already full. The entire garrison knew the danger to Dafydd in Ireland, and Gwenllian had seen the pity—as well as grief—in their eyes when they looked at Lili. Now, people buttressed her on all sides in their attempt to give her love and support.

Having followed Lili up the stairs to the battlement, Gwenllian searched the sky for the plane and didn't immediately find it until she looked west and realized it wasn't as close as she'd thought. Avalon was full of noise, but the loudest thing at Dinas Bran was the bell in the chapel tower and the wind in the trees, so they'd been able to hear the engine from miles away.

Dinas Bran sat on its mountain a thousand feet above the valley floor, allowing them to see for miles in every direction. Over the next minute, they watched the plane come towards them, descending with every second as it approached. The people around Gwenllian were dumbstruck at the sight.

Cadell, however, was a child of both worlds. "Come on, Gwen!" He ran for the main gatehouse tower, and then up it. Having left Arthur with his mother, Gwenllian huffed behind Cadell, glad she wasn't twelve yet so her skirt still ended above her ankles and didn't hinder her running.

They reached the highest tower of the castle and came out with gasping breaths. Cadell clambered up onto the lip of the wall, reaching for the pole upon which Dafydd's banner hung.

Gwenllian grabbed his belt at the back, panicked he was going to fall, and then with the help of one of the guards, once he understood what Cadell wanted, they pulled one of the long flagpoles from its rest.

Cadell was only eight, so the pole was too heavy for him, but with the same man-at-arms steadying them, she and Cadell waved it above their heads in welcome.

Another minute passed before the plane reached the castle and circled directly overhead. The pilot responded to the flag by dipping the wings in greeting, and Gwenllian hugged Cadell jubilantly.

"Get off!" Cadell elbowed her in the stomach, but as she pulled away, he was laughing. The plane flew east, fat tires extended, and Gwenllian didn't see how it could possibly stay up in the air, though she'd done the calculations for flight in her physics lessons.

The guard behind Gwenllian asked, "Where is it going?"

"The pilot needs a flat place to land." Gwenllian handed the pole to the guard. "Thank you."

"We don't do flat here very well." Cadell stood on tiptoe to lean over the battlement. "It looks like they're going try by the Dee." He dashed for the tower door again, this time heading down the stairs, and by the time Gwenllian had followed, everyone else had descended from the wall-walk.

"Did you see where they landed?" Math asked his elder son. In his arms he held four-year-old Bran, who had a death grip around his neck.

Cadell nodded earnestly. "Right by the river in old Gruffydd's field."

Math strode towards the stable, Cadell and Gwenllian on his heels. Padrig and Elisa raced after them. "We're coming too!"

Gwenllian caught their hands, and when they reached the stables, she threw Elisa up in front of Cadell, who was old enough to ride a horse of his own, and then once she'd mounted, Math helped Padrig up behind her. He kept Bran with him.

"I wish I could fly myself!" Lili laughed as Arthur, who was astride in front of her, shouted, "Yah!" and brandished his little sword. Alexander was the only family member not to come, since he'd been handed over to his nanny.

Constance was riding escort, back to her usual duties as Lili's bodyguard, though like the Norman barons, Edmund and Humphrey, far more subdued than the family. Of course, Constance's husband was imprisoned at Beeston Castle, his life in the balance, along with Venny and the others, so even the arrival of the plane couldn't make up for his absence.

It took far too long to descend the road down from the castle, but they did eventually get there. As they approached the plane, which seemed impossibly huge compared to when it was flying above them, the door opened, and one by one everybody Gwenllian cared about spilled out, including her parents, Dafydd ... and Anna.

Bohun had been riding his horse just behind Gwenllian's, and now he swore, which wasn't exactly the reaction Gwenllian would have expected. It was apparently a curse of joy, however, because as he dismounted he wore a smile a mile wide—which was almost terrifying on Bohun's face, since he smiled so rarely.

Humphrey's son, William, had dropped to the ground to stand before his father. The two men looked at each other, so much alike in their features and height, though William was far more slender. Then Humphrey reached for his son. "By God, I'm glad to see you."

He scooped him up in a hug that eventually had William saying, "I'm well, Father. Let me go!"

"His assistance was crucial to saving my kingdom," Dafydd said helpfully from behind them, his arms full of Lili and Arthur.

Humphrey turned. "I am not surprised, not in the least." He draped his arm across William's shoulders and squeezed him again. "He is a Bohun."

William, for his part, appeared stunned by his father's exuberance.

Gwenllian herself had been hugged and kissed and hugged again before finally ending up in her brother's arms. "I liked the flag," he said.

"It was Cadell's idea."

"It was a good one. It made your mother cry."

"Am I never going to stop being afraid for you?" Gwenllian said.

"No," he said simply and kissed her temple.

Then Dafydd loosened his hold, and Gwenllian turned to see that everyone had formed a semi-circle around them.

Dafydd gazed at his friends and family, taking in the face of each one in turn, though his eyes rested for the longest on Anna, who stood next to Math, holding hands with her boys. "Thank you. I cannot thank you enough." Then he looked at Bohun. "You took a great risk."

Bohun scoffed, but Gwenllian could tell how pleased he was by the attention. "My life was never in danger. I fear for the poor Venables boy, however. How are we going to get him and the others out?"

"Your kingdom isn't saved yet, my lord. We don't know how far the contagion has spread." Edmund's expression was not quite as joyful as everyone else's—but then, it was his brother at the heart of the conspiracy.

"I don't have a plan right now," Dafydd said, honest as always, almost to a fault, "but if I have learned anything in the last weeks it is that *I* don't have to." He reached for Gwenllian and pulled her close to him again. "I have all of you—and we are going to figure this out together."

36

21 March 1294

Anna

Medieval beds were often built big, but Anna and Math's was even bigger than normal, seeing as how they'd had it built when Anna was nursing Bran, and they'd wanted it spacious enough to accommodate the whole family. Tonight, Bran was snuggled up to Anna, who herself lay in her husband's arms. Cadell had started out with them, but he was big enough that he'd learned not to like sleeping while anyone was touching him, and he'd taken himself off to his own room.

"I'm proud of you," Math said. "Terrified, but proud."

Anna had been almost asleep, but she raised her head to look at her husband, whom she could see by the moonlight shining through the half-open window. It was March, but she'd wanted it open. She'd told Math it was because it was too warm in the room, but really, she had wanted to smell the rain. It was Welsh rain, and tonight it stood for everything she'd almost lost.

"Time travel is the price I pay for being who I am."

Math lifted her hand as it lay on the covers and kissed it. "I know that. I accept what I cannot change, and I suspect it's time both worlds knew what an amazing woman you are."

Bran stirred, allowing Anna time before she answered. She eased her son away from her so her movements wouldn't wake him. Then she rolled all the way over so that she and Math could face each other.

"It's better they don't know."

"I can't see how."

Anna shrugged one shoulder. "Because then you and I can go on being underestimated."

Math's expression turned thoughtful. "It is easier to protect those we love when your enemy has no idea what you're capable of."

"Exactly." She nodded. "It's impossible to protect against everything. In Avalon, they're obsessed with security, and even there, danger slips through. Here, it's even harder, especially when the threat is from a Norman baron like Roger Mortimer, who's good at keeping secrets."

Math bent his head so his forehead touched hers. "He should never have threatened you, *cariad*." He breathed deeply through his nose in the way he did when he was trying to control his temper.

"No, he should not have." She stroked a hair from his forehead. "But my going to Avalon turned out to be a good thing. I made a difference. We can be glad of that."

Math pressed his lips together for a moment, clearly considering his next words before he spoke. "I know now it would never occur to you to stay in Avalon without me, but if you wanted, we could all go. Seeing Christopher with his family—" he shook his head, "—I don't ever want to experience this kind of separation again. I certainly don't want what happened to Christopher to happen to Cadell. It could, you know."

Anna herself was shaking her head before he'd finished speaking. "I don't want to live there—and I certainly don't want you to try to. I hope it's many years before any of us have to go back."

"It's your home."

"Not anymore. This time it felt like I was visiting the moon." She paused. "No, it's worse than that. To me, it's as if Avalon is the land that is back in time. I feel I should know how to function there, but I don't. Sometimes it's almost as if I catch a glimpse of the woman I would have become if I'd stayed, but she keeps just out of sight, only visible out of the corner of my eye. I can never look at her directly. Truthfully, I don't know her anymore. I certainly don't want to *be* her."

"That's just fine by me." He paused. "I overheard you saying something different to Dafydd, though, something about being a goose when you're there?"

She laughed. "The goose that lays the golden egg. It means that because I was valuable to the people chasing me, nobody was going to harm me. I don't like the metaphor, but once I thought about it more, it gave me a measure of confidence, in dealing with the people there, which I hadn't had going in."

"Did you say as much to Dafydd?"

"I did."

Math laughed under his breath. "That's why he was smiling. I've seen him look like that only a few times. His smile was almost ... wicked."

"Wicked? Are you sure we're talking about the same David?"

Math grinned. "Inordinately pleased, then, and certainly proud of you. I think our king has finally come to appreciate the strengths and gifts his family and friends bring to the table."

"Oh, I think he's known for a long time. It's been harder for him to exploit them because he hates putting anyone at risk other than himself."

Math grunted. "Plenty at risk over the next few days and weeks. Avalon is the least of our problems. Unravelling Balliol's plot is quite enough of a puzzle to be going on with."

"We'll solve it. Mortimer and Balliol think they're clever and planned for everything, but look what's become of their plan to conquer Ireland!"

"As your mother tells it, making peace there was a feat for the ages. Defeating these conspirators will be as well."

As she looked into her husband's face, Anna's expression turned serious. "John Balliol and Roger Mortimer have broken the peace and threatened the security of everyone who lives in

England, Scotland, Ireland, and Wales. They tried to murder not only David but his parents and his friends. Despite all that, if they were willing to lay down their arms, David would have forgiven them because we have grown to hate war. But Mortimer had to go after me—"

"If Balliol knows what's good for him, he will run as far away from your brother and me as he possibly can." Math gently stroked a finger down Anna's wounded arm, and she knew he was hating again that she'd been hurt.

Anna snuggled against him, more happy than she could say to be home safe. "Mortimer has set in motion people and events he has no hope of controlling. He and Balliol—" she shook her head, "—they have no idea what's coming."

Acknowledgments

First and foremost, I'd like to thank my lovely readers for encouraging me to continue the *After Cilmeri* Series. I have always been passionate about these books, and it's wonderful to be able to share my stories with readers who love them too.

Thank you to my husband, without whose love and support I would never have tried to make a living as a writer. Thank to my family who has been nothing but encouraging of my writing, despite the fact that I spend half my life in medieval Wales. And thank you to my posse of readers: Lily, Anna, Jolie, Melissa, Cassandra, Linda, Brynne, Carew. Gareth, Taran, Dan, Olivia, Mark, and Venkata. I couldn't do this without you.

About the Author

With two historian parents, Sarah couldn't help but develop an interest in the past. She went on to get more than enough education herself (in anthropology) and began writing fiction when the stories in her head overflowed and demanded she let them out. While her ancestry is Welsh, she only visited Wales for the first time while in college. She has been in love with the country, language, and people ever since. She even convinced her husband to give all four of their children Welsh names.

She makes her home in Oregon.

www.sarahwoodbury.com

Made in the USA
Middletown, DE
09 September 2017